GW00865215

797,885 Books

are available to read at

www.ForgottenBooks.com

Forgotten Books' App
Available for mobile, tablet & eReader

Download on the
App Store

ANDROID APP ON
Google play

ISBN 978-1-331-57639-6
PIBN 10208028

This book is a reproduction of an important historical work. Forgotten Books uses
state-of-the-art technology to digitally reconstruct the work, preserving the original format
whilst repairing imperfections present in the aged copy. In rare cases, an imperfection in
the original, such as a blemish or missing page, may be replicated in our edition. We do,
however, repair the vast majority of imperfections successfully; any imperfections that
remain are intentionally left to preserve the state of such historical works.

Forgotten Books is a registered trademark of FB &c Ltd.
Copyright © 2017 FB &c Ltd.
FB &c Ltd, Dalton House, 60 Windsor Avenue, London, SW19 2RR.
Company number 08720141. Registered in England and Wales.

For support please visit www.forgottenbooks.com

1 MONTH OF
FREE
READING

at
www.ForgottenBooks.com

By purchasing this book you are eligible for one month membership to ForgottenBooks.com, giving you unlimited access to our entire collection of over 700,000 titles via our web site and mobile apps.

To claim your free month visit:
www.forgottenbooks.com/free208028

* Offer is valid for 45 days from date of purchase. Terms and conditions apply.

English
Français
Deutsche
Italiano
Español
Português

www.forgottenbooks.com

Mythology Photography **Fiction**
Fishing Christianity **Art** Cooking
Essays Buddhism Freemasonry
Medicine **Biology** Music **Ancient**
Egypt Evolution Carpentry Physics
Dance Geology **Mathematics** Fitness
Shakespeare **Folklore** Yoga Marketing
Confidence Immortality Biographies
Poetry **Psychology** Witchcraft
Electronics Chemistry History **Law**
Accounting **Philosophy** Anthropology
Alchemy Drama Quantum Mechanics
Atheism Sexual Health **Ancient History**
Entrepreneurship Languages Sport
Paleontology Needlework Islam
Metaphysics Investment Archaeology
Parenting Statistics Criminology
Motivational

Margaret Davis, Tutor

BY

ANNA CHAPIN RAY

Author of "Half a Dozen Boys," "Half a Dozen Girls,"
"The Cadets of Flemming Hall,"
"In Blue Creek Cañon"

———•o❍❀❍o•———

NEW YORK: 46 East 14th Street

THOMAS Y. CROWELL & CO.

BOSTON: 100 Purchase Street

COPYRIGHT, 1893,

BY T. Y. CROWELL & CO.

Typography by J. S. Cushing & Co.

Presswork by S. J Parkhill & Co,

TO

MY TWO REAL CHARACTERS

Danforth

FRIEND, PUPIL, AND CRITIC

AND

Laddie

THE FAITHFUL COMPANION

WHO FELL ASLEEP JUST AFTER THIS

LITTLE STORY WAS WRITTEN

2072272

CONTENTS.

MARGARET DAVIS, TUTOR.

CHAPTER I.

THE TWINS.

"'He may have been little, or he may have been tall,
But his tale is so sad, you will weep for it all,
And it happened along of a bat and a ball.
Boo-hoo! Boo-hoo!'"

sang Jack teasingly. "That fits your case pretty well, Dan; but I don't see any use in your being so mortally glum about it."

Danforth Spaulding had been lounging in one of the deep window-seats of his room, moodily twisting the fringe of the dimity curtain; but at his brother's last words, he abruptly sat up and faced him, as he said, with a sudden flash of anger, —

"Can't you let me alone one single minute, Jack? There's no use in hitting a fellow when he's down; and I'm in enough of a scrape as 'tis, without your crowing over me."

9

"There isn't any scrape about it, only you do take things so hard," declared Jack, who sat on the edge of the table, swinging his heels as he talked. "'Twas nothing but a frolic, and old Duffy ought to know it wasn't. You aren't the fellow to mean to chuck a ball through his window and upset all the things on his desk, and you'd have told him so, if you'd had half the spunk of a baby mosquito." Jack brought his heels together with an emphatic click; then he went on, in a tone of mingled annoyance and accusation: "But that's the way it always is; as soon as Duffy went for you, you turned all colors at once, and stammered, and acted scared out of your seventeen senses. Of course he came down on you all the worse, after that, for he thought you were a sneak that wouldn't take the couse-quences of his sins; and I don't much blame him, I declare I don't."

"Oh don't, Jack!" remonstrated the culprit feebly, while his face flushed and his eyes grew large and dark, as if the tears were not far away.

"Yes, I know; but it's so, every word of it," said Jack rather impatiently, for he was often sorely tried by his twin brother's lack of self-assertion. "You don't do half the things, the rest of us can, and come out all right; but you always will get rattled in the wrong place, and let Duffy see just what you've been about. Then when he gets after you, you act as if you were frightened to death. Now, I think the only way for a fellow to do, when he gets into a corner, is to hold up his head like a man, and take what's given him, without a grumble. Old Duffy likes you better, if you do, and he isn't half as apt to go for you next time. He's sort of used to scolding you, somehow, and he keeps at it. If you wouldn't be so everlastingly meek about it, he'd let you off easier; but now he's given you a thrashing, and sent a note home to grandpa."

The charge was in part deserved, and Jack felt that right was upon his side, so he rounded out his criticism with the unsparing frankness of boyhood. Then, when he glanced at Danforth again, his conscience suddenly smote him. The two boys, as unlike as twins often are, were as fond of each other as brothers could possibly be; and although Jack never hesitated to express his own opinion of his brother's doings, he was quick to resent even the suspicion of blame or reproof from anyone else. And now Danforth sat curled up in a corner of the window-seat, biting his lips to

steady them and digging his clenched hands deep
down into his pockets, to keep from showing, by
some involuntary motion, how he was writhing
under the scorn in Jack's voice, while he looked,
as he felt, a picture of abject misery. Jack
watched him, for a moment, out of the corners of
his eyes; then he slid down from the table and
began to wander up and down the room in a
series of curves which gradually brought him
nearer and nearer his brother in the window. At
length he paused at Danforth's side.

"I didn't mean to be hard on you, Dan," he said
more gently, as he rested one small brown hand
on his brother's shoulder. "I only hate to see
you keep getting thrashed for something that
isn't your fault. You need more bones in you,
somehow; that's all. It's because you're such a
good fellow that I care, you see. But how that
ink did fly, and how funny Duffy did look, mad
as a yellow-jacket, and with a great black smooch
on his cheek!" And Jack laughed so uproar-
iously at the recollection, that even his brother
smiled. It was a pale and watery smile, but
Jack heralded it with rapture, for it was a sign
that the cloud was passing. "'Twas no end of a
shame," he continued, as his hand closed upon

his brother's palm which was red and swollen, as if from a recent bruise; " 'twas a perfect shame for him to hit you so. He never knows what he's about, when he's mad, and he lays it on harder than he means to. But, I say, I'll go and get some of that stuff of Uncle Jerry's, and maybe 'twill feel better."

"I don't mind the hurt," said Danforth sturdily, as, yielding to his brother's encouragement, he sat up and shook himself; "that will be all right by to-morrow; but I hate to go back into school again, for grandpa says I must apologize before all the fellows, and I know Duffy will read me a sermon."

"Grandpa's all upset over it," observed Jack not too consolingly. "He says no Atherton was ever whipped in school before, and it's brought disgrace on the family name. I shouted at him that we weren't Athertons, we were Spauldings; but he didn't hear, for he'd dropped his trumpet just then, and grandma looked so shocked that I didn't dare say it over."

"I wish grandpa wouldn't be quite so hard on us," said Danforth, turning despondent once more. "He always acts as if boys in his day were never in a scrape; and I heard him telling grandma that he didn't see what to do with us next. If only papa —"

"But papa isn't," responded Jack promptly. "Papa's in India, and we're here. And even if he weren't, Dan, we've come to where we must fight our own battles; we aren't babies any longer, we're almost men. But wait till Uncle Jerry gets home, and then he'll straighten it all out," he added hopefully, for Uncle Jerry was the refuge of the boys in times of trouble.

But in the meantime Uncle Jerry had come home, and a council was even then being held down-stairs. Bobbie, as the boys called their younger sister Roberta, had been ignominiously dismissed from the drawing-room; not at all to her own satisfaction, however, for she was curious to hear what was to be the outcome of "poor Dan's awful scrape," as she termed it, and moreover she was loyally desirous of speaking a word for her brothers, if the tide of feeling seemed to turn against them. But Grandpa Atherton had ordered her from the room; and Bobbie was too honorable to linger in the hall, where she could easily have overheard all that was said, thanks to her grandfather's extreme deafness, which effectually put an end to the privacy of the family conclaves.

It was a strangely assorted family circle who lived in the old Atherton house. Years ago, the old place had been gay with the busy life of a large family of children. Then, for a time, the childhood had gone out from it, and it was not until a new generation came on, that the echoes of past days were wakened once again. Life in an old family house, even the plainest, is fuller and richer, oftentimes, than in the finest mansion of last year's building. Each nook and corner has its unspoken story, and each chair and table can set one dreaming of the past. If we but think of it, the very air of the rooms about us is haunted with the shadows of former days, who walk over and guard us, their children of later years.

Old Captain Atherton had built this house for his bride, when the present century was still young. In those far-off days, it was no matter of a few weeks to plan and execute the building of a house; but when at last it was done, and the furniture, ordered from France and England, was arranged in its place, no bride could have been brought home to a richer, more sumptuous dwelling. But not even the beauty of her home, not even her young husband's devotion could prolong the life of the poor little bride. The same day

which brought a son into the house, took away
the young mother; and before he realized that
the blow was about to fall, Captain Atherton
found himself alone in the great house, alone,
for neither the servants nor his tiny son could
be companions to him in his loss.

However, the years which looked so long, as
they stretched out before him, that stormy Decem-
ber day, hurried by, and once again a bride was
brought to the home. Captain Atherton lived
to welcome his son's wife; then, only a few weeks
later, he quietly passed away to join his own bride
of years ago, leaving his house filled anew with
the gladness of young married life.

Fifty years had passed since then, and the bride
and groom had become old people, though they
were still living in the unchanged home. They
were Grandpa and Grandma Atherton, now; and
the years which had brought them a flock of children, had taken them away again, — all but two.
Grace, the oldest daughter, had gone abroad for
a year, and soon afterwards she had married an
English army officer; while Gerald, the youngest
of them all, was living in the old house, unmar-
ried.

Three years before, the Atherton house, so long

quiet, all at once wakened into new life. A letter had come from far-away India, where Colonel Spaulding was in service, to tell them that Grace and the children would start for home by the next steamer, to make them a long visit.

"I want the children to get acquainted with their home and friends," Grace wrote. "They have never known any grandparents, and they are disgracefully ignorant about America. Perhaps, if I can find courage to leave them, I shall ask you to take charge of them until they are educated. But I can talk about that later, when I see you."

To see Grace again, and perhaps to have Grace's children for their own! The old people went about in a happy dream, while they waited for the days to pass until the steamer should reach New York and Gerald could meet his sister. Then came a sudden shock which left them wondering how they could ever have been so happy, wondering even what happiness meant. On the P. and O. steamer, soon after leaving Bombay, Grace had been taken seriously ill, and, from the first, the ship's doctor had declared that there could be but one result. The poor little woman had made a brave fight, for she was determined to reach America alive, and herself place her children in her parents' care; but it was all in vain. She lingered until England was passed, and she was on the Cunarder, with New York almost before her eyes; but when the steamer came into port, Gerald only found three motherless children who looked at their stranger uncle, with fearful, awe-stricken eyes, and then turned away, to cling to each other and sob, in all the freshness of their loss.

The home-coming had been a sad one to them all, and for weeks the old house had lain under a heavy cloud; but little by little they took up the threads of life again and resumed their former ways. It had been arranged that until the children were ready for college, they should remain with their grandparents; and, with the easy adaptability of childhood, they had quickly settled into their new surroundings of home and school. Long before their first year was over, their Indian life was a vague dream to them, and they were as loyal little Americans as if they had always dwelt under the stars and stripes. The twins were fifteen now, and Roberta a year and a half younger, a bright, headstrong, wilful little woman who was at once the torment and delight of her brothers. She was as fond of them as they were of her, loving Danforth with all the fervor of her nature, while she adored Jack as a superior being, in spite of their frequent contests. When Jack teased her beyond endurance, she fled to Danforth for sympathy. When she was in disgrace for assaulting Danforth's sensitive points, which happened at least five times a week, she betook herself to Jack, and together they plotted fresh mischief. But when an outside enemy threatened any one of the trio, then they ranged themselves shoulder to shoulder, and fought for each other and for themselves as gallantly as their soldier father would have done, in their places.

And now the outside foe had made an attack, for Duffy, as the children irreverently termed Mr. Dufferin, their teacher, had not only whipped Danforth for a mere accident, but had carried war into the enemy's camp by sending a note to Grandpa Atherton, requesting the old man to uphold his discipline, and add a private punishment to the public one. No wonder that the boys had fled to their room, and that Bobbie had been summarily dismissed from the drawing-room, while Grandpa and Grandma Atherton talked it over with Uncle Jerry.

"He'd be a hopeless young scamp if he weren't

such a baby," Grandpa Atherton was saying tes-
tily. "In my day, boys used to mind their
teachers, and treat them with some respect."

"But there wasn't any disrespect in this case,
father," urged Uncle Jerry, stretching himself up
to his fullest height, to bring his lips up to the
ear-trumpet of the tall old man before him.

Uncle Jerry was very small, no larger than a
boy of fourteen should have been. Nevertheless,
no one who knew Gerald Atherton ever referred
to him as a dwarf; it was always as "the little
man," with a half-tender accent upon the words,
since to meet him once was to be won by his bright
manner, his unvarying courtesy and his cheery
unconsciousness of his physical disadvantages.
Except in the matter of size, nature had been kind
to Gerald, for his little body, though far too small
for the great, generous heart within it, was perfectly formed, and his handsome face with its blue
eyes, dark hair and crisp brown mustache, with its
look of perfect health and its ready smile, gained
the liking of the very strangers in the streets.
He had been the favorite at school; he had been
the most popular man of his college class; and
now, at thirty, Gerald Atherton had more friends
than any other man in town, and was generally

acknowledged to be one of the most promising young lawyers of his state.

"No," he said again; "I can't see that Danforth was in the least to blame for anything but his carelessness."

"Then why couldn't he have said so like a man, and not whimpered like a baby?" retorted Grandpa Atherton, abruptly shifting his ground for the attack.

"Don't you know that isn't Danforth's way, John?" asked Grandma Atherton gently.

"What?" And Grandpa Atherton swung hastily around, and brought his trumpet to bear upon his wife who sat knitting by the fire, a dainty picture of sweet old age.

She repeated her question. This time, her husband heard her.

"It's time it was his way," he responded curtly. "I've no patience with that boy. He hasn't any spirit, and never will have; and I believe it ought to be thrashed into him. His mother spoiled him, when he was almost a baby, all because he wasn't as strong as Jack; but he'll never make a man unless it's taken out of him, and I hope Mr. Dufferin will do it," he added irascibly, as he freed his mind by marching up and down the room in his favorite attitude, with the long skirts of his dressing-gown drawn forward over his arms, and his hands clasped in front of him.

It was plain that Grandpa Atherton was in a bad humor.

In the meantime, Uncle Jerry had been hastily collecting his thoughts. For a long time, he had been convinced that Mr. Dufferin's rule, with its unreasoning alternations of tyranny and indulgence, was as bad for wide-awake, mischievous Jack as it was for sensitive Danforth. However, there was no other good school within reach, so he had held his peace and waited until some emergency should bring him the opportunity to suggest his long-cherished plan. The golden opportunity had come; but it would be no easy task to influence Grandpa Atherton in his present mood. Uncle Jerry felt that some concessions might be necessary.

"Yes," he agreed; "Danforth is too sensitive, too easily frightened, and unless he changes soon, he never will bear the hard knocks he'll get, when he goes into college. The worst of it is, he is growing more and more so, with every day he's under Mr. Dufferin."

"Needn't be such a baby, then," growled Grandpa Atherton. "Look at Jack! He's worth ten Danforths; and he knows as much in a minute as Danforth does in all day."

"Dan can't tell half he does know," said Uncle Jerry. "He has a better mind than Jack; but Mr. Dufferin frightens it all out of him. Jack is one of his favorites, and slips along easily; but it will spoil him the other way, and make him conceited and headstrong before we know it."

"He has plenty of that, as 'tis," answered Grandpa Atherton, with a short laugh. "But even if Mr. Dufferin isn't the best man in the world, what are you going to do about it? There's no better school in town."

"Why not hire a tutor?" proposed his son, with a promptness which suggested its coming from no sudden impulse.

Grandpa Atherton frowned in thoughtful disapproval. In his young days, tutors were not so common as they are now, and it took him a few moments to accustom himself to the new idea.

"Well," he said at length; "whom would you have? I don't know of anybody."

"Neither do I," Uncle Jerry was beginning, when he was interrupted by his father who had forgotten to adjust his trumpet.

"What?" he demanded. "Begin again."

"I said that I didn't know of anybody now," repeated Uncle Jerry; "but we could easily find some one."

"How?" Grandpa Atherton asked the question with the air of having offered a poser.

"Advertise," responded his son. "Our best way to get the kind of man we want, would be to send right to one of the literary weeklies. There are plenty of college men who would be glad to take a position with us, for a few years, as resident tutor for the children. What do you say about it, mother?" he asked, turning with a gentle deference to address Grandma Atherton.

"If only it were not for his having to live here, Jerry," she said doubtfully.

"But we might all of us enjoy that part of it, mother," he urged quickly. "If he were a bright, gentlemanly fellow, you and father wouldn't much mind him, and he'd be good company for me, evenings. Perhaps I'd better advertise for one who plays whist," he added, laughing. "Then we could have our evening rubber without calling on the children. Jack and Bobbie won't learn how to play, so it all falls on poor Danforth who doesn't dare tell how cordially he hates it." Then he turned back to his father once more. "It would

be so much better for the boys," he said persuasively; "and it might be a good thing for Roberta.
The child isn't learning anything in that school
where she is, — anything that's of any use to her, I
mean. They teach her a little German and a little
French, and some music and drawing, and a great
deal of society nonsense that she ought to know
nothing at all about, for years to come. If you
will agree to my plan, I'll save you any care about
the matter. I can't teach the children, myself,
for I haven't the time; but, at least, with a tutor
right here in the house, I can see that he's doing
good work for them, and send him off, if he
isn't."

Nobody, least of all Gerald Atherton himself,
knew just how it was that Grandpa Atherton was
invariably brought around to his son's way of
thinking. No matter how much their opinions
might clash at first, the result was always the
same; so it was no surprise to Grandma Atherton,
who had long ago been coaxed into agreeing with
her son, to hear her husband, at the end of a half-
hour's discussion, eagerly urging upon Gerald the
advisability of a tutor for the children, without
having the faintest doubt but that the suggestion
had originally come from himself.

Then the children were called back into the drawing-room, to hear the result of the conference. The boys were to go back into school, for the rest of the month, and were under strict bonds to behave themselves like gentlemen and Athertons; while Danforth was ordered to make a public apology to Mr. Dufferin for the mischief done by his ball. When the first of October came, they were all three to be taken out of school and put in charge of a tutor, who should prepare the boys for Yale and Bobbie for Smith. The news was received with disgust by Jack, who was the acknowledged leader of the school; with secret misgivings by Danforth, who regarded it as only the beginning of fresh troubles; and with open exultation by Roberta, for she hailed with delight the prospect of abandoning her present rather old-maidish teacher, since even thirteen years' experience of life had taught Miss Bobbie that one sidelong glance of her roguish brown eyes could bring to her feet the most obdurate of mankind.

So Uncle Jerry went away to write the letter, and Grandma Atherton followed him, to make sure that the library was not too warm, and that his desk was in order. Grandpa Atherton was soon deep in his paper, and the children were free to express their opinions upon the sudden change in their prospects.

"Who wants a horrid old tutor around in the way, all the time?" grumbled Jack, in a low tone, for Grandpa Atherton's ears were never so sharp as when he was particularly desired not to overhear some mutinous remark.

"He can't be much worse than Duffy," said Danforth uneasily; "and I'm glad to get out of that school and start fresh. Duff thinks I'm a fool and a sneak; but maybe this new fellow will give me some show."

But Bobbie could not forbear giving one little frisk of sheer triumph.

"Don't worry, boys," she said saucily, as she caught up her skirt in both hands and made a sweeping courtesy, "I'll manage him for you; you needn't be afraid."

CHAPTER II.

THE MESSAGE OF THE ROSES.

LATE the next Saturday afternoon, Margaret Davis was walking home from a meeting of the A. C. A. She had been unusually interested, for there had been an address by an earnest young Englishman from Toynbee Hall, followed by a discussion of the proper aims and employments of a college woman. Now she was thinking it over, as she walked along the city streets, crowded with the usual Saturday afternoon throng; and her face, meanwhile, expressed a vague dissatisfaction either with herself or her surroundings. At the post office she stopped for a moment, to see if her favorite weekly had come in, too late for the afternoon delivery. When she came out on the steps again, she held it in her hand and was eagerly running her eye up and down over the delightful gossip notes which close each number. Then, as she folded it again, her glance rested upon the opposite page. The next moment, her face lighted with a

sudden thought and she nodded decisively to herself, as she quickened her pace towards home.

On the steps, she was rapturously received by a
shaggy black and tan collie who, finding that his
low whines and taps on the door had failed to give
him admission to the house, had patiently settled
himself to await the coming of his mistress, that
he might go in with her.   Now, from his vantage-
ground of the top step, he plunged forward upon
her, in all the fervor of his joy.

"There, there, Laddie!" she exclaimed, as two
rough paws descended upon her two shoulders
with a precision of aim born only of long practice.
"Yes, I've come home.   Was he glad to see me?"

Laddie gave one short, sharp bark in reply; then
he dropped back again and stood with the tip of
his nose pressed hard against the door, waiting to
push his way through the first crack which offered
itself.   Once inside the house, he allowed his mistress to take the lead, and went soberly trudging
after her up the stairs and into the large front
room, where Mrs. Davis and her other two daugh-
ters were trying to coerce the folds of a home-
made gown into looking as if they had just come
from a tailor.   They glanced up expectantly as
Margaret burst in upon them, with all the breezy

energy developed by her long walk in the open
air.

"Oh, Peggy, I'm so glad you've come!" exclaimed her younger sister, who was temporarily
acting as lay figure. "Can't you put this on for a
while? I'm so tired of standing here." And she
cautiously stretched out her long arms and yawned.

"Do stand still, Molly," interposed her mother
hastily. "When you move, you throw these back
folds all out of place. This doesn't seem quite
right, though, Elinor," she added, turning to her
oldest daughter who was sitting on the floor, in a
sea of brown tissue paper and breadths of blue
serge.

"But it must be all right," said Elinor firmly.
"I've put it together just exactly like the pattern.
Peggy, do call Laddie away! He will tear this
paper all to pieces, if he rolls on it. Now listen,
mother, while I read, and see if it isn't right. Let
me see." And she referred to the paper in her
hand, running her finger down along the closely-
printed sheet. "'Cut the front gore with'—no,
it's the back we want. Here 'tis. 'Gather the
top of the back from the triple perforation to
the second notch from the middle, and apply it
to the belt, adjusting the fulness to fit the figure.'

There, you see it is right," she concluded triumphantly.

"Perhaps you haven't adjusted the fulness to
fit the figure," suggested Margaret, who had
dropped into the nearest chair and was surveying
them with unmixed scorn. "Do you know," she
added, after a pause, "I'd rather never have a
new gown than go through such a performance
to get it."

"Nobody would ever doubt that who saw you,"
answered Elinor, laughing in spite of herself, as
she rescued a half-finished sleeve from Laddie's
mouth. "You are chronically out at elbows.
Now, I'd rather have a few more gowns and make
them myself, instead of putting all my money into
dressmakers."

"I wouldn't though," returned Margaret placidly,
while she took off her hat and ran her fingers
through her front hair. "It takes more brains to
puzzle out a paper pattern than it does to write a
book. Some day I may want to use my mind, you
know, and then I should be so disappointed to find
that it had all gone into my clothes. I'm willing
to live on one frock a year, if it's necessary; but I
positively decline to make that one." She was
silent for a moment; then she said coaxingly,

"Mammy dear, let that old gown go, and come into my room for a talk. I know you're tired enough now, and it's too dark for you to see much longer. Besides, I want to consult you about a new idea I have."

"What is it, a treatise on ancient history, or an entertainment for your boys' club? It's sure to be something stupid," observed Molly, with all the pertness of sweet sixteen.

"Neither, this time," answered Margaret good-naturedly. "Mother can tell you by and by, when she's ready." And throwing an arm about her mother's waist, she drew her away into her own room and put her into a chair by the window. Then, hat in hand, she dropped down on the side of the bed, where she sat silent, as if not knowing how to proceed.

"Well?" said her mother interrogatively.

"I know it," answered Margaret irrelevantly; "but —" She hesitated.

"What is it, Peggy?" her mother asked again.

Something in the old-time name and in the motherly tone gave Margaret courage, and she said, with an odd little catch in her breath, —

"Mammy dear, may I go away for a few months?"

Mrs. Davis's face fell; she had been dreading the day when this should come. For the past few months, she had seen that Margaret was growing restless, as if the daily routine of home life were pressing too closely about her and cramping her. A change would be good for the girl; and yet, bright, tempestuous, impulsive Margaret was her favorite child, the one who entered most deeply into her mother's life. How could she give her up? A whole battle was fought and won, in the silence which followed Margaret's question. Then Mrs. Davis said gently, —

"If it is really best for you, Peggy, I could let you go. What is it you want to do?"

"It's this." And Margaret thrust the paper into her mother's hand.

"You'll have to read it to me," Mrs. Davis said; "I haven't my glasses on." She was perfectly well aware that her glasses were lying in her pocket, but her eyes had grown too dim to allow her to use them.

"It's only an advertisement I saw to-day," said Margaret more quietly. Then she read, "*Wanted, a resident tutor for a family in New Hampshire. Must be a college graduate, Yale pre-ferred. For particulars, address G. A., care of*

——. May I try to get the place, mammy, just for this one year?"

"But it says 'Yale preferred,'" answered her mother, vainly clinging to this one hope.

"Yes, I know; but our degrees are as good as Yale's. I have my A. M. too, and that would be a help; besides, I can refer to ever so many of the professors here. I know the chances are against me, but I do want to try." And Margaret paused expectantly.

"Why is it that you want to go, dear?" asked Mrs. Davis. "Can't you be happy, here at home?"

Margaret dropped down on the floor at her mother's feet, and rested her chin on her hands.

"I am happy here," she said slowly; "very happy; but — can't you understand it, mammy? — I want to try my wings. I've been at home for four years now, ever since I was graduated; and it's time I took a year of work, if only to prove that I can do something useful, if I try. Besides, I'm getting tired of being snubbed as a do-nothing. Every new member that comes into our A. C. A. asks me if I'm not teaching, and when I confess that I'm not, she looks at me reproachfully and says, 'Of course, then, you're studying here at Yale.' When they find that I'm a mere cumberer of the ground, they turn their backs upon me, only," she added, with a little laugh; "they waggle their heads and point all their morals at me, when they discuss the proper relation of college women to the community. And then I want to taste the sweets of independence. I'd like to be able to be rashly extravagant, once in a while, and not have to decide whether I'd forego the next symphony concert, or wear my old gloves a month longer."

" You can easily have a larger allowance, Margaret," her mother was beginning; but Margaret interrupted her, —

" Truly, it isn't that, at all. I want to feel that I'm really earning my own money, not living on what you give me. But that is only a half-reason. Back of it all, I am getting a little uneasy and want a change. I'm fond of children and always get on well with them, so no work could be pleasanter. It would only be for this one year, and that is such a tiny little bit of a time."

"But how could I let you go?" And Mrs. Davis looked regretfully down into the eager face before her.

"That's just it. If you really needed me, I

wouldn't say a word; but you have Elinor and
Molly to do the useful and ornamental for you,
and I'm the extra one. Of course, if you truly
disapprove, I'll give it up at once and forever."
Margaret tried to speak bravely; but the unconscious change in her tone showed how her heart
was set upon this sudden desire.

That settled the matter; and after a long talk
too full of mother-love to be set down here for
stranger eyes to read, Margaret seated herself at
her little oak desk, to write a formal letter of application to the unknown G. A. of the advertisement.

"It's rather awful to have to make an inventory
of one's personal attractions and mental attain-
ments," she said to herself, as she abstractedly
inked the nose of the grotesque face carved in the
top of her desk. "I do hope I haven't been selfish; but I really don't think I'm needed here, and
I do want to go. I don't believe mother cares
much."

How much her mother cared, Margaret never
knew.

Great was the dismay of her sisters, half an hour
later, when Margaret came in with her hat on, and
announced that she had just been out to mail a

letter, asking for a tutor's position in a strange family.

"If that isn't just like Margaret," groaned Elinor; "to take up with every new whim that comes into her head! Do you realize, Margaret Davis, that you'll be nothing more than an upper servant, or a nurse-maid? You'll have to live in one or two little tucked-up rooms, and to eat at second table, and play for dancing when they have company? How are you going to like that?"

Margaret's face fell. This was a new view of the case to her, and it was not an encouraging one.

"Well, you needn't be alarmed," said Molly, who had possessed herself of the paper and was studying the advertisement. "It's a man they want, and he must be from Yale, so Margaret won't stand any chance of getting it. I hope she won't, either," she added, as she threw the paper across the floor. "What will the girls at school say, when they know my sister has gone out as nursery governess?"

"Is it girls or boys?" asked Elinor.

"I don't much care," answered Margaret, catching up the paper again, to hide her annoyance at Elinor's tone of disapproval. "I like them both; but it is probably boys. I shouldn't think they'd

want a Yale graduate for a girl. Dear me, I wish
they would hurry and answer my letter! I am so
afraid it will be the kind of a place that I don't
want to take."

"But what about Laddie?" inquired Molly
suddenly. "Even if you don't mind leaving us, I
shouldn't think you could stand it to be away from
him."

And Laddie, as if to add his voice to the general
remonstrance, rose, walked slowly across to Margaret's side and laid his nose in her lap, with a
profound sigh.

"It's too bad of you, Molly, to talk in that
way," protested Margaret. "You know it isn't
because I want to leave you; but — well, mother
understands," she added desperately, as she bent
over to stroke the head in her lap. "But what's
the use of talking about it any more? Most likely
they won't want me at all, and we shall have had
this tempest in a teapot all for nothing. Come,
Laddie, we must go and smooth down our ruffled
plumages before dinner.' And she escaped to her
own room, leaving her mother to defend her course
and quiet her sisters' objections.

No one who knew Margaret Davis would ever
have thought of her as the victim of an unhappy

love affair; yet she had known her one little romance, and now, at twenty-five, she regarded that side of life as being ended for her. It was one of those vexatious little mistakes for which neither one is at all responsible, but which apparently destroy the happiness of two people, and send them drifting far apart just at the moment when they are about to come together for life.

The second winter after she left college, Margaret had met a young electrician, with whom she quickly formed an easy, off-hand friendship. They were in the same whist club and the same oratorio society, they attended the same church and were invited to the same parties; so, long before the season was over, they had come to depend upon their frequent meetings, although as yet the thought of love had not come to either one of them. They had the same tastes and the same interests, that was all, and they enjoyed coming together and talking over their doings and their plans. But this state of affairs could not last indefinitely, and before the second winter was over, it had become evident to every one that matters were growing serious for both Margaret and Mr. Thornton.

Mrs. Davis was quite content, for the young man's character and family were all that she could desire. Moreover, he had a good salary, and Margaret would some day have a little money of her own, so that question need not stand in the way of a prompt engagement.

Then came the end, so suddenly and unexpectedly that the friends who were only watching for the time to offer their congratulations, knew not what to think. It was during the previous winter, just before Lent, when•city life is always at its gayest, that Hugh Thornton came, one afternoon, to call on Margaret. Just what he said to her was never known; but Molly, who inopportunely appeared to them in the parlor, saw him hastily start up from her sister's side, as he said, with an evident effort to act as if nothing unusual had occurred, —

"Very well, Miss Davis, I shall see you to-morrow night, at Mrs. Sutherland's, and we'll finish our talk there." And he had gone away, leaving Margaret in a strange state of excitement and elation.

The next day, Margaret had received a large box of flowers, but she had hunted in vain through and through their fragrant masses, for the card which should be there. She was sure they were sent by Hugh Thornton, and she longed to carry some of them to the reception that evening; but she dared not do so, for fear they might chance to come from some other friend. Still, it was with happy anticipations that she dressed herself, that night, for she knew so well the nature of the talk which she and Hugh were to finish, and she felt that it could have but the one ending.

However, the evening proved to be one of bitter disappointment. As she stood at her mother's side, responding vaguely to the greetings of her hostess, she had glanced quickly about the room until she caught sight of Hugh's face looking steadfastly at her from a distant doorway, with a strangely downcast, questioning expression. It was only for a moment; then she lost sight of him, and during all the rest of the evening, she waited in vain for him to join her. Hurt and annoyed, she covered her feelings as well as she could, and talked and laughed as usual, while the time slowly dragged away until she could go home and hurry to her room.

There on the table lay an envelope addressed to her. She snatched it up and tore it open, sure that it must in some way explain Hugh's strange behavior of the evening. It only contained a note from the florist, saying that the enclosed card had been accidentally omitted from the box which he had sent her that morning. In a dazed fashion, Margaret stooped to pick up the card which had fallen to the floor at her feet, and turned it over and over, staring at it as if slow to read its meaning. Below the name was written, " Carry some of these roses this evening, and I shall know what your answer will be." Then she understood it all. Two days later, the papers announced that Hugh Thornton had resigned his position and gone to New York. Margaret's romance was ended.

It was not like Margaret to make any demonstration of her sorrow; in fact, she never once alluded to it. As spring came on, she grew a little thinner and paler; but, to all appearances, she was the same bright Margaret they had always seen. Her mother knew better; but even she was ignorant of the nights when Margaret lay awake and lived over and over again the happiness of the past winter. But brave as the girl was in making the best of it and trying to forget, the wound still remained, and she often longed to go away for a time, to drop out of the associations with the past, into a new life where all was fresh and untried. For weeks this feeling had been growing upon her, when she came upon Gerald Atherton's advertisement for a tutor, and she hailed it as an offer of escape, little dreaming that it was the first thread of the new web which the fates were weaving for her life.

By the next morning Margaret had persuaded herself that she had done a foolish thing in offering her services for a position which was so evidently designed for a man; and she regretted her letter of application which could only bring her the mortification of a prompt refusal. So sure was she of the truth of her new view of the matter that, when the postman stopped at the door, four days later, and handed her, among others, a letter addressed to herself in a plain, legal hand, she opened her other mail first, before she had the curiosity, or the courage to examine the one which was to decide her fate. When at last she took it up, she turned it over and over, as if trying to gain, from the outside, some idea of its contents. It was a square, thick letter, written on heavy paper of a bluish tint, and the flap of the envelope bore a tiny crest in blue.

"I don't like crests, here in America," she said to herself critically; "I think they're snobbish; but the writing is plain and refined, without any flourishes. That's one comfort."

Deliberately she cut the envelope and opened the letter within. Then, as her eye ran down over the first page, she gave a little gasp of surprise. Instead of the curt refusal which she had expected, the letter contained a cordial acceptance of her application, with the offer of a salary so generous as to make her almost doubt the reality of the whole affair. For a moment, she stood gazing at the letter in her hand, as if expecting to see it suddenly vanish from before her eyes ; then she rushed excitedly into her mother's room, exclaiming, —

"Rejoice with me, mammy! The fates are propitious, and G. A. wants me as much as I want him."

The hurry and excitement of the next ten days of preparation were broken by two more letters from Mr. Atherton, letters so friendly in their tone as to remove even Elinor's doubts in regard to the position which her sister was to take. Then, before Margaret realized that she was going out from her old home corner, the farewells were said, and she found herself seated in the train which was rushing away northward, to meet the new life before her.

During her five-hour ride, Margaret had plenty of time to think of the future. The past few days had been so full, that she had only lived in the present; but now, as she realized that she had suddenly started out into the world upon her own account, she had a momentary longing to take the first south-bound train which she met. But she laughed at herself for her inconsistency, and busied herself in arranging her umbrella and wraps to her liking. Then she opened her bag and took out the letters she had received from her future employer.

"Gerald Atherton isn't a bad sort of name," she said to herself; "but, as Molly says, he's probably a fussy old bachelor of sixty-five or so. I do hope the children won't be too sinful. They evidently don't mean to make a servant of me, for Mr. Atherton says he decided to take me, instead of that Yale '89 man, because I'd be such a pleasant companion for his mother. Wonder how he knows, for I'm not always so pleasant. I suppose I must wait till I see his lordship before I can find out anything more."

Then, with one last glance out at the Hanging Hills lying blue in the early afternoon sunshine, she settled herself to the new *Century* and forgot all that was passing around her, until the twilight forced her to abandon her book and fall to musing again

The darkness had quite fallen when the train stopped at the little city where Mr. Atherton had agreed to meet her; but, as she stepped out on the platform she saw the dim outline of a rugged mountain rising close at hand, and heard the dull roar of the river, as it thundered over the falls, a thousand feet away. A moment later, Gerald Atherton stood before her, hat in hand.

"Miss Davis, I think?" he said questioningly. "I am Mr. Atherton. If you'll give me your checks I'll hand them to an expressman, and then take you across to the carriage."

With a momentary feeling of pity and dismay, Margaret's eyes had rested upon the little figure before her. However, as she met his smile, she forgot all that; and she answered with perfect ease to his kindly inquiries about her journey, while Mr. Atherton led the way across the platform to a low, open carriage, with a coachman in plain green livery on the front seat, helped Margaret to her place and seated himself by her side. Then, as they drove away, he asked if she had received his last letter, and went on to tell her more of the family life to which she was so soon to be introduced.

"I thought if you didn't care," he added; "that

it would be better not to have the lessons begin until next week. That will give you two or three days to get acquainted with the children, before you have to take charge of them."

"They are your sister's children, I think," said Margaret. "Two boys and one girl, you said, didn't you?"

"Yes; they are good children, too," answered Mr. Atherton quickly. "I hope they won't make you any trouble. They weren't getting much good at school, so I thought it would be better to have a change. Jack and Roberta are bright, wide-awake children, perhaps a little too self-willed; but I fancy that your greatest care will be with poor Danforth."

"Why so?" asked Margaret, a little puzzled at his way of alluding to his nephew.

"Don't be alarmed." And he smiled at her evident fear. "Dan is one of the dearest and best fellows in the world; but he's a sensitive boy that we all have to handle with gloves. He is the real cause of your coming here. Jack would have done well enough in school; but Danforth was constantly in disgrace, for his teacher had no mercy on his weak points, and simply bullied the life out of him. If it had gone on much

longer, he would have been so discouraged that
he would have given up trying to amount to
anything. I think you'll be sorry for the boy,
Miss Davis, and I hope you'll like him. If you
do, you will have no trouble, for while he has a
will of his own and can't be driven an inch, he
can be led anywhere. If he trusts you as a friend,
you can do what you please with him. Forgive
my speaking so plainly," he added; "but I am
fond of Danforth, and I wanted you to understand
him from the first. Strangers always take to Jack,
for he's a good-looking boy; and Danforth steps
into the background, as a matter of course. But
there are the home lights, on that hill ahead of
us, and I am glad, for I can see that you are very
tired."

They had driven rapidly through the city streets
and across a long covered bridge which throbbed
with the rushing of the water beneath; then they
turned into a narrow country road, which ran
along, close to the base of the shadowy mountain.
A mile up the valley, they turned abruptly, wound
up a steep hillside and stopped at the steps of a
great brick house with a broad, hospitable porch
over the front door, and a bright shaft of light
shining out from the fanlight above it. Before

the carriage had fairly stopped, Mr. Atherton had leaped out and offered his hand to Margaret.

"Come in," he said hospitably; "my mother is waiting to welcome you."

Feeling as if she were in a dream, Margaret followed him into the wide hall which ran through the 'middle of the house. She had just time to give a passing glance at the paneled walls, the quaintly-carved banisters, the ancient settees ranged along the side wall and the marble Cupid on its ebony pedestal in the corner; then she found herself upon the threshold of the drawing-room, with a beautiful old lady coming forward to meet her. It needed but one look at the trim, upright figure, at the sweet face, with its white curls surmounted with a tiny square of choice old lace, to assure Margaret that this was the mother of whom Mr. Atherton had spoken so often and so lovingly. A second look told her that the faces of mother and son were much alike, both in feature and expression.

"You are welcome, Miss Davis," Grandma Atherton said gently; then, as she looked at the fresh young face before her, she suddenly forgot her more formal greeting and, leaning forward, she pressed her lips to Margaret's cheek, in a motherly caress, while she added, "I hope you may be very happy here with us, my dear."

The rest of the evening was always a vague dream to Margaret. Already she found herself reacting from the excitement of the past two weeks, and she felt strangely tired and dull. She knew that she was introduced to deaf old Grandpa Atherton; she knew that the children were brought forward and presented to her, and she realized gratefully that kind Grandma Atherton and Gerald were trying to make her feel at home; but as soon as she could, she excused herself, and asked to be shown the way to her room.

Grandma Atherton went with her, to see that all was in order; then, when the last good-night was said and the door had closed behind her hostess, Margaret dropped into the nearest chair and stared blankly about her, trying to realize the sudden change in her surroundings. She looked at the unopened trunks, at the high mahogany bedstead with its graceful canopy and soft white draperies, irresistibly reminding her of an altar raised to the god of sleep; and, for one short moment, she had a twinge of homesickness, the first and the last which she was ever to know in that house.

"I wish mother and Elinor could see me now,"

she thought to herself a little later, as, after one
or two vain attempts to climb into bed, she drew
up a chair and stepped into that, preparatory to
mounting higher. "I don't believe they would
feel so sorry for me, and say I was to be a nurse-
maid. There!" she added, as she finished her
toilsome ascent and lay down among the feathers,
which surged high about her; "if this is a sample
of the bed I've made, I'm perfectly willing to lie
in it — if only I don't smother before morning."
And in another five minutes, she had drifted away
into a quiet, restful sleep, only broken by happy
dreams that once more she and Hugh had met.

CHAPTER ·III.

NEW FRIENDS.

BOBBIE and the boys were unusually prompt in answering the summons to breakfast, the next morning. As a rule, it was no easy matter to get them up in time for the meal. Little short of an earthquake could rouse Bobbie from her sound sleep of healthy childhood; and Jack had an exasperating fashion of answering, " Yes, we're 'most ready," to the maid who rapped at his door, and then rolling over and falling to sleep again, while Danforth dozed away, in happy unconsciousness of any interruption to his dreams. However, curiosity is often a powerful stimulant; and, on this particular morning, the children were gathered in the dining-room fully half an hour before the breakfast-bell.

"She isn't so bad for a woman," Jack was saying, with infinite condescension. " I don't see what struck Uncle Jerry to take her, when he started for a man; but there's one good thing, we shall have an easier time of it."

"Don't be too sure," counselled Bobbie sagely. "Miss Pond was ever so much worse than Mr. Dufferin. She used to scold us, 'most every day."

"You most likely needed it oftener than we did," suggested Danforth unkindly. "I never noticed that Duffy was any too mild; did you, Jack? I like the looks of Miss Davis, though."

"She isn't really pretty," said Bobbie critically. "Her mouth is too large, and her nose is sort of puggy. I think it must be her gown that makes her look so well; that makes all the difference in the world." And this acute observer of woman-kind smoothed down her brown camel's-hair, with perfect content.

"Trust a girl for knowing all about clothes!" said Jack scornfully. "I don't know a thing she had on; but I think she's pretty, and she looks as if she had some fun in her. She can't be worse than Duffy, at any rate, and I believe we're going to like her."

In the meantime, the subject of these remarks was already stirring in her own room. Her long night's sleep had left her feeling rested and re-freshed; and as she stood before the mirror, braid-

ing her yellow hair, she felt fully prepared to
enter upon her new duties. When she finished
dressing, she crossed the room and stood by the
open window, gazing down the valley before her,
at the lovely views of hill and river, and at the
white smoke which hung over the city across the
water that went bubbling and foaming and rushing over the rocks in the ravine, close at her feet.
Captain Atherton had made a wise choice when
he selected the site for his house. It stood alone
upon a little bluff commanding the valley and
the group of simpler houses clustered about the
foot of the hill; and it reminded Margaret of
the castle of an old feudal lord, surrounded by
the houses of his vassals.

But the breakfast-bell rang to call her from the
picture; so she turned away and slowly went
down the stairs to the dining-room. It was a fine
old room, with its great open fireplace, its oak furniture dark with age, the rare line engravings on
the wall, and the table, covered with its snowy
cloth and set with the finest old blue china, not
an odd piece here and there, but a complete ser-
vice⁻ of arching bridges and kissing swallows.
Grandma Atherton was already in her place
behind the huge silver coffee-urn which had done

duty for four generations of Athertons; but
Grandpa Atherton was still lingering before the
fire, toasting himself until the room was filled
with the odor of singeing wool.

No one who looked at Grandpa Atherton would
have thought him the descendant of one of the
oldest and best of New Hampshire's fine old
families, which traced its ancestry to the May-
flower and across the seas into England. At a
first glance, he was not imposing; in fact, he
bordered upon the ridiculous. He had been tall
and straight, in his early manhood, with a proud,
clear-cut face under a mass of dark brown hair;
but old age had left many a mark upon his face
and figure, while the brown hair had fallen away
until the crown of his head was as bare and
smooth as a sheet of ice, and only gained an
artificial covering by the long locks over his ears,
which were drawn up to meet above, and carefully braided into a little close knot.

Moreover, Grandpa Atherton had a strong affection for long-tailed, flowered dressing-gowns of gor-
geons tints, which he wore continually, both at home
and upon the street, and only laid aside on Sunday
for the short hour when he was in church. Added
to this was his extreme deafness, and his invariable

habit of forgetting his ear-trumpet until the conversation was well under way, when he would break in upon the full tide of argument, and remorselessly force the speakers to begin again at the very beginning and repeat it all to him, bit by bit.

Quick-tempered and tyrannical as Grandpa Atherton certainly was at times, he was honorable and just to the last degree; and was moreover, though unknown to himself, ruled and guided by the lightest word of his one living child. What Gerald said and thought and did, was to Grandpa Atherton the only right thing to say and think and do. Unfortunately he was not of the same mind in regard to his grandsons. It had been very hard for Grandpa Atherton to give up the traditions of his own boyhood, and adopt the more progressive point of view of Young America; and he had only partially succeeded in doing so. And yet, in spite of himself he was often moved to a quick admiration for Jack's spirit and independence, even though their wills constantly clashed. At heart he was conscious that Jack was his favorite; and he could never explain his son's liking for Danforth, whose shy sensitiveness was a source of continual irritation to Grandpa Atherton's mind.

As Margaret took her place at the table between Grandma Atherton and her son, she was both amused and slightly embarrassed to find herself under the close scrutiny of three pairs of eyes; for the children, just across the table from her, appeared to be bent upon determining what sort of a person this was, who was to have the charge of them. But, little by little, they became interested in their breakfast, and in the talk which was going on about the table, until at length Margaret could take her turn to study them, unobserved. Bobbie who sat directly opposite, had a dark, pretty little face and an eager, wide-awake manner peculiarly her own. She was never shy, and there was a bright decision in her ways which was as amusing as was her ready independence of thought and speech.

From Bobbie, Margaret's eyes moved to her two brothers, seated one on either side of her. To Jack she was attracted at once, and it was not long before they were exchanging smiles and an occasional word or two across the table. Jack looked at least a year the older of the brothers, for he was more strongly built, a sturdy, rollicking boy of fifteen who appeared to be on excellent terms with the world and all that was therein. He was an un-

usually handsome boy, with a rich, dark beauty that
told of abundant health and activity, as if he were
the child of a more tropical region, who had but
lately strayed to rugged New Hampshire. There
was a strong resemblance between Jack and his
sister, while Danforth, at Bobbie's other hand,
looked like the child of another race. Though as
tall as Jack, he was much slighter and more delicate looking, graceful in figure and refined in face,
although without a hint of Jack's proud beauty.
His freckled, oval face, with its straight, closely-
cut yellow hair and thin red lips, was only saved
from being actually plain by a pair of dark violet
eyes, which looked deprecatingly out upon the
world from behind a pair of round-eyed, gold-bowed
spectacles. These spectacles were at once the woe
and the joy of Danforth's soul. Six months before,
Uncle Jerry, after watching the boy for a few
weeks, had carried him off to a New York ocu-
list who had proclaimed him abnormally near-
sighted, and had promptly put him into glasses.
It had been a wise measure; but Danforth was
even now unable to decide whether his present
ease of vision was enough to balance the mortification of having to go back to school, on his return,
and answer to the manifold questions and com-

ments of the boys. But after Jack had valiantly cuffed the first two or three of these who had ventured to express their disapproval, Danforth was left in peace once more, except for the occasional teasing of Bobbie, who declared that she would never forgive him for making such a grandmother of himself.

"Now, children," said Uncle Jerry, as they rose from the table, "I leave Miss Davis in your care to-day, and you must see that she isn't homesick. Let her get acquainted with you and with the place here; and then, next week, you can begin your lessons."

"All right. What would you like to do first, Miss Davis?" inquired Jack comprehensively.

"Everything, all at once," she answered, with a gay little laugh which promptly ranged Jack upon her side.

"Then come out and see our ponies; and Dan and I have a fine trapeze under the shed. Do you like athletics?"

"That depends," she replied, much amused by the boy's eager friendliness. "I don't do much but skate and play tennis, though I did bring a pair of Indian clubs with me. But I know enough to keep a score-card at a ball-game."

"Honestly?" And Jack stared at his new tutor with undisguised admiration. Then he went on, with striking frankness, "Why, I don't see but you're about as good as the Yale man that wanted to come. Dan and I were no end disappointed when Uncle Jerry didn't take him; but if you care for such things, you'll be just as well. We'll show you how to perform on the trapeze, and you can do it just as easy as anything."

"Oh, Jack," interrupted Bobbie; "do stop talking such nonsense. Miss Davis doesn't want to go gymnasticating with you; she'd much rather see the house and the old pictures; wouldn't you, Miss Davis?"

For a moment, Margaret hesitated; then she reflected that Jack's frankly-offered friendship was not to be thrown away, so she answered, —

"Jack spoke first, Bobbie; so suppose we all go with him now. We can see the house later, for I truly do want to go over it," she added kindly, as she saw Bobbie's disappointed face.

"Ah ha, Bob; you've lost your innings!" said Jack triumphantly. "Come on, Miss Davis." And he led the way out to the lawn in front of the house, with Margaret following close at his side.

It was hard to say just wherein lay Margaret's attraction for children. Perhaps it came from her perfect understanding of them, her perfect sympathy with them and with their interests. She was rarely conscious of making any effort to meet them upon their own ground, or of trying to gain any control over them; and yet, wherever she went, she was usually surrounded by a flock of children, and was the central figure in all their fun.

"Margaret is just like Castoria," Molly used to say; "children all cry for her."

Margaret herself often regretted her lack of dignity. At twenty-five she was at heart as much a girl as she had been at sixteen, and nothing but the consciousness of her quarter of a century kept her from indulging in all sorts of school-girl pranks. Nevertheless, her child friends never took liberties with her. They treated her like one of themselves, yet far above themselves, and her simple, "I wouldn't do so, dear," outweighed many a parental lecture.

Children are close critics of us older people, quick to see through sham dignity and false standards of right and wrong; and if any one of us is able to bear the test of their searching scrutiny and come out of it with their respect and love, we may feel that

we have gained one of the honors of the earth.
They have their own standards, and they weigh
us by them. If we pass their examination, and
once win their friendship, we find it true and
lasting.

Jack had been the first to feel Margaret's
charm. During the past week, he had become
somewhat resigned to the idea of a tutor, since
it could not fail to give him greater freedom than
he had known in school where, though he had
been a favorite with Mr. Dufferin, he had hated
him cordially for his injustice to his more timid
brother. His one regret, that Margaret was not a
man, had quickly vanished at her coming; and by
the time breakfast was over, that morning, he was
ready to swear allegiance to this bright-faced
little woman who had met his advances so warmly.
There was a hearty sincerity about the boy, which
Margaret liked, and she had felt attracted to him
at the first; so it seemed perfectly natural that
they should stroll off across the lawn together,
talking like old friends, while Bobbie and Danforth followed them at a little distance.

"Here's Bobbie's swing," Jack was saying, as
they paused under a great arching elm; "and
over there, on that bank, we had a toboggan chute

last winter; but Dan ran off it and was 'most killed, so grandpa made us have it taken down. Perhaps, if you're very fond of tobogganing, he'll let us have it put up again this year, though," he added roguishly, as he smiled suggestively up at his companion.

"I don't think I care enough about it to run the risk of Dan getting his neck broken," she said laughing. "But what a dear pony!" she exclaimed, as her escort led her across the lawn and, stopping at a low fence, called to a little brown pony that was nibbling the grass in the field beyond.

"Yes, this is Brownie Bell, my own pony," said Jack proudly, while he stroked the pretty creature's neck. "Just notice that white star in her forehead; they're the only white hairs she has anywhere on her. Duke, the black one over there, is Dan's. He's prettier than Brownie; but he's cross sometimes, and grandpa wants Uncle Jerry to sell him. Dan isn't a bit afraid of him, though."

"What does he do?" inquired Margaret curiously, as she turned to Danforth who had come forward and was leaning on the fence at her other side. "I've never had anything to do with horses, myself, and I don't know much about them."

"Oh, he rears a little sometimes; and once he was cross when I took him out, and bolted," he answered shyly. "That was ever so long ago; but it frightened grandma, and she and grandpa have never thought he was quite safe, since then."

"And aren't you ever at all afraid?" asked Margaret, trying to draw him on to talk with her, for she liked the boy's gentle manner, and she suddenly recalled his uncle's speaking of the matter-of-course way in which he took his place in the background. Whenever she had looked at him that morning, she had found him gazing at her intently; but he had made no advances. Now she reproved herself for having given all her attention to Jack, when she had been warned that Danforth was to be her especial care.

"Oh, no; why should I?" he answered, with a little look of surprise. "Duke knows that I'm his master, and that he must mind me. He won't let Jack ride him at all; but I can do anything with him that I choose. See here!" And Danforth stepped to the top of the fence, called the pony to him, vaulted on to his bare back and went gallop-

ing away across the field, followed by the other
ponies in hot pursuit.

"The little gray one is mine," explained Bobbie.
"She's old, and I mean to have a new one, some
day; but Uncle Jerry says I must wait till I'm
older and stronger. The other three are all carriage horses; we haven't but six in all."

"Oh, Miss Davis, don't you want to try Lady
Jane?" asked Jack eagerly. "She's a splendid
woman's horse, and Dan or I could go out with
you, if you don't know the roads round here."

"What fun!" she answered quite as eagerly.
"I wish I could, but I've never tried riding in my
life, and I don't know anything at all about it."

"Lady Jane is perfectly safe," said Danforth,
who had trotted back to them once more, and
guided Duke up to the fence to let Margaret
stroke his nose, an attention which he returned by
promptly snapping at her. "You'll feel comfortable with her as soon as you get into the saddle."

"But I never was in a saddle," protested Margaret, though she looked with longing eyes at the
demure little gray pony who had strolled across to
the fence. "I'm afraid I should fall off; but I'd
like to try."

"How funny that you never rode!" remarked

Bobbie, with a little air of superiority. "Every-body does here."

"No; they don't either, Bob," said Jack, nettled at his sister's tone. "And even if they did, it's no sign that they do it everywhere. I'll tell you what, Miss Davis, we'll go round and see the barn and trapeze and things; then Bobbie can put you into her riding skirt while we saddle Lady Jane, and we'll give you a lesson in the noble art of rid-ing. It's only fair," he added, with a laugh. "Your turn is coming, next week, and then we shall have to put up with lessons from you, the whole time."

Then he led the way into the vast barn, with its large mows piled high with the summer's hay, and out into the low, square corn house where the golden and red ears peeped out between the cracks in the bins. Grandpa Atherton owned a rich old farm which stretched far across the plain at the back of the house, and his head farmer was as proud of his orderly barns as a young housekeeper would be of her well-kept china-closet. Jack was a thorough host, and every nook and corner had to be visited before he could feel that his duty was done; but at length he brought Margaret out by a little door which led into the carriage shed, and allowed her to pause for breath, while he explained to her their somewhat complicated trapeze.

"But what do you do with it?" she asked vaguely, at the end of a long and minute explanation.

"Wait and see. You sit down there; or no, you'd better get up here, for you can watch us better." And Jack pointed to an ancient chaise, which might have been the Deacon's Masterpiece, returned to its original unbroken condition.

"It was the one Great-grandpa Atherton had when he was married," explained Bobbie, as she helped Margaret to climb into the tall, swaying old carriage, and took her seat beside her. "I've heard grandpa tell all about it, how his father wore a blue velvet coat with lace ruffles in the sleeves, and the horses — they had two, one in front of the other, for the wedding — had long white ribbons hanging from their ears. Just think how lovely!" And Bobbie gave a rapturous wiggle, which set the old chaise to rocking upon the leathern straps that served as springs. "Did any of your grandfathers fight in the Revolution?" she asked suddenly.

"Only one, and he was nothing but a great-uncle," replied Margaret, smiling as she watched

the child's face change at the admission. "But
my great-great-grandfather signed the Declara-
tion," she added mischievously, for she was much
amused by this small disciple of America's aristoc-
racy.

"Oh, come off there, Bob!" exclaimed Jack
irreverently. "What do you suppose Miss Davis
cares about our ancestors' best clothes? She'd
much better ask what their children can do. I
don't want to live on my grandfather's greatness;
I'd rather have some new bones of my own."

"Is that the reason you're trying to break those
you have?" inquired Bobbie, in no wise ruffled
by Jack's scorn. "Remember how you fell down
and scraped the skin all off your nose, the last
time you tried the parallel bars, and be a little
careful to-day."

For half an hour longer, Margaret sat there in
state and, all regardless of the hayseed which had
sifted down into her hair, and the wisps of straw
that fringed her dark blue gown, she watched the
two boys while they went through a series of evo-
lutions which, to her untutored eye, appeared to
be especially designed for the purpose of dislocat-
ing their necks. To her surprise, she discovered
that Danforth was quite as energetic and daring

as his brother; and she soon found that, when
once he became interested in his sport and unconscious of himself, his face lighted and grew almost
handsome. The longer she studied the boy, the
more she liked him. Underneath all his shy awk-
wardness of manner, she could see a native refine-
ment and delicacy; and his face, though a little
weak, was true and good. She was still wondering how she could best make friends with him,
when Jack came leaping down to the floor again,
and paused before her, cap in hand, looking glori-
ously strong and rosy and alive.

"The show is ended, ma'am," he said. "Don't
you see what good fun it is? Now, Bobbie, you
go and get your riding-skirt for her, and we fellows will have Lady Jane ready by the time you
are."

"Be sure you buckle the saddle tighter than
you did for me, last time," cautioned Bobbie. "It
slipped, when I was over in Riverton, and I had
to get a man to tighten it for me. Lady Jane
doesn't like to have her saddle on," she explained
to Margaret, as she led the way back to the house;
"so she holds her breath and swells out, to keep
the girths from being tight enough to hold."

Ten minutes later Margaret stood on the steps,

bareheaded and with Bobbie's green skirt slipped
on underneath her own blue waist.

"I think I must be a remarkable spectacle," she
confessed, in an apologetic aside to Grandma
Atherton, who had come to the door to watch the
mounting; "but I've given myself unreservedly
into the children's hands, this morning. I thought
it was the best way to get acquainted with them."

Grandma Atherton smiled in perfect approval.

"It's just what they need, Miss Davis," she said;
"and the more you can be like an older sister to
them, the better we shall all be pleased. 'Tisn't
for the lessons alone that we want you; I hope
you'll make little men and women of my children,
not mere scholars. Jack, is that saddle all
strong?"

"It's all right, grandma, I've looked out for it,"
he answered, turning instantly with the pretty
deference which both the boys always gave her.
"Come, Miss Davis." And he led Lady Jane up
beside the low block of stone in front of the
steps.

"But how do I get on her?" asked Margaret,
looking anxiously up at the saddle which appeared
to be several rods above her reach.

"Put your foot in the stirrup, and swing yourself up," instructed Jack. " Here, Dan, you hold the stirrup for her, so. Now, one, two, three ! "

Obeying his tone and gesture, Margaret put her toe into the stirrup, clutched Lady Jane's white mane and attempted to leap into the saddle as she had seen Danforth do. She only succeeded in bumping herself against Lady Jane's smooth flank, and scraping her elbow on the edge of the saddle.

" Once more," said Jack encouragingly. " You'll get there this time. Now ! "

This time she sprang a little higher and landed, face down, across the saddle. She clung there for a moment, and then slowly slipped down again to the ground.

" See, Miss Davis ! " And with one little wriggle and spring, Bobbie was in her place. " Now," she added, as she jumped down again ; " put your foot in here, so, and your right hand up, like this. Then give a little jump, not too hard a one, for you might go clear across her, and fall down, the other side. I did once."

" I'm afraid it's no go," said Jack ruefully, after he had watched Margaret through several more attempts. " If you could only get on board, I know you'd stay there; but I don't just see how to get you up, in the first place."

"You might take her out to the barn, and she could climb up on a hay-mow and slide down into the saddle," suggested Bobbie, who was unable longer to conceal her amusement.

"Why not bring out a chair?" proposed Grandma Atherton from the doorway, where she made a pretty picture, with her white curls just stirred by the breeze, and a chuddah shawl wrapped closely about her shoulders.

"I know the very thing," said Danforth suddenly. "Wait just a minute." And he rushed into the house, to reappear again with a low step-ladder in his arms.

"But won't Lady Jane resent such a proceeding?" asked Margaret, looking distrustfully at her ladyship, who was growing impatient over this prolonged operation of mounting.

"Oh, no; she's a dear, and used to anything," said Bobbie, while Danforth planted the ladder firmly in the middle of the driveway, and Jack led Lady Jane forward to this improvised mounting-block. "Now, Jack, you hold her head, and I'll keep her from backing round sideways. Dan, you get Miss Davis across into the saddle."

With an amused glance back at Grandma Atherton, Margaret mounted the ladder and, clinging to

Danforth's sustaining hand, she cautiously crawled across into the saddle. The next moment, she gave a little mortified laugh, and backed off on to the ladder again; for she had found herself seated upright with her face pointed straight towards Lady Jane's tail.

"Laugh, if you want to," she said gayly. "It doesn't hurt my feelings a bit, and I'm going to get the knack of it in time."

"You're all right," said Danforth hopefully. "Try it again."

She did try it again, and landed devoutly on her knees, sideways in the saddle, with her flowing robe so twisted about her feet that she was unable to turn around into her place. However, the third attempt proved to be successful, as it usually does; and after all her struggles, Margaret at last found herself seated properly, with her eyes on Lady Jane's ears, and one hand clutching her mane so fiercely that it threatened to be torn from the skin. With one or two deft touches, Danforth drew her skirt into place, and settled her foot in the stirrup.

"Thank you, Dan," she said gratefully, as she bent down as far as she dared, and let go her hold upon Lady Jane long enough to rest her bare hand

lightly on the smooth yellow head beside her.
" You are a most devoted young squire."

The color rushed to the boy's face, as his eyes
met hers in one quick glance; but he made no
other answer.

" All ready? " asked Jack.

" Oh, don't let her go! " And she clutched
the reins again.

"She's as safe as a meeting-house," said Jack,
laughing; " but if you're afraid one little bit,
we'll lead her, this time." And the cavalcade
moved off, with Margaret on her lofty perch, rocking to and fro as unsteadily as a yacht in a heavy
sea, while Danforth walked at her side, to be
within reach in case she slipped.

They took a few turns up and down the lawn;
then Jack started off down the long drive.

"Where are you going, Jack?" she asked
anxiously, as he turned out into the road.

"Only down to the corner, to meet Uncle
Jerry," he answered. "It's time for him to be
coming home to lunch, and I want him to see how
splendidly you're getting on."

"Oh, don't!" she begged, with a sudden reali-
zation of her undignified appearance, after her
morning's explorations. What would Mr. Ather-

"Here we are, Uncle Jerry."

—Page 75.

ton think of her ability as a tutor, if he beheld her in her present position? "Don't you see I haven't any hat?" she urged.

"That's all right; this isn't the city," said Jack composedly. "Here, take my cap," he added, tossing it back to Bobbie who handed it to Margaret. "There he comes, now! Here we are, Uncle Jerry!" he announced, pausing before his uncle while Margaret longed to hide her blushes, as she tried to smile down with unembarrassed ease upon the little figure in the road before her.

To her surprise and relief, Uncle Jerry did not seem at all shocked at sight of her. Man-like, he was quite unconscious of the discordant colors of her composite gown, and of the spikes of hay still clinging to her head and shoulders. He only saw her bright, flushed face, with its wealth of golden hair all loosened about it, under Jack's light gray cap which was cocked on the back of her head; and he appeared to be perfectly satisfied to find the prim duenna, who usually poses as a model teacher, resolved into a pretty young woman, surrounded by a trio of eager children.

CHAPTER IV.

MARGARET AND HER PUPILS.

THE following Monday morning, Margaret entered upon her new work. Her knowledge of the children had made rapid strides, during the past three days; and she quickly discovered that this knowledge would be of great help to her in arranging their studies, and suiting them to their habits of thought and their interests. All in all, she liked Jack the best. Even his faults, the faults of a hot-tempered, self-willed boy, were rendered attractive by a frank manliness which made him ready, after the first explosion, to listen to reason, repent of his manifold sins and take their consequences.

Bobbie, though the brightest, was less interesting. She had all Jack's faults, but not all of his virtues, for she was a little vain and self-conscious, and lacked her brother's jovial unselfishness. Moreover, she was undeniably lazy, and she had a vexatious fashion of skimming over the surface of her world, picking up a catch-word, here and there, which she had the tact to treasure up in her mind, and bring out at the exact moment when it was calculated to impress the listener with her unusual fund of information. In fact, Bobbie's tact often stood her in good stead, for it saved her from many a well-merited lecture; and many a duty unperformed was accounted for with a little word of explanation and apology which carried its point, in spite of its evident lack of sincerity. It was not that she was untruthful. Bobbie never lied; but when she was in disgrace, she had a trick of cocking her head on one side and casting down her eyes, which usually disarmed her opponent. But when Bobbie's temper· was really roused, it was like the sweep of a young tornado; and even Jack was forced to stand aside and let the hurricane rush past him.

Danforth was still Margaret's unsolved problem. The more she studied him, the more she admired him and the less she became acquainted with him. From the first, he made few advances, but stood back and allowed Jack to take the lead; yet, every now and then, he would surprise Margaret by some sudden glance or gesture which showed his shy liking for her, and his evident

wish to have her like him. By nature he had a
much more even temper than his brother; and he
had a way of making the best of things, with a
quiet optimism which rendered him a most agreeable companion. This came partly from his
habit of reasoning everything out to his own
satisfaction, for both in his books and his home
surroundings, he was never content to leave
anything unexplained or unaccounted for. In
his way, too, he was quite as affectionate as Jack
and much more unselfish. Indeed, his lack of
self-assertion was his worse fault, and he fell an
easy victim to Bobbie who, finding it impossible
to quarrel with him, devised endless ways to
tease him, ridiculing his weak points and oppos-
ing his pet interests until poor Danforth was
nearly distracted, and Margaret longed for her
authority to begin, that she might protect him
from the assaults of his sister.

On Sunday evening, Gerald had called Margaret away into the cosy little library, the one
modern room in the old house, where the walls
were lined with rows of well-selected books, surmounted by a fine collection of modern etchings,
broken here and there by an ancient wood-en-
graving whose coarse crudeness was only equalled

by its value. A Turkish carpet covered the floor and dull-hued draperies concealed the doors, while a great table littered with the latest magazines, a well-stocked desk and three or four luxurious-looking chairs drawn up before the open fire, completed the furnishing of the room and made it look what it was, the favorite retreat of a man who loved what was best in art and literature, and had the means to indulge his tastes to the utmost.

"What a charming room!" Margaret had said half involuntarily, as Mr. Atherton drew aside the portière and stood waiting for her to pass in before him.

"I'm glad you like it," he answered, with a smile; "for this is to be your future sanctum, and every morning it will be given up to you and the children. Sit down here by the fire, and we'll arrange a little about their work. Then, after they are started, I shall leave them to your care. You certainly have a gift for managing them; but, tell me, how do you like them?" And he turned to look at his companion with a little feeling of pleasure, as his eyes rested on her animated face and slight, graceful figure.

"Shall I tell you what I really think?" And Margaret met his gaze frankly.

"Do, please, and then we can tell better how we are going to start."

"I like them all," said Margaret slowly, as the color came into her cheeks; "but I like the boys better than I do Bobbie. She is an attractive little thing; but she is less frank and generous than they are, and I don't think she is always quite considerate enough of Danforth. Jack is a dear boy. He has plenty of faults; but they are all manly and honorable ones, and he will outgrow them with time and the proper training. I don't know Danforth, and I doubt my ever really doing so; but he is very interesting, and I believe that, down under all his shyness, he's the flower of the family, but whether you or I will ever live to see it proved to the world at large, is an open question. There," she added, laughing; "have I passed a satisfactory examination on my three days' study?"

"Good! You have said just what I've been thinking for the past three years; and now, the next thing is to plan how, between the two of us, we can make the most of the children. Their training will largely depend on us, for neither my father nor mother are strong enough to have the care. I'm too busy to have more

than a general oversight of them, and they've
been running wild of late. And now about
your work."

For more than an hour they sat there together,
talking over different plans for the winter's work.
Then, as they rose to go back to the drawing-
room, Mr. Atherton said suddenly, —

"By the way, Miss Davis, Danforth tells me
that you own a fine dog ; — a collie, isn't he ? "

"Oh, yes." And Margaret's face brightened at
the thought of her pet. "Laddie is a beauty, and
he has a pedigree reaching back into Scotland,
for generations and generations. Dan is so fond
of pets that I was telling him about the dog
yesterday."

"If he's your own dog, why not have him sent
up here to stay with you?" suggested Mr. Atherton, smiling at the enthusiasm of her tone. "I'm
not quite unselfish in proposing it, for I've been
meaning to get a dog for the boys, as soon as I
could find one that I liked. Dan came to me, last
night, with a long face, and told me a pitiful tale
of how you had been forced to leave your pet, and
how you were probably mourning for each other.
I strongly suspect that he spoke one word for you,
and two apiece for himself and Jack; but I told

him I would ask you what you thought of sending
down for the dog."

"Really?" And Margaret gave a little gasp
of gratitude. "I wanted to bring him up here
and have him board somewhere near, so I could
see him; but my sisters made fun of me, and I
was afraid you would find it out and think I was
silly. But he isn't always a good dog," she added
conscientiously. "Sometimes he barks, and once
in a while he eats up stray shoes and gloves. He's
only two years old, and hasn't much dignity
yet."

"No matter." And Gerald laughed. "Send
for him to-morrow. His pranks will amuse the
children, and mother is like Dan in her love for
all pets, so unless he is very sinful, we shan't
mind him in the least." And he led the way back
to the drawing-room, quite unconscious of the
happiness of which he had just been the cause.

By the end of the next week, Margaret had settled into a well-established routine which made
her feel quite like a daughter of the house, so
warmly had she been welcomed by them all. For
the first few nights, she had gone to bed with a
conviction that this could not last and that, as soon
as the strangeness had worn off, she would be

gently reminded that her position was that of tutor, not of guest; but day after day passed by, and she was still occupying her same place in the family circle, a place of many privileges and pleasant duties.

Her daily routine was unvarying, for the most part. After breakfast, as an especial mark of favor, she was allowed to retire to the great china-closet with Grandma Atherton, and help her by wiping the old blue dishes which no profane hands were ever permitted to wash. It was a half-hour of keen enjoyment to Margaret, for she already loved the sweet, motherly woman, and their quiet talks over the steaming dish-water often gave her a help and inspiration which lasted far on into the day. Promptly at nine o'clock, Margaret gathered her little flock into the library, and then, for four long hours, hard work was the order of the day. As a general rule, the children did work with a will, though Bobbie was occasionally a little inclined to be idle, or Jack demoralized them all with his pranks; but Margaret contrived to keep them busy, and to force into their minds their daily allowance of Greek and Latin, English or Mathematics, without their knowing just how or when they learned it all. After their mid-day lunch,

she was free to pass the time as she chose, except-
ing the hour before dinner when she read aloud
with the children, usually some history or travels.
This last was so successful that, before the first
week was over, they had agreed to go back to the
library for an hour after the meal, and read the
best fiction of the day.

All in all, it was a pleasant, easy life for Margaret, who fully realized that she had been fortunate
in coming into this charming home. It was hard
for her to decide whether she more enjoyed her
leisure hours spent out of doors, or sewing by the
fire, while she chatted with Grandma Atherton,
or her work with the children, who were always
ready to linger over their lessons as long as she
would keep them with her. It was no uncommon
thing for them to claim her afternoons for a long
walk or drive over the mountain roads; or, on
stormy days, to tempt her up-stairs into the great
room where they held sway, kept their treasures
and received their intimate friends. Here Margaret made the acquaintance of Bobbie's other self,
Penelope Stoddard, a pretty, yellow-haired young
girl whose quiet face and gentle manner were the
imperfect mask of an impishness equal to Bobbie's
own; and of Ellsworth Pierson, a slight, dark little

fellow of thirteen, who frequently came to the house, nominally to see the boys, although he made no secret of his devotion to Bobbie, who alternately snubbed him and tyrannized over him, with a perfect unconsciousness of the real state of his feelings.

Of Gerald, Margaret saw but little, except at meal-times and late in the evenings, for he was much in demand in a social way, and after a long day at his office, he was frequently out in the evening. But when they met she always found him the same cordial, kindly host who had welcomed her on her arrival; and she quickly learned to look forward to his coming, for he never failed to bring with him a new spirit of genial optimism. There are some people who never enter a room, without being met with a smile from every person in it.

No atmosphere, however, is altogether cloudless, and Grandpa Atherton was the one dark spot upon Margaret's horizon. In an unguarded moment, she had confessed to a liking for chess, and, after that, Grandpa Atherton considered her his lawful prey. Whenever he became weary of the interminable games of solitaire, with which he beguiled his leisure hours, he pounced upon

Margaret and demanded a fight at chess. Worst of all, he was really a fine player, and in Margaret he believed that he saw unusual promise, so he promptly devoted himself to her development.

There is no doubt but that Margaret's character and patience were increased by his training, for Grandpa Atherton was as hot-tempered as his grandson and namesake, and now lectured Margaret upon her mismanagement of her pawns, now scolded her for risking her queen in dangerous positions, and on one occasion, when she had put into practice his precepts and had succeeded in checkmating him, he jerked the board, men and all, to the floor, and stalked out of the room with the very tails of his dressing-gown quivering with ill-suppressed indignation. After that, she dared beat him no more, but spent long, tedious hours bending over the board, planning how to keep up a brave fight to the last, then suddenly fall a victim to some one of his favorite plays.

On the second Saturday afternoon in her new home, Margaret was up in the Wilderness, as Gerald called the children's room, helping Jack to cover over his favorite ball with the long wrists of a discarded pair of her gloves, when Bobbie suddenly appeared upon the scene. Jack glanced up and gave a low whistle, before re-marking, —

"Hullo, Bobbie; why this elegance?"

"What elegance?" she asked unconsciously, though with a sidelong glance down at her best gown, the Eton jacket of which she regarded as being particularly successful. "I only changed my gown because Grandma just told me that Mr. Huntington is here, and she's going to keep him to dinner. She likes to have us neat, you know."

"And so you put on your store clothes," said Jack, finishing her sentence for her. "Turn around very slowly, Bobbie, so we can see them all, and then you'd better run away again. Miss Davis and I are busy."

"It's time you stopped, though," responded Bobbie, sitting down on her brother's knee and running her fingers through his wavy dark hair. "It's almost five, and time to read. Besides, I want to stay here; I'm lonesome. They're talking about all sorts of stupid things, down-stairs, and Pen wouldn't stay any longer, so she's gone off home. I like you best, anyway. Can't I help you?" she concluded artfully.

"Not a bit," said Jack promptly, for Bobbie had interrupted Margaret's account of the last

Yale-Harvard race, and he was anxious to get his sister out of the way, so that he could hear the rest of the story. "Where's Dan? you'd better go and hunt him up."

Bobbie's lips took on a little disdainful curve, and she let one arm rest caressingly on Jack's shoulder, as she answered contemptuously, —

"Oh, he's down in the library, and doesn't know anything but his stupid old book. I tried to stir him up; but he was cross, and sent me off. Say, Jacky, can't I stay here? I can cover your ball as well as Miss Davis can."

"Suppose you try it," suggested Margaret, not at all to Jack's satisfaction. "It is almost time to have our history, and I've something to do first. Come down to the library in about half an hour."

"All right." And Bobbie slipped into the chair from which Margaret had just risen. "Are you going to change your gown, Miss Davis? If you do, please put on the pretty red one you wore the other night."

Margaret laughed, as she made her escape into her own room. Then, after pausing a moment to see that her hair was in order, she softly opened the door, and went down-stairs and into the library. From Bobbie's sudden affection for Jack, Margaret suspected that she had been having a disagreement with her other brother; and, from her week's observations, she was perfectly well aware that such disagreements were usually all on one side, so she had resolved to go down and see for herself wherein Danforth's crossness lay. Pushing aside the portière, she entered the room so quietly that the boy was quite unconscious of her approach; and she stood resting her hand on the back of his chair, studying his face for a moment, before he discovered her presence.

The contest, whatever had been its nature, had evidently proved disastrous to Danforth, for he had dropped his book to the floor and clasped his hands behind his head, as he sat scowling moodily into the fire. His cheeks were flushed, and his small white teeth were shut over his lower lip; while one lock of his yellow hair stood aggressively erect. Obeying some sudden impulse, Margaret gently smoothed it down into its accustomed place. At the first touch, Danforth shook himself impatiently.

"Do go away, Bobbie," he said, without looking up. "I've stood about all I'm going to, to-day."

"But I'm not Bobbie," said Margaret's voice in his ear.

"Oh, Miss Davis!" And Danforth started up hastily. "I honestly didn't know 'twas you; I thought it was Bobbie, and — and —"

"Yes, I know," said Margaret, drawing a chair up beside his and seating herself. "I knew you were all alone here, so I thought I'd come down and have a little visit with you, before Jack and Bobbie should come. Sit down again and let's enjoy the fire for a while before we have to have a light. Bobbie says that a Mr. Huntington is going to be here to dinner," she added. "Who is he?"

"Really? How jolly!" And Danforth's face grew suddenly bright and interested. "He's the new minister that came here last fall, a first-rate sort of a fellow. Bobbie doesn't take to him, because she says he wears his clothes too long, till they get shabby; but Jack and I think he's about the right sort, not one of your long-faced kind, but likes boys and knows what they like."

"For instance?" asked Margaret, smiling at the boy's eagerness.

"All sorts of ways. He knows us all and,

last winter, he had a club of us; but he had to drop that, because he had so much else."

"A boys' club; that is in my line. You know I used to have one at home, such dear boys, too! Tell me about yours."

And Danforth told, forgetting himself and even Bobbie's teasing, as he gave Margaret a glowing description of the good times they had had in their meetings. She watched him closely, fascinated by his ease of expression and by his animated, changing face. Why could he not always be as unreserved with her, she asked herself; and she determined upon a bold stroke. As he paused, she leaned over and rested her hand upon his, which lay on the arm of his chair.

"Dan," she asked abruptly; "I like boys just as well as Mr. Huntington does, and I know a good deal about them, too. Why can't we be as good friends as you and he are?"

"I don't know." And Danforth retreated into his shell as promptly as an offended box-turtle.

"That's not a fair answer," she responded, laughing. "I'm really in earnest, Dan. I've been here more than a week now, and I'm getting on beautifully with Jack and Bobbie; but I don't know you any better than I did the very first

night. I don't think it is all my fault; but we
don't seem to be getting at each other at all."

Danforth was staring into the fire again, and
Margaret began to fear that she had made a mistake in trying to take him by storm; but it was
too late to draw back.

"Truly, Dan," she urged; "Jack informed me
to-day that I wasn't half bad, and you really ought
to give me the benefit of the doubt. I want to be
friends with both my boys, for then we could have
so much better times together. I don't ask you
to like me, only to trust me and to believe that I
really care for you, instead of being here just to
teach you your lessons."

Danforth turned a little in his chair, and looked
up at her with a mute appeal in his great blue
eyes. No woman's voice had taken just that tone
in speaking to him, since his mother left him;
and, except for Grandma Atherton and Uncle
Jerry, no one had cared to try to win his liking.
At heart the boy was very lonely, and hungry
for a word of sympathy and understanding from
some one. Even Jack failed at times, for his animal spirits and love of fun made him slow to
appreciate all the moods of his more sensitive
brother. Moreover, Margaret's face was very

sweet and gentle as she bent towards him, with a little, half-shy smile trembling on her lips.

"What I want, Dan," she went on slowly, "is that you shall feel as if I were a cousin or something, so that you can come to me when things go wrong, and talk it over together, and let me have a share in your interests, when things go right; to grow to be friends through thick and thin. It won't come all at once, I know; but let's try for it, because," she hesitated; then she went on, in a lower tone, "because I could be very fond of you, Dan, if you'd only let me."

The clock struck five and Jack's voice was heard in the hall outside. The next moment, he and Bobbie came into the room, but not before Margaret had felt the boy's fingers close upon hers in a firm, close grasp.

When they adjourned to the drawing-room, after their hour's reading, Margaret was introduced to the minister of whom Danforth had spoken so warmly. She found him a slight, dark young man, with a pale clear-cut face and a little manner of boyish shyness which reminded her of Danforth himself. Accustomed as she was to meeting strangers, she was secretly amused by this young man's downcast eyes, and an odd little fashion he

had of irresolutely laying the tip of his forefinger
against his mustache, as if to steady his sensitive
lips. But when the talk went back from society
nothings to the real interests of life once more,
she was surprised to see the man's whole manner
change, while his face grew animated and his
great dark eyes lighted up, without any trace of
his former embarrassment. In spite of the shabby
black coat, worn white at the seams, which had
roused Bobbie's dislike, in spite of the nervous
forefinger, Margaret knew and liked him for just
what he was, an earnest, kindly young worker,
who had neither the time nor the inclination to
become a mere society man, so absorbed was he in
the real needs of his calling.

As they took their places at the table, Grandma
Atherton said to Margaret in a low tone, —

"Just for to-night, I have put Danforth between you and Gerald, to make room for Mr.
Huntington."

And Margaret answered, with a smile for the
boy who stood waiting at her side, —

"Why not let him stay here all the time? It is
the best place for him."

It was growing late, that evening, when the
maid came to the door and spoke to Gerald. He

rose from his place in the midst of the group before the fire, and went out into the hall. A
moment later, he opened the door a crack and
announced, —

"A young gentleman is here, who would like to
see Miss Davis."

Then he threw the door wide open ; there came
a rush and a scramble, and Laddie, dragging his
chain after him, bounded into the group. Straight
to Margaret's chair he raced, leaped up and put
his paws on her shoulders, where he stood, barking
madly in his joy at once more finding his beloved
mistress who had so faithlessly deserted him. But
when at length he was quieted and brought to
order once more, they found that, in his wild
gambols about the room, Laddie's chain had tied
Margaret and Danforth together in a firm, close
bond.

CHAPTER V.

BOBBIE'S EXPLORATIONS.

"Come, Dan," urged Bobbie; "Uncle Jerry said I mustn't go alone, and I think you might come with me, just this once."

"But I don't want to, Bob. I told Jack I'd find out how to rig up our telephone. There's something wrong about it, and I borrowed this book, just for this afternoon, so I could find out the trouble. I'll go with you to-morrow; won't that do?" he pleaded, for Bobbie stood over him, with her lip curled in scorn.

"You are getting to be a perfect old poke, Dan," she said impatiently. "You never were half the fun Jack is; and, this fall, you've been worse than ever, just won't do anything I want you to."

"But don't you see I can't? Why won't Jack go with you?"

"Because he won't. He has taken Lady Jane and gone for a ride with Miss Davis. He's with her the whole time, afternoons." And Bobbie pouted.

Danforth leaned back in his chair and looked up at his sister, with a gleam of amusement in his dark blue eyes.

"Do you know, Bob, I believe that you're jealous of Miss Davis, and that's where the shoe pinches."

"Danforth Spaulding, what an idea! I'm not jealous of anybody; only," she went on, a little illogically, "it seems too bad that, when I need my brothers, they should be going off with somebody that isn't their sister one bit."

"It's hard luck, Bobbie," said Danforth sympathetically, as Bobbie dropped down on the arm of his chair.

"Then why won't you go?" And Bobbie smiled her sweetest, as she rested her head against her brother's shoulder.

"I can't, honestly, Bobbie. I must do this now. I haven't much time anyway, for it's almost three. If you'll wait till to-morrow, I'll go."

"How selfish you are, Dan." And Bobbie straightened up suddenly. "I should think you'd be ashamed of yourself, so there! You and Jack are both just as mean as mean can be." She

stood facing him angrily as she went on. "All
you care for is to sit over the fire and read, like
an old grandfather. But if you won't do what I
want you to, you shan't do what you want."
And before Danforth could divine her intention,
she darted forward, pulled off his glasses with one
hand, seized his book with the other, and ran
away out of the room.

He rushed after her; but she was too quick for
him, and before he was half-way up the stairs, he
heard the key turn in her door. Accordingly, he
was forced to abandon the pursuit, and, after a
few warning words, the effect of which was
marred by their being delivered through the key-
hole to a silent room beyond, he went back to the
library where, since reading was out of the question for him, he meditated upon vengeance.

"What a little wretch she is, when she gets
wild!" he remarked to Laddie, who lay before the
fire. "I wouldn't mind, if she'd left my glasses;
but now our telephone must wait a while longer.
I believe I'll go out for a ride; there's nothing
else to do." But he was still sitting there, half an
hour later, when Margaret came into the room,
dressed for a walk.

"Do you know where Bobbie is?" she asked,

coming forward to the fire, as she slowly drew on
her gloves.

"No; I'll be hanged if I do," answered Danforth with unwonted impatience.

"I didn't know but you might have seen her,"
said Margaret, a little surprised at his tone. "I've
looked everywhere for her since I came back, in
her room and in the Wilderness; but I can't find
her at all. She wanted me to get some ribbon for
her, when I went over to Riverton."

"I honestly don't know where she is, but maybe
I can find her." And Danforth rose reluctantly,
to go in search of his sister.

"Never mind, Dan; if she isn't here, she can
wait till another time. What are you doing in
the house, this lovely day? You ought to be out
in the air, not drying up your brains in this warm
room. Come over to Riverton with me, if you've
nothing better to do. I've only one errand, and
then I shall come right home again."

"All right." And Danforth stretched himself
and buttoned his coat. "I promised Jack and
Ellie that I'd get our telephone straight, this afternoon; but Bob has run off with my glasses, so I
can't finish the book, and I'd like to go."

"So that's it! I had been wondering what

made you look so odd to me," said Margaret, with a smile. "But what is Bobbie doing with your property?"

Danforth gave an uneasy laugh.

"Oh, we had a little row, and she went for me and came off first best, that's all."

"But Bobbie had no right to meddle with your glasses, no matter what you did." Margaret's tone was a trifle indignant. "I wish you'd tell me what was the real trouble, Dan. This ought to be stopped."

"I don't want to tell tales of Bobbie, Miss Davis." And Danforth met her look squarely. "'Twasn't much, anyway; and I'm glad to get rid of my spectacles for a while. You know I hate wearing them. Besides, I brought it on myself; I wouldn't go nutting with her, and she thought I ought to."

"I'm sorry, Dan. We shall have to give Bobbie a talking-to. But now let's be starting, before we lose any more of this splendid day." And privately resolving to give Miss Bobbie a lecture upon her sins, she followed Danforth into the hall, and stood waiting while he took down his overcoat and plunged his arm into the sleeve.

The next moment, he gave a short exclamation of disgust, and shook it off again.

"What is it?" asked Margaret curiously.

"Something is wrong with the sleeves; I believe Bobbie has been monkeying with the lining. Yes, see there!" And he pointed to a row of hasty, uneven stitches which drew the lining together into a little untidy knob of satin. "She must be in no end of a temper, for she hates to sew, and she'd never have taken so much trouble."

In spite of herself, Margaret laughed as she saw the stitches. Bobbie's fun and originality showed, even in her naughtiness, and she certainly devised striking methods of taking revenge upon her brothers. The child was wily enough to know that, no matter what she did, if she could only get the laugh on her side, the punishment which followed must of necessity lose much of its severity; and when she was not so angry as to lose her head, she never failed to add the saving touch of comicality to her worst sins.

"Just run up to my room and bring me my scissors, Dan," Margaret said, after a moment's amused contemplation of the sleeves which she had turned inside out. "I'll set this right in a minute." And she was as good as her word for, five minutes later, Danforth's coat was on, and they were leaving the house.

It was about two weeks after Margaret's little talk with Danforth, and ever since that night, she had been conscious of a slight difference in the boy's attitude toward her, as if he were beginning to trust her friendship, or had entered into some secret alliance with her. He no longer watched her out of the corners of his eyes; but he met her advances more frankly, although a quick, unconsidered word would send him back into his old reserve once more, until Margaret could succeed in drawing him out again. It was rather exhausting, she said to herself at times, and she was occasionally half-inclined to give up the effort.

Then her conscientious wish to make the most of the boy, and a feminine desire to please led her to make still another attempt; and she would be rewarded with some shy mark of liking, a quick look of understanding which gave her courage to go on. Little by little she became interested, then fascinated by the quiet, undemonstrative boy who at first had seemed to her the least promising of her pupils; and although Jack and Bobbie monopolized most of her time and attention, she found that her rare half-hours alone with Danforth were among the pleasantest memories of her day. Once or twice he had mustered courage to ask her to go for a ride with him, and he had shown himself quite ready to accompany her, in the one or two little expeditions she had proposed.

They started off gayly enough to-day, with Laddie trudging at their heels; and it was no surprise to Margaret to have Danforth suggest, after their errands were done, that they should prolong their walk down the valley, and across the bridge at the lower end of the town. Accordingly they strolled along, enjoying the pleasant October sunshine and talking of this matter and that, for Danforth was in an uncommonly social mood, that day, and Margaret wondered to herself to find him so interesting and companionable. Always sympathetic and easy in her manner with boys, she was often conscious that she utterly failed in her efforts to interest them; but with Danforth in his present mood, there was no such effort. He showed himself so intelligent and bright that she forgot the difference in their years, and met him as she would have done a friend of her own age.

"Let's stop here and take breath, before we go home," he suggested suddenly, as they paused on the bridge leading across a rocky gorge where a little stream tumbled over the boulders below.

"I know a fine place on the bank down here, and we've plenty of time, I'm sure."

He led the way along the bank to a moss-grown ledge which overlooked the clear depths of the stream, and pointed to a sunny nook facing the west. Margaret sat down there, and he threw himself on the rock at her feet. Before them, the gorge opened out into a little round basin, like the bed of a former lake, and at its western edge lay the scattered buildings of a solitary farm, while along the top of the bluff beyond ran one of the main drives of the city, bordered with stately houses and well-kept lawns. It was Margaret's first visit to the spot, and she gave a little exclamation of delight, as she saw the pretty picture before her. When at last she looked down again at the boy at her feet, she found that he had rolled over on his back, and was gazing up at her with a curiously intent expression in his blue eyes.

"Well, Dan, what is it?" she inquired.

"Nothing, only I was thinking," he began; then he asked abruptly, "Has anybody here ever said that you look like my mother, Miss Davis?"

Margaret shook her head.

"No; nobody has spoken of it. Do you think I do, Dan?"

"I don't know as you really look like her; but you've made me think of her, ever since that first night you came, and I wondered if anybody else had thought of it."

"What was she like?" asked Margaret gently. "I think I've never seen a picture of her."

For his only answer, Danforth took out his watch, opened the back of its case and held it up to Margaret's outstretched hand. She took it from him and looked long at the picture fastened inside the case, a picture of a pretty, delicate young face, in all the freshness of early womanhood.

"You are like her, Dan," she said, after a moment; "very much like her. I had always supposed that you were the odd one; but now I understand it. Was this taken long before —?"

"No; only a month before we started. She wanted to leave it with papa. There were only a few of them, and I had this one. I always keep it in here; but nobody else knows about it, so maybe you'd better not say anything. I wanted to show it to you though, somehow."

"Thank you, Dan," she answered quickly. "I only wish I might remind you of her, a little; not to take her place, but to help to fill it, if you'd let me."

Danforth straightened up, and sat with his eyes fixed on the valley at his feet.

"I don't say much about it, it's no use; but it seems as if the others didn't need her, quite so much as I did. Bobbie was too little to mind much, and Jack used to be off with papa a good deal; but I was with her more, and it's been so lonesome since we came here."

"Poor, mother-sick boy!" thought Margaret; but she said nothing. She only bent forward and drew the lad's head over against her, with an indescribably gentle, womanly motion.

"I was alone with her, you know," he went on, after a little pause. "Bobbie was afraid and cried, and Jack took her away; but I stayed there, and she held on to my hand all the time. Seems as if I could feel it now. Then we came here, and grandma and Uncle Jerry are just as good as they can be; but nobody's hand ever felt just the same to me, till you came into the library, that night. It hasn't been nearly so lonesome, since then."

Margaret stooped and passed her hand caressingly across the boy's low, broad forehead and freckled cheek.

"You make me very glad I came here, Dan,"

she said. "I feel as if perhaps I'd found my proper place."

In the meantime, Jack was searching the house for his sister, whom he wished to have go out with him for a continuation of the ride which had been cut short by Margaret's errands. But Bobbie was nowhere to be found, and Jack was forced to give up the quest and take the ponies away to the barn to unsaddle them. Danforth too had mysteriously disappeared; so Jack, finding the bright, bracing October air too fine for inaction, resolved to go over to Riverton for a call on Ellsworth Pierson, whom he had seen but twice before, that day. Accordingly, he sauntered away down the hill, and on towards the bridge leading across the river. He had no especial desire to see Ellsworth; it was only because he seemed, for the moment, the one available source of entertainment, and because, to Jack's restless activity, there was need for constant occupation.

On the bridge he paused for a moment, and stood with his elbows on the rails, gazing down at the seething water below him where the river, dashing over the dam just above the bridge and splashing down on the rocks beneath, was churned into a mass of white foam. Behind him, above

the dam, the water lay smooth and quiet; before
him, it went tearing through the narrow gorge
where whirlpool and rapid followed one another
in quick succession, until it swept around an
abrupt turn, half a mile below, raced under the
two bridges, tumbled over a second dam and then
went sliding away through the fertile meadows, on
and on until it reached the sea.

The river always had a peculiar fascination for
Jack, and he invariably chose the narrow footpath
along the edge of the upper railroad bridge by
the dam, instead of the safer and longer route of
the covered bridge below. Here he loved to linger, watching the spray dancing up and down in
the sun, or counting the eddies circling about the
rocks in mid-stream. To-day he waited there
while a long freight train went slowly by him;
then, when the bridge had ceased to throb with
the moving weight, he started to go on again,
when his eyes suddenly fell upon two little figures passing around the point of rocks, far down
the stream. Jack stared at them for a moment;
then he gave a long, low whistle.

"Scott!" he remarked comprehensively. "Those
girls must have level heads. Any slip there
would be sure death for them, with such a slant

on the rocks and that rapid below. That's Bobbie's doing; Pen never would have had pluck
enough to go down there alone. Wonder what
Uncle Jerry would say. I believe I'll go down
and look after them; I don't suppose they're in
any danger, but it makes me squirm a little."
And he hurried back to the river bank once more,
and started down the gorge.

Bobbie was the first to see him coming.

"Pen! Pen!" she called, raising her voice to
be heard above the roar of the stream. "Here
comes Jack."

"Good!" And Penelope turned a welcoming
glance up the valley to the spot where Jack could
be seen, cautiously picking his way along over the
pile of boulders in his path.

"But 'tisn't good, a bit," protested Bobbie.
"He'll make us go back home, and I wanted to
get down as far as the lower bridge. We're more
than half-way there now, and it's too bad to have
to give up, after all this."

Penelope had dropped down on a tempting
point of rock.

"I don't care so very much," she confessed a
little wearily. "We've gone about far enough
for one day, and I'd just as soon rest a little,
before we try the rest."

"I wouldn't," returned Bobbie undauntedly. "Nobody else ever did it, I 'most know, and I want to be able to tell of it. If we go home, somebody will be sure to find it out and say we mustn't do it again. Besides, I'd rather not see Jack just now."

"Why not?" asked Penelope curiously, as she took advantage of the opportunity to tie up the ribbon, fast slipping from the end of her long yellow pigtail.

"Because I don't. You see I cut his old telephone wire, just before I left the house; and he's probably after me now."

"Why, Roberta Spaulding! How did you ever dare do such a thing?" And Penelope looked up in surprise, for not even three years' intimacy with Bobbie had accustomed her friend to her sudden tempestuous outbursts.

"I wanted to," explained Bobbie, with impenitent dignity. "The boys cared a good deal more about it than they did about me, and I thought 'twas time it was stopped. But let's get out of the way before Jack gets here. It will take him ever so long, and I'd rather not see him here. He'll be cross, and it will be better for you not to hear what he says," she added crushingly.

"Where shall we go?" inquired Penelope meekly, for she never failed to be awed when Bobbie assumed that tone.

"Come round the point back here, and we'll hide somewhere," suggested Bobbie. "If he can't find us, he'll give up and go home, and then we can go on down to the bridge." And suiting the action to the word, she led the way back up the bank and took refuge behind a jutting point of rocks, where she stood looking about, in search of a suitable hiding-place. "I'll tell you," she said suddenly: "you know we saw those two great pot-holes way up there, when we went down. Let's climb up and get into them. They're 'most dry and plenty large enough to hold us, and Jack would never find us."

Climbing with the light, sure step of a young chamois, she quickly made her way up the slippery cliff to the spot, only reached by the spring floods, where the rushing waters had worn two round, deep holes in the living rock. In a gorge noted far and wide for the number and size of its pot-holes, these two had been the wonder and admiration of generations of geologists, who had marvelled that the little round stones inside could have ground away the rock to a depth of four feet

and more. No better hiding-place could have
been found, and it was but the work of a moment
for the two lithe, active girls to let themselves
down into the cool, brown hollows. There was
plenty of room for them to stand on the stones
which rose out of the stagnant, shallow pools in
the bottom; and by crouching down a little, they
were completely hidden from the sight of any one
walking along the rocks below. They stood with
their heads rising above the edges of their stony
nests, like a pair of pretty Jacks-in-the-box, talking softly to each other, until they heard Jack
scrambling over the rocks just around the point;
then they cuddled down and waited.

They could hear the boy's steps coming nearer
and nearer, till he paused on the rock below them,
so near that it seemed as if he must detect the
quick beating of their hearts. They could fancy
just how he looked, standing there with his cap on
the extreme back of his head and his hands in his
coat pockets, as he turned to gaze this way and
that, wondering where they could have vanished.
In the silence, Penelope could hear a little giggle
from Bobbie's hole. Jack, nearer the rushing
water, heard nothing. Then he went on again;
but presently he retraced his steps, and once more

took his stand below them and called their names, once, twice, three times. Even thoughtless Bobbie could hear the little note of alarm in his clear young voice; but she remained obdurately silent. Again he called them; then, turning slowly, he went back around the point and up the bank. Bobbie waited until she lost the last echo of his footsteps; then she cautiously raised her head to the surface again.

"It's all right, Pen," she said, in a low voice. "Didn't I tell you he'd never find us? Come on, now; we'll get out, and go on down to the bridge."

Penelope stood up, and clutched the edge of the rock with both hands, as she said, —

"I shan't be sorry to get out, either, for my hole was a tight fit and my foot went fast asleep. I thought he'd never go."

"He was a little bit scared," said Bobbie, laughing. "He didn't know where we were, unless we'd ridden off on a pair of broomsticks." And she too grasped the rock, preparatory to climbing out to the surface once more.

For the next five minutes, the silence was only broken by the sounds of scraping and sliding, and by little gasps of exhaustion. Then Bobbie's voice was heard again, but it was in a minor key and very plaintive.

" But I can't get out, Pen.'"

" Neither can I." And Penelope's tone was even sadder than Bobbie's.

"But we must." And Bobbie made another prolonged struggle to escape from her self imposed trap.

Pen's courage began to fail.

" It's no use, Bobbie," she said disconsolately, " I've stepped down into the water, and kicked all the patent leather off the toe of my new shoe. Shall we have to stay here always ? " And her voice died away into a sob.

" Don't be silly, Pen. Let's call Jack back again. I hate to, for he'll laugh at us forever; but we can't stay here all night. We'll call together, to make more noise."

They did call, again and again; but only the rushing water answered them as it swept on its course, mocking their cries with its hoarse murmur. Jack, who had climbed up the bank to the road and was rushing towards home as fast as his feet could carry him, was too far away to hear their voices.

" It's no use," said Bobbie valiantly, as she

rubbed away the red drops from a long scratch in her rosy palm; "but crying never did anybody any good. We must try again."

For a long half-hour they struggled on, now raising themselves for a few inches, now falling back again, now hopeful, now despondent once more. At length they stopped, exhausted, and looked at each other, then out at the yellow sunshine which was beginning to slant along the water in pale, horizontal beams.

"It's dreadful, Bobbie. What shall we ever do?" And Penelope began to cry again, this time from sheer nervousness and fatigue.

"I'm so sorry, Pen. I was the one to blame; but I never meant to get you into such a scrape," said Bobbie consolingly, for in any real trouble, she was always honorable in taking her share of the blame.

"I should think it was a scrape." And Penelope laughed hysterically through her tears. "I've scratched all the skin off my hands, and torn my jacket, and made an awful hole in my stocking. I don't 'see why we were such geese as to get in here."

"You'd better say mice," returned Bobbie, with a giggle, for even in the present crisis, her sense of fun did not desert her. "I never saw any mice in a better trap; and grandma and Uncle Jerry will eat me up, like a pair of cats, when we do get out. I wish we never had started; but, now we're here, we must make the best of it as well as we can. Jack saw us here, and if we don't go home, somebody will come to look for us before long."

Jack, meanwhile, was more alarmed by the sudden disappearance of his sister than he cared to admit, even to himself. When he had first caught sight of the two girls, they were in a most dangerous place, for the smooth, slippery rock slanted directly down into the boiling, racing stream below, and any misstep, as he had said, meant certain and instant death. What had sent the girls wandering into that particular spot, he could not imagine; but now he was far more occupied in trying to fancy what could have become of them. Except for the one nook hidden behind the point, he had not lost sight of the river bank nor of the road above, so he had been confident that they were concealed beyond the point. However, when he reached the spot, no girls were to be seen. They both were too substantial to have vanished into thin air; but how else could they have escaped him? It was like Bobbie to hide; but he could see no place for her, and, strange to say, he never thought of the pot-holes.

For an instant, a sudden sickening fear made him look down at the green water below, and brought a note of terror into his voice as he stood calling them. He waited for the answer, which did not come; then he turned away and hurried home, sure that he would find Bobbie standing on the steps and mocking at his fears. Instead, he only found the dangling wires of his telephone, and, on the hall table, the scissors left by Margaret after she had opened Danforth's sleeve. Margaret and Danforth had not yet returned; Grandma Atherton was in her room, and there was no use in frightening her, for it might be a false alarm. Still, where were the girls? His fears mounted with every moment.

Half an hour later, Gerald Atherton looked up from his writing, to see his nephew standing on the threshold of his office, his face pale and his dark eyes shining with excitement.

"Uncle Jerry, I can't find Bobbie!" he began breathlessly.

"Bobbie? Well, she isn't here, Jack."

"Yes, I know; but she's somewhere," urged Jack incoherently. "She isn't at home, and I've just been to Pen's for her; but I can't find her anywhere."

"Sit down, Jack, and get your breath." And Uncle Jerry pushed a chair towards him; but Jack was too restless to take it.

"You don't see what I mean," he went on desperately. "I'm afraid something has happened to them. The last I saw of them, they were on the rocks just beside the long rapids, and I went to tell them to look out; but when I came there, they weren't, and I hunted everywhere before I came to you, and now——"

"What? On the rocks in the gorge!" Uncle Jerry sprang to his feet. "Tell me again, Jack, whom do you mean by 'they'!"

"Bobbie and Pen," said Jack more quietly, for he was half-frightened by his uncle's sudden pallor. "They were climbing down through the gorge when I saw them from the bridge, and I went after them, for I was afraid they'd get into a scrape. Then I lost sight of them, and when I came to where I'd seen them, they weren't anywhere round. I went home and looked, and then to Pen's; but I didn't tell why I wanted them. I thought I'd better come to you."

Uncle Jerry was tossing his papers into his

desk, preparatory to closing it; then he caught up his hat, saying briefly, —

"Come with me, Jack. We'll look in the gorge again before we alarm anyone else." And he went hurrying away towards the river.

The sun was just dropping behind the hills as they crossed the bridge, scrambled down the bank to the water's edge and started on their toilsome climb over the boulders and along the shelving cliffs. Once in a while Jack spoke a word or two, as he turned to give his uncle his hand over some unusually wide crevasse; but, for the most part, they went on in silence, peering this way and that through the deepening twilight, in the vain hope of seeing the two girlish figures. As they neared the point of rocks, and saw no sign of life Jack's heart was heavy with the same old nameless dread, and Uncle Jerry's thoughts were busy with men and grappling-irons and ropes. All at once Jack stopped short.

"Listen!" he exclaimed. "What's that?"

For a moment they stood breathless. Then, above the roar of the tide, came two high-pitched cries, —

"Help! Somebody help!--Co-o-ome he-e-e-ere!"

"It's Bobbie!" And the color rushed back to

Jack's face, as he shouted, with the full power of his lungs, "All right; we're coming. Where are you!"

"In the big po-o-o-ot-ho-o-o-ole." It was Penelope's voice which replied.

"Why don't you get out?" called Jack again.

Hurrying in the direction of the cries, Jack and his uncle rounded the point of rocks, and discovered the pair of heads sticking up from their holes just as the answer from two throats came wailing back to them, —

"We can't."

It was hard-hearted of them both, surely, but the revulsion of feeling was so great, and the sight and sound were so absurd, that together the boy and the man dropped down on the rocks and burst into a roar of laughter, while the imprisoned girls before them begged and remonstrated and wept in vain. The laugh was against them; and by the time they had been fished from their slimy depths and firmly planted, shamefaced, cramped and bedraggled, on top of the rock, Jack felt he could forgive the severed telephone wire, and Uncle Jerry knew that he needed to add no word of reproof for their rashness.

CHAPTER VI.

LADDIE'S CHAMPION.

"Is there anything I can do for you, before I go over to Riverton?" asked Margaret, one November afternoon, as she came into the Wilderness where Jack sat curled up over the fire, reading and nursing a cold which had kept him housed for a day or two.

"No, I don't think there is, unless you take my head along with you and chuck it into the river," responded Jack, yawning and stretching himself. "It feels larger than an empty trunk, and not half so light. I wish you'd bring me back something to do, though. I might just as well be out, this splendid day."

"Where are Bobbie and Dan?" inquired Margaret. ·

"Bob is over at the Stoddards' and Dan's fussing around the barn with the ponies. Duke has a lame foot, and he's trying to find out where the trouble is. I say," he added, as Margaret turned

121

to the door; "if you see Ellie anywhere, send him up here. Tell him I'm dying for something to do."

"I can go round past his house, just as well," suggested Margaret kindly.

"Never mind that; 'twill take you out of your way too much. I only meant if you happened to see him; that's all."

Privately making up her mind to make a point of happening to see Jack's friend, Margaret went down-stairs and out of the house. It was one of the first warm days of Indian summer, when the haze lay soft upon the hills, throwing a silvery light over the ruddy brown oak leaves which still clung to their branches. At her feet, the river tossed and tumbled along, showing clear green spots mingled with the white foam. And at her other hand rose the mountain, sheer and straight.

"'And a very high mountain overhung the way,'" she said to herself, with a whimsical memory of Jack's struggles with his Cæsar, that morning. Then she smiled at the absurdity of associating the majestic progress of the Roman army with the quiet New England road along which she was strolling, with Laddie frisking by

her side. Jack was getting along well in his
Latin, she thought. It was only the fifteenth of
November, and he was already well on in his
year's work; Danforth, too, for that matter; only
he never made the show that Jack did, and —
The fifteenth of November!

Just a year ago that very afternoon, she had
driven up to the park with Hugh. She remembered it all so well, the little bay horse and light
wagon, the long drive through the city and up
the winding road which led to the top of the
park. Hugh had stopped the horse at the top,
and they had sat there for a long time, gazing
down upon the city with its elm-fringed streets
and smoke-capped factories, and on the sail-dotted
harbor beyond, with its long breakwater flanked
with the red lighthouse and the tall spindles,
and, far, far away, the faint blue outline of the
distant island. Even now, it was all so fresh in
her mind that she half-believed that she could
smell the faint, spicy fragrance of Hugh's inevi-
table carnation, and she could see the long shadow
thrown across the ground at the foot of the monument.

How she and Hugh had laughed at the position of one of the figures on that monument!

Hugh was in an unusually gay mood, that day.
He had just got back from a long business trip,
and was as happy as a boy in the fine weather, and
the drive, and the pleasure of seeing her again.
Why —

Turning suddenly, Margaret called to Laddie
who was investigating a neighboring hen-house,
to the manifest discomfort of its inmates. There
was a little strained note of irritation in her voice,
and Laddie thought it best to obey promptly,
while his mistress drew a long, slow breath, shut
her teeth hard together and quickened her pace
toward the bridge.

Once across the river, she turned aside from her
regular route and went up the long, hilly street
leading to the Piersons'. Mrs. Pierson herself
met her at the door, and insisted upon her coming
in for a little call.

"I'm so sorry that Ellie isn't at home," she said,
as she led the way into her pleasant parlor. "I
hope Jack isn't going to be ill."

"Oh, no; it is really nothing but a cold," Margaret replied, as she sat down. "He was out in
the rain all last Saturday morning, and then, boy-
fashion, he kept on his wet shoes through the
afternoon. Sunday and yesterday he felt rather

forlorn; but to-day he's a good deal better, and had his regular lessons again. Mrs. Atherton thought he'd better not go out for a day or two longer, and he looked so lonely that I said I would stop here and ask Ellie to go over to see him for an hour."

"I think Ellsworth is over at the Stoddards'," said his mother, with a little laugh. "He sat here doing his examples for to-morrow morning, too busy even to let me speak to him, till all at once he saw Bobbie going home with Penelope. Then he remembered that I had spoken of wanting to send a message to Mrs. Stoddard, and was off like a shot."

Margaret laughed too.

"Such devotion ought to be rewarded," she said. "I really can't tell whether Bobbie is just playing, or whether she really is so unconscious of Ellie's adoration for her. They have certainly begun at a most tender age."

"What can you do?" asked Mrs. Pierson helplessly. "Anything that I can say would only make it worse, for it would seem as if we regarded it as a serious affair, and they would pose as a pair of persecuted lovers. It's contrary to all my ideas; but I am hoping that, if we don't take any notice of it, and if Bobbie goes on snubbing him as vigorously as she has done, Ellie's love-affair will die a natural death. It is funny, though, in spite of everything; and I have to laugh, even when I long to put him to bed without his supper, as a gentle reminder that he is nothing but an infant."

"Poor little fellow, he is so in earnest and has so little idea of his own comicality!" And Margaret smiled, as she recalled certain scenes between the two children. "My only fear is that Bobbie will catch the disease from him, and I shudder to think of the teasing they would have to endure from Jack and Danforth, for they neither of them are of a particularly sentimental turn of mind, and they regard girls as an unmitigated bore."

"I wish Ellie did," said his mother fervently. "But I wonder why it is, Miss Davis, that our own love-affairs are always so tragic, and other people's so comic. It's as true with children as it is with grown people." She paused for a moment; then she went on, with an utter change of subject, "I am very much delighted to-day over a bit of family news, and while it can't interest you, I am going to be egotistic enough to tell you about it.

You know, I suppose, that there has been some trouble about putting in our new electric road; and the president of the company has sent off the head electrician and all his men. I don't know enough about it to understand the justice of the matter; but what interests me is that my favorite cousin has just been put in chârge of the work."

"How delightful for you!" And Margaret's voice showed a sympathetic pleasure which her hostess was quick to feel.

"Yes, I am very happy over it, for Hugh is a dear fellow, one of those intimate cousins who seem almost like brothers."

"And when will he come?" asked Margaret, conscious that her heart gave a quick throb, at the unexpected coincidence of names.

"Very soon, for he is to finish putting in the road, and to stay here for a year, as managing electrician. I had hoped he would make his home with us; but he was here a day or two ago, and he said that, for the present at least, he must be farther down town, within reach of the power-house."

"But you will see him so often."

"I know that, and I am delighted to have so much. Please tell Mr. Atherton — the younger

one, I mean — that I shall want him to dine here
soon, to meet Mr. Thornton.   He will be here the
first of next week.   But tell me, Miss Davis," she
asked, pausing suddenly; "aren't you working too
hard with your pupils?   It seems to me that you're
not looking quite as well as you did when you first
came up here.   I didn't notice it when you came
in, after being out in the air."   And Mrs. Pierson
put on her eye-glasses, and stared at Margaret's
white face with a close scrutiny which was almost
impossible to bear.

With a strong effort, Margaret rallied.

"I'm quite well," she said, with a forced laugh.
"Your hill air is agreeing with me splendidly; I
have a most remarkable appetite, and I sleep like
a dormouse.   I've only a little headache to-day,"
she added, seeking refuge in woman's one excuse for every unexplained mood and tense of her
being.

"I'm glad if that is all," said the older woman
kindly, as Margaret rose to go.   "I thought you
looked a little tired.   Gerald has told me how
much time you are giving to those children, and I
never see Jack without his quoting Miss Davis in
some connection or other.   Must you go?   Come
again."

Once out in the street again, Margaret walked rapidly onward, without knowing nor caring in which direction she turned. She only felt the need of prompt physical action, until she could tire herself out and grow quiet enough to allow herself to think connectedly. She told herself over and over again that there was no possibility that her old friend and Mrs. Pierson's cousin were one and the same person. And yet, it did seem strange that there should be two men named Hugh Thornton, and occupied in the same professional work. And if it should really be her friend, what then? Living so far out of Riverton, she might not see him at all. Moreover, she was not at all sure that she wished to see him, unless he would give her the opportunity to explain the misunderstanding which had come up between them. Even then, he might not be of the same mind that he was eight months ago.

"It's too bad!" she said to herself forlornly. "I was just learning to forget all about it, and now it is worse than ever. What's the use of trying?" The last words came with a little half-suppressed sob; but fortunately there was no one to hear it but Laddie, who showed his sympathy by abandoning the pursuit of an inoffensive kitten and coming to frisk about his mistress, leaving the prints of his dusty toes all over the front of her gown.

"Do you remember him, Laddie?" Margaret asked half-involuntarily. "Listen, Laddie; where's Mr. Thornton?"

For one short instant, Laddie stood still, with his ears cocked forward and his face turned inquiringly up toward his mistress, who was watching the workings of his canine mind.

"Go find him, Laddie," she added, after a moment.

And Laddie gave one wild bark of perfect comprehension, as he dashed away up the street, not in search of his old friend, but in joyous pursuit of the kitten who had taken advantage of the temporary cessation of hostilities, to descend from the tree to which her foe had driven her.

Unconsciously Margaret had taken the same direction that she and Danforth had done, a month before; and now, finding herself so near the spot where they had sat and rested, she walked on again until she reached the self-same rock. There she dropped down and, resting her elbows on her knees and her chin in her hands, she sat for a long time, gazing out across the little basin with dreamy, sad, unseeing eyes, while Laddie, at last reading something of her mood, sat down by her side and rubbed his cold nose against her cheek.

Half an hour later, she was walking toward home again, with her usual quick, firm step, although her cheeks were a little pale and her eyes suspiciously bright. She was just passing through one of the small streets at the lower end of the city, not far from the factories which filled the point between the two rivers, and Laddie, all his antics exhausted, was trudging soberly by her side, when Margaret gave a sudden shriek of terror.

Rushing out from a little yard close by, a white bulldog which to Margaret's excited imagination looked as large and ferocious as a lion, had pounced upon the unsuspecting Laddie who, all unused to this kind of an attack, had abjectly rolled over on his back and helplessly extended his four legs in the air, in a mute appeal for assistance. His adversary, not slow to see his advantage and to follow it up, had seized him by the throat in the unrelaxing hold of the bulldog kind; and for the next few moments, there followed the mingled growls of anger and yelps of pain, so terrible even to the impartial observer, so doubly terrible where one's own dog is the under one in the fight. Margaret, unusually excitable after her call and her lonely half-hour on the rock, and seriously alarmed for her pet, ran frantically forward for a few steps, ran back again; then, bursting into tears as a prolonged howl from Laddie, and an angry snarl from the other dog showed but too well how the contest must end, she rushed forward again and seized Laddie by his fluffy golden tail, in a vain attempt to free him from the iron grip upon his throat.

"Let 'em alone! You'll get bit; and he's my dog, so I'll see fair play," shouted a voice in her ear.

Turning, she saw a short, stout man in shirt-sleeves and slippers, whose face alone might have told the story of his relationship to the white dog.

"Do help me!" she begged.

The man laughed impudently.

"What for? Let 'em fight it out. You didn't have to come by here, you know. I aint·a-goin' to touch my dog, and you'd better let yours alone. That dog of mine is a daisy."

Terrified at the face and words of the stranger, Margaret fled to a little distance; then, as she saw her pet being demolished before her very eyes, she lost all self-control. Regardless of the crowd rapidly gathering in the street, she sobbed aloud while she hopped up and down on the pavement, and incoherently informed an elderly Irishwoman standing near, that Laddie was her dearest friend and that some one must save him.

Poor Laddie's struggles were growing faint and fainter, and Margaret had turned away that she might not see the end, when a carriage came in sight, around a corner a little way up the street. As it drew nearer, Margaret looked up; then, recognizing the pale, calm face and great dark eyes of the driver, and realizing that here was a friend at last, she dashed out into the middle of the street, crying, —

"Mr. Huntington, save my dog!"

Under some circumstances, it might have been a dramatic situation; but to call upon a minister of a most unworldly temperament and an undeniably delicate physique to interfere in a serious dog-fight, would have presented certain incongruities to Margaret's mind in her calmer moments. However, no such idea occurred to Mr. Huntington, who reined in his horse just as that astonished animal was about to step on the excited, tearful young woman in his path, and exclaimed in amazement, —

"Miss Davis! Is it possible?"

"Save Laddie!" she begged again. "He's my own dog, and I do love him so. Do save him! Help me!"

Without stopping for a word, Mr. Huntington passed the reins to his companion, leaped to the ground, whip in hand, and walked straight to the scene of action. There is no record that any of King Arthur's knights ever championed the cause of a victim of a dog-fight; but no knight of the Round Table ever showed a greater spirit of chivalry than did the quiet little minister, when he replied to the threats of the angry owner of the dog, with the simple word, —

"This lady has asked me to help her, and I shall do so."

Then came an exciting interval while Mr. Huntington remorselessly battered the dog's head with the heavy handle of his whip, and the dog's irate master vainly shook his fists and vowed vengeance. Margaret, meanwhile, had squeezed herself between the wheels of the carriage, and buried her head in the lap of Mr. Huntington's elderly housekeeper, as she sobbed forth the minutest details of Laddie's pedigree and accomplishments. At last it was ended, and Margaret,

alarmed at the sudden silence, looked up to see
Mr. Huntington drawn to his fullest height and
delivering a few plain truths to the owner of the
bulldog, who was examining the head of his favorite with apparent anxiety. Then the minister
turned on his heel and came back to the carriage,
with Laddie limping along beside him. Forgetful
of all else, Margaret dropped down on her knees
by the dog, and caught his yellow head in her
arms. Then she seemed to come to herself, and
she rose again, with a blush of shame, as she realized her behavior of the last fifteen minutes.

"Oh, Mr. Huntington, I'm so grateful!" she
said, while the deep color came up over her cheeks
and brow. "Please don't think me too great a
baby; but it was all so dreadful, and if it hadn't
been for you, Laddie would have been killed.
How can I thank you?"

"It was nothing," answered the young man
kindly; "I am only too glad that we chanced to
be passing. We had been out to see some people
across the river, and we took this way home because it was late and we were in a hurry. But I
hope that Laddie will be all right now," he added
cheerfully. "He was more frightened than hurt."

"But I hate to have him have such nervous

shocks," said Margaret, with a quick rush of tears which prevented her seeing the little involuntary smile on Mr. Huntington's lips.

"I am much more afraid that you will be the worse for the shock," he said gravely. "But, at least, you must ride home with us. There isn't much room, and I would walk; but I think you are in no condition to drive this frisky horse."

"I can't leave Laddie," protested Margaret. "He is too lame to run and keep up with us, and I dare not leave him. The other dog might come back." And she glanced apprehensively over her shoulder.

Mr. Huntington hesitated. He saw that she was completely unstrung and nervous from the sudden fright, and that she was in no condition to take the long walk home in the gathering twilight. On the other hand, his carriage was small and was already well-filled, with only himself and his plump old housekeeper, together with several pails and baskets, emptied in the course of his pastoral calls. He dared not trust either woman to drive the gay little horse he was using, that afternoon, nor could he well ask his aged companion to give up her place to an invalid collie.

"Perhaps," he suggested at length, "perhaps, if we pack ourselves in very closely, we can all ride."

"Oh, I couldn't allow that; let me walk home with Laddie. I'm not afraid,— at least, not very," said Margaret falteringly.

"I really dislike to leave you in this part of the town, so late and alone," he answered, with a gentle insistence. "I think we can manage very well, if you will forgive a little crowding. Come." And stretching out his hand, he helped Margaret to climb into the carriage. Then, seizing Laddie in his arms, he put him on the floor, between the baskets, stepped in after him and, all together, they started for home, with Margaret sitting in the housekeeper's lap and embracing a vast tin pail, while Mr. Huntington's foot and Laddie's tail dangled out at the right side of the narrow little carriage.

CHAPTER VII.

LADDIE STUDIES THEOLOGY.

IF Margaret had feared that her manner, at
dinner that night, might betray any of the agitation caused by her call on Mrs. Pierson, she had
reason to be grateful to Laddie for saving her
from all comments. In their excitement over
her account of the contest and her rescue, the
family neglected to give any but a passing attention to Margaret, and attributed her pale face to
the result of the fright. But after Laddie's
wounds were dressed, and he was put to bed in
a corner of Margaret's own room, when the family
finally gathered about the table, Margaret told
over again the whole story of the fight, sparing
herself in no way, but dwelling with a mischievous
frankness of detail upon her frantic appeal to Mr.
Huntington, his valiant coming to her aid, and his
final benevolence in packing them both into his
little carriage and bringing them home.

"'Twas dreadfully ignominious," she confessed,

as soon as she could make herself heard above the shouts of the boys. "I had always supposed that I should be a model of calmness in an emergency. I have a dim idea that I cried out loud, and I know that I informed Mr. Huntington that Laddie was my only friend on earth, but that he might have him, to pay for saving him. What must the man think of me?"

"When he drove up to the house, he looked as if he thought you took up a good deal of room," said Jack, laughing again at the recollection. "The poor man was half out of the carriage, and Laddie looked ready to tumble out, too, perched up on top of that basket. I hope you had a pleasant ride."

A week later, Mr. Huntington called to inquire for the invalid and the invalid's mistress. Margaret, by that time, had fully recovered from the shock and excitement, and she apologized so merrily for her misbehavior that Mr. Huntington gained the impression that it was rather an accomplishment than otherwise for a young woman to lose her self-control under trying circumstances, and demand the protection of a comparative stranger. Then Laddie was brought in to make friends with his preserver, who, influenced as much by Laddie's mistress as by Laddie himself, petted the dog in a way which he repented later, for Laddie had an excellent memory and rarely forgot a friend or a foe.

It would be hard to say just what caused the luckless combination of circumstances which took place, the next Sunday morning. Margaret had announced her intention of staying at home from church with Grandma Atherton, who was not feeling quite well, so the three children had gone away with their uncle and grandfather, leaving the house in perfect quiet.

Much as Margaret enjoyed the ministrations of Mr. Huntington, who was always at ease and at his best in his desk, she found the Sunday-morning hour spent in church rather a trying one, owing to the eccentricities of Grandpa Atherton. On account of his extreme deafness, the family occupied one of the front pews of the large church, where, Sunday after Sunday, Grandpa Atherton took his place and followed the opening services of the day with profound interest. Then, as soon as Mr. Huntington, sermon in hand, advanced to the desk, Margaret knew that the time had come when she must use all her self-control to keep from laughing. During the early part of the

sermon, Grandpa Atherton sat with strained attention and uplifted trumpet, to catch the words which
fell from the lips of the young clergyman, nodding
violently from time to time, in vigorous approval
of his sentiments. This was bad enough for any
one not used to his peculiarities; but unfortunately
Grandpa Atherton did not stop here. On the
contrary, as soon as the minister let fall some
opinion with which the old man did not quite
agree, or when Grandpa Atherton thought that he
had listened long enough and it was time for the
sermon to be ended, he had a fashion of suddenly
dropping his trumpet, whirling around in his pew-
corner until he could fix his eyes far back on the
side wall of the church, and sitting there in an
attitude of stolid unconcern most disheartening to
his youthful spiritual adviser.

It had taken the children a long time to get
used to the demonstrations of their grandfather,
and even now Uncle Jerry found it necessary to
put Jack at the extreme inner end of the pew,
and to have Bobbie sit at his other side, in order
to prevent an explosion. But for Margaret, who
lost her self-control far too easily, there was no
such way of escape. She found herself watching
for the dreaded moment with such anxiety lest she

should disgrace herself, that when it really did come, she was farther than ever from being able to meet it with calmness. On this account, she made the most of every excuse to absent herself from church, whenever Grandpa Atherton was going to be present. Moreover, since her late adventure with Mr. Huntington, she felt that it would be more than usually difficult to sit un-moved under his preaching, for they both were conscious of an almost irresistible desire to laugh outright, whenever they came face to face.

This particular morning was one of those bright, breezy days which seem to arouse a spirit of hilar-ity in everything which is young and alive. While she was dressing, Margaret had seen Danforth racing up and down the lawn with Laddie who, in spite of an ugly wound just back of his yellow ruff, had quite recovered his spirits, and who was already nearly as fond of the boy as he was of his mistress. Later, she had stood in the door, watch-ing them as they set off for church, and laughing at the antics of Jack and Bobbie who brought up the rear of the little procession. Fortunately for her peace of mind, she was unable to see what followed.

The opening invocation and anthem were ended,

and Mr. Huntington had just risen to read the scripture lesson, when there was heard a little creak from the light, swinging door at the entrance, followed by a soft *pad*, *pad*, coming up the aisle. A moment later, Grandpa Atherton was aroused from his devotions by a violent push against his knee. As he involuntarily moved a little to make room for the supposed stranger, Laddie wriggled past him into the pew, wagging his tail in rapturous welcome. He sniffed at each member of the family in turn and, mounting the seat by Danforth's side, he pressed his cold nose against the boy's neck, with a suddenness which called forth a half-stifled exclamation from Danforth and a giggle from Jack. Then, as the dog settled down upon the cushion, his wandering attention was caught by the sound of Mr. Huntington's voice, and he cocked up his ears in glad recognition. Here was surely a friend, and one who had been good to him, reasoned Laddie, and he had neglected to express his joy at the unexpected meeting. Before Danforth could divine his intention and lay a restraining hand upon his collar, Laddie had jumped from his seat, pushed his way out into the aisle again, and gone rushing forward to the desk, swinging his tail round and round, in a series of circles symbolic of his complete happiness in once again beholding his preserver.

In the midst of his reading, Mr. Huntington had been following the dog's performances, with amused eyes; but he was not prepared for the greeting which followed, and he tottered in his place as Laddie, rising on his hind legs, plunged forward upon him, resting his paws on the ministerial arm, and stretching up to caress the ministerial cheek with fervor. It was only the work of a moment; then, as the dog dropped back again, Mr. Huntington gave a sigh of relief, and breathed up a voiceless petition that Laddie might be moved to go away. Nothing, however, was further from Laddie's mind. His new position at his friend's side was quite to his liking. In spite of Danforth's suppressed calls and snapping of his fingers, Laddie sat immovable beside the desk, with his soft yellow ears turned expressively forward and his tongue lolling out of his mouth, as if in perfect derision at his temporary master, while he turned now and again to glance up at Mr. Huntington with a deprecating yawn, which was even more trying to the young clergyman than were the demonstrations of Grandpa Atherton.

Already there were signs of an outbreak on the part of the younger members of the congregation, and Uncle Jerry was just bending over to tell Danforth to go forward and remove the dog by force, when the final catastrophe occurred. During some moments, Mr. Huntington's increasing nervousness had been evident to all, for the color in his cheeks had grown bright, and again and again his finger had sought his unsteady lip. At length, in his confusion, he made a little hasty gesture which knocked down from the desk his carefully-written sermon.

Now at home Laddie's chief amusement had consisted in what Mollie called " reading the paper"; and she never wearied of giving him a loosely-folded newspaper, and watching him while he wildly flapped it to and fro, to enjoy its rattle, or plowed it along the floor, worrying it as he would have done a sleepy kitten. But since he had come to live at the Athertons', no papers had been offered for his perusal, and Laddie's puppy soul was longing for an old-time frolic. Here and now was his chance, and he determined to make the most of it. Darting forward, he caught up the loose sheets of manuscript and went galloping across the platform, growling and shaking his head

with a violence that sent bits of paper flying far
to the left and right, while he flirted his tail in
contemptuous defiance of his pursuant who dodged
about the desk, vainly seeking to catch him. The
unsanctified game of tag lasted for some moments;
but the limits of the platform were too narrow and
Laddie felt that he needed a wider field; so,
leaping down to the floor and scurrying past the
horrified occupants of the Atherton pew, he went
plunging down the aisle, with his nose, sermon
and all, rooting along on the carpet and leaving
behind him a trail strongly suggestive of hare and
hounds. Then the swinging doors creaked and
clattered as he dashed through them, and the
astonished congregation could only join their
pastor in an ill-suppressed laugh, while Laddie
went capering away toward home, bearing in his
mouth their weekly portion of exhortation and
encouragement for their spiritual needs.

From her seat by the front window, Margaret
saw him come leisurely strolling up the hill with
a solemn air of preoccupation which was in
perfect harmony with the day, while from his
mouth there dangled a few dingy shreds of paper.
Experience had taught her, that, with Laddie, this
subdued mood was always an infallible sign that

he had been in mischief, so she hastily dropped her book, and went out on the steps to investigate. At sight of his mistress, Laddie paused and abstractedly contemplated the fleecy white clouds above his head; then, seeing that there was no way of escape, he came forward and deposited his trophy at Margaret's feet. Margaret looked at the soiled, crumpled paper before her, and picked it up gingerly; the next moment she sank down on the step, with a little groan of mortification. She had easily recognized the writing as that of Mr. Huntington, and on the scrap of paper in her hand, she read the words, —

"And finally, my brethren, the apostle tells us that we ought to be strong and steadfast in the pursuit of the enemy. But who is the enemy, and how shall we overtake him?"

If it had been difficult for Margaret to face Mr. Huntington after her excited appeal for his help, it was doubly so now, since Laddie's latest escapade; and not even the minister's courteous answer to her note of apology could entirely remove her feeling that her pet had brought everlasting disgrace upon her head. However, within a few days Margaret forgot all else, in her anxiety about the dog who suddenly began to droop in an

inexplicable way and grew rapidly weaker, in
spite of the constant attentions of his mistress
and Danforth. At length, yielding to his nephew's
entreaties, Uncle Jerry sent up a doctor to look
at the invalid, and, after a careful examination,
Laddie was pronounced to be suffering from the
effects of his still unhealed wound.

"The best thing for him," said the doctor, just
as he was going away from the house; "the best
thing for him would be to take him down to the
river, some warm morning, and let him have a
good bath. The more water he has, the better
for him, provided he doesn't take cold."

Accordingly, on the next clear day Danforth
started off to give Laddie his prescribed bath in
a little, still cove in the river bank, not far above
the dam. Jack and Bobbie stood looking after
them as they walked away down the hill, with
Laddie, too weak for any puppy pranks, trudging
along dejectedly at the end of his lead, and Danforth carrying a pair of tall rubber boots tied
together and slung over his shoulder, so that, if
need be, he could encourage Laddie by wading
into the water ahead of him. It had been perfectly characteristic of the three children that,
while Jack and Bobbie had been loud in their

expressions of pity for the dog, and anxious that he should have the best of care, Danforth had been the one to come to Margaret's help, and offer to go with him upon the somewhat disagreeable errand. In fact, Margaret had soon discovered that it always seemed so much easier for Danforth to do the unpleasant things, that his brother and sister usually stood aside and allowed him to take the lead.

Three quarters of an hour later, Grandma Atherton came hurrying into the library where Margaret was helping Jack to stumble through the first page of the Anabasis. Her face was pale, and her dainty lace cap was pushed slightly to one side, an evidence of great excitement in the precise little woman.

"Oh, Miss Davis!" she began, as soon as she reached the threshold; "there's a man coming up the hill, a strange man with Danforth's boots in his hand. Can't you come and speak to him? I know something terrible has happened, and I can't listen to it. Do come quick!"

For the past two or three weeks, Grandma Atherton had not been quite well, and this was doubtless the cause of the unreasoning alarm which had broken down her usual calmness.

Without stopping to convince her that, if anything very serious had occurred, the man would have brought home, not Danforth's boots, but Danforth himself, Margaret hurried out to the porch. With the volubility of his race, the man hailed her, the moment she appeared.

"Do these boots belong to the b'y as lives here, Miss?" he asked, waving his burden in explanation of his words. "'Cause, if they does, I'm to say that the dog's took sick, in the road by the bridge, and he wants the man to come and help get him home."

"Is the dog worse?" inquired Margaret anxiously.

"'Deed an' he is; he's most dead," was the encouraging answer. "The boss and me found 'em together by the side of the road, the dog just coming out of a fit, and the b'y's arrm round his neck, and him cryin' like a girl. He's got sand in him, though," the man added admiringly. "We told him 'twasn't any use, and he might as well let the dog lie there and die; but he stuck to it he'd stay, so the boss told me to come up here and leave word about it."

Margaret heard no more, for she hurried away to the barn in search of the coachman, whom she

sent to the rescue, with a wheelbarrow to serve
as an ambulance.   Then she went back to the
house to reassure Grandma Atherton, and to
wander restlessly from window to window, watching to see 'Laddie brought home to her, still and
lifeless.   They came in sight at last, Danforth
leading the way, followed by the man trundling
the wheelbarrow; and as she beheld them, Margaret felt tempted to rub her eyes, to make sure
that she saw clearly.   Bolt upright in his novel
chariot sat Laddie, smiling broadly and evidently
enjoying his ride to the utmost, while the sand in
his full ruff and the tangled hair on his back were
all the traces left that he had just been passing
through the crisis of his illness, and was now on
the way to recovery.   The dog himself was in a
much better condition than poor Danforth, who
came dragging himself wearily up the hill, looking
tired and dejected.   As soon as she could free herself from Laddie's exuberant caresses, Margaret
went forward and took the boy's hand in hers.

"They told me he was going to die," he said
simply; "but I wasn't going to leave him till you
came."

Later, in the midst of the recital of his adventures, Danforth broke off abruptly, saying, —

"But wasn't it funny about the man, Miss Davis?"

"What man?" she asked.

"The one that sent the Irishman up here. I believe he thought I'd stolen the dog.' You see, he came along when I was sitting on the grass beside the road, and he asked what was the matter. I told him, and be bent down to look at Laddie; then, all at once, he turned and stared hard at me. I didn't know what to make of it at first, till he began feeling around in Laddie's ruff for a collar. Then he asked if the dog belonged to me, and I said yes, — at least that he lived at our house. I didn't mean to lie about it; but he acted so queer that I didn't know what to say. He looked him all over again, and I heard him mumbling something to himself about having been sure 'twas the same dog."

Margaret rose abruptly and walked to the window, where she stood looking out, while the boy went on, —

"He told me that he thought the worst was over, and Laddie might be better again soon, and he sent his man up here for me. He was as kind as he could be, if it hadn't been for his acting so funny about my having the dog. He said he was at church last Sunday, and he asked if this wasn't the same collie that stole the minister's sermon," added Danforth, with an irrepressible giggle.

"What sort of a looking man was he?" asked Margaret slowly, without turning her face from the window.

"A good-looking one; not handsome a bit, but sort of splendid, somehow," answered Danforth promptly. "He was a gentleman and not so very old, with dark hair and a little brown mustache. I remember noticing a little red and white button in his coat, when his overcoat slipped sideways once. 'Twasn't anybody I ever saw before, and I know almost everybody here."

"I don't see what business 'twas of his, whose dog Laddie is," said Jack resentfully. "Good for you, Dan, for not letting on that he wasn't yours! You'd better look out for Laddie, Miss Davis, for a while. Most likely the man's a sneak-thief, dressed up as a gentleman."

But Margaret made no reply. She had silently left the room.

CHAPTER VIII.

IN THE FIRELIGHT.

To enter the drawing-room at the Atherton house was to feel that one had suddenly stepped out of this over-decorated end of the nineteenth century, and into an age when be-ribboned chairs and meaningless bric-a-brao were alike unknown. It was the room which old Captain Atherton had prepared for his bride, and except for a grand piano at one end of the long room, and the little tokens of every-day use which lay scattered about on chairs and tables, the place was left just as it had been on the day it was completed.

Above the panelled wainscoting, the walls were covered with a priceless paper, showing a Venetian landscape. Here a gondola floated down a wide canal before a row of marble buildings; there the Bridge of Sighs spanned the stream, and there again a group of gorgeously-dressed women chatted idly upon the steps of a lofty palace. At one side of the fireplace, some blooming maidens and their wasp-waisted swains were having a picnic, under the trees on an island; on the other, a vicious-looking goat was nipping the grass by the roadside. It was evident that either the paper had been made for the room, or the room had been designed with reference to the paper, since each picture fitted its own particular space between door and window, while the whole effect of the four walls was as complete and harmonious as any modern cyclorama. Arranged in each corner, with the old-time love of symmetry, was a marble bust of rare workmanship; and scattered about the room was an array of spindle-legged chairs, claw-footed tables and dainty footstools, enough to dazzle the eye and satisfy the longings of the most rapacious of collectors.

Early one evening, a week or two before Christmas, Margaret was sitting by the drawing-room fire. Except for Laddie who, fully recovered from his recent illness, was snoring on the floor at her feet, she was quite alone, for Grandpa and Grandma Atherton were in the library with their son, and the children were up in the Wilderness, busy with their preparations for the coming Christmas. Margaret was feeling a little tired, that night. The lessons had gone hard in the morning, for Bobbie had been in one of her perverse moods, and would neither work herself nor let the boys work, until her tutor had spoken to her more sharply than she had ever done before. Now Margaret was wondering whether she had been too severe, and half reproaching herself for her own lack of patience; but Bobbie's pranks and the boys' idleness' had driven her nearly distracted. Their work must be done, and done before one o'clock; and what else could she do? Still, she regretted her reproof almost before it was uttered. No true lover of children ever gives them even the most needed rebuke, without suffering from it much more than they do.

She picked up her book again to go on with her reading. It was a series of light essays, a curious mingling of fun and earnest, which Gerald had brought home, a few days before; and Margaret had been hastily glancing through it, that evening. But the blue flame dancing lazily above the wood on the andirons, proved more attractive than the book, and Margaret dropped the little volume into her lap, and fell to musing again. It was almost Christmas, she thought, and in a few days more she would see the dear home faces again. All in all, her experiment was proving a success. For the past three months she had been very happy; and the children, in spite of the naughtiness of the morning, were children quite after her own heart, simple, natural and, best of all, alive. The family, too, was a most delightful one, so free from all false ambition and social sham, but with an atmosphere of reality and genuineness which formed a refreshing change from the social struggles of too many of the people whom she met. She had made a few pleasant acquaintances in Riverton, and she almost regretted that her promised winter of freedom was nearly half ended.

Fate had been kind to her, very kind, if only it had not sent Hugh to be quite so near her. She had heard of him repeatedly, of his efficient work on the electric road, of his genial manner in meeting new friends. She rarely heard of him in society, however, and she wondered a little at that, when he used to be so gay, and so fond of a variety of interests to keep him occupied outside of business hours. She had not met him at all; but that was scarcely strange since she lived so very quietly, and only went out occasionally, at the invitation of some of the Athertons' intimate friends. She marvelled at herself, that she never wearied of this life which would have seemed so monot-

onous to her, only a year ago. Now she enjoyed it, and she found that her one absorbing
interest lay in the children and their doings. Was
her life narrowing, she asked herself.

Then, by an involuntary change of thought, she
went back to what Grandma Atherton had been
telling her, that morning, about Mr. Huntington.
She regretted now her amusement at his shabby
coats and his various makeshifts to keep himself
dressed properly for his calling; for she had heard
the story of his life, the old familiar story of the
father living beyond his income, and dying just
as the son was completing his studies, to leave
that son burdened with his debts and with the
support of his mother. Little by little, by eking
out his small salary with tutoring and doing hack
work on an insignificant magazine, the debts were
being paid, and his mother was able to keep her
old home. No wonder that the son looked pale
and shabby; but, after all, what a glorious life to
live, a life whose only luxury lay in hard work
done for the sake of conscience, and in countless
little kindnesses to his fellow-men who were worse
off than himself! But even the denial and the
drudgery brought their own blessing, Margaret
thought to herself as she remembered the man's

face and manner. No one would ever have called Mr. Huntington an unhappy man; and his life among people spent in doing good, in extending the cheery word and the helping hand to all whom he met, was bringing him in a rich harvest of love. The very children in the streets used to stop him for a few words; and Margaret smiled as she remembered how she had seen a little urchin, one day, stretching up to offer Mr. Huntington a bite of his rosy-cheeked apple, and how pleasantly the young minister had bent down and tasted the fruit, though he knew that he was in the middle of a crowded street.

"I used to think that I should like to marry," he had told Grandma Atherton, with unconscious pathos; "but now I know that it is impossible, at least, as long as my mother lives."

Was it so with everybody, she wondered. Then she roused herself with a little impatient shake, and looked at her watch. Half past eight! She had been dreaming there by the fire for an hour. How disgraceful for an active, energetic young woman, living in the end of the nineteenth century, to waste her time in any such fashion! She rose, and walked restlessly up and down the room; then, obeying some sudden impulse, she sat down at the piano and began to sing. Three minutes later, Jack appeared on the threshold.

"I say," he remarked so suddenly that Margaret gave a little start of surprise; "why didn't you say so before?"

"Say what?" she answered, as she dropped her hands from the keys and turned to face him.

"Say you could sing, of course," responded Jack, coming forward to her side.

"I can't, much," she said, laughing at his aggrieved tone. "I've taken lessons for the last two or three years; but I haven't any especial talent for it. Besides, I thought you said you hated music."

"So I do, Bobbie's everlasting scales and that rubbish," he answered frankly. "Yours isn't like that. Go ahead and sing some more; I like it."

Margaret sat for a moment, silently running over her small repertoire. Her teacher had been a man of strictly classical tastes, and his selections for her voice were scarcely of a nature to interest a boy like Jack. At last she drifted into a little French love song, to which her young auditor listened in silence.

"Don't you know something a little more cheerful than that?" he demanded, as soon as the last note had died away. "That gives me the blues, it's so doleful."

Margaret laughed outright. Evidently Jack had not a sentimental soul.

"How will this go?" she asked, as she broke into the prelude of a rollicking German student song which Hugh had taught her.

She sang the song through to the last of its many verses, throwing herself into it with an abandonment which made her quite unconscious that Uncle Jerry was softly opening the doors between the library and drawing-room. At the end, she was saluted with a double burst of applause, for Danforth had followed his brother into the room, and stood leaning against the mantel.

"That's just fine," said Jack approvingly. "Give us another like it."

"I'm afraid that I don't know any more," she said, as she rose and came forward to join the boys by the fire. "I have a whole book of those student songs at home, though, and if you wish, I'll bring it up here, when I come back after the holidays."

"Why, are you going home for Christmas?" And Danforth looked up at her, with disappointment written on every line of his face.

"Didn't you know it? I supposed that it was all understood, long ago," she answered, with a keen sense of pleasure at the boy's tone of regret.

"No; I thought of course you'd be here," he said. "'Twon't be half so much fun without you; and we had our plans all made —"

"Shut up, Dan!" said his brother so warningly that Danforth's color came, and he relapsed into silence again.

"I am so glad, if you are going to miss me," said Margaret. "But I shall leave Laddie to represent me, and it will be for only two weeks; that isn't very long."

"Well, if you're through singing," said Jack restlessly, "I'll go back and help Bob with her pastry. She and Pen have used more than a barrel of mucilage, this Christmas, and now Bobbie has taken to paste. She says it's easier than 'tis to sew things; she'll be pasting together her clothes, yet." And he departed, whistling " Danny Deever " at the top of his lungs.

There was silence for a moment after he had gone; then, as Margaret dropped into a chair and looked up at Danforth who was still leaning against the mantel, with his foot resting on one of the andirons, she said interrogatively, —

"Well, Dan?"

"I was trying to count up how long 'twas since you came here," he answered. "It seems kind of long and kind of short, you know."

"No; I don't think I do know exactly," she replied, laughing at his explanatory tone.

"Why, it doesn't seem but a few days since you came, and yet I feel as if you'd always lived here, for you fit in, somehow. Only you aren't a bit of a teacher."

"Thank you, Dan," she responded gravely.

"No; I don't mean that." And Danforth blushed at his own stupidity. "But you truly aren't like any other; they're mostly poky and cross. Don't you know what I mean?" he added despairingly. "I haven't said it at all as I started to; but there is a difference. You aren't schoolma'amish, like the others."

"Perhaps because I never was a schoolma'am before this," suggested Margaret laughing. "I'm so glad if I'm not, Dan, for it proves that one can teach without being too much demoralized; and I've heard ever so many people say that they could always tell a teacher by her voice and manner."

"You mostly can," said Danforth reflectively;

"only you aren't like the usual run of them. It's fun to work with you, somehow; you make it so much easier than Duffy did."

"You certainly are getting along well," said Margaret thoughtfully. "At this rate you and Jack will easily be ready for college a year from this fall."

"And then you'll go away?"

For her only answer, Margaret put out her hand, and drew the boy down into a low chair by her side.

"You'll spoil me, Dan, and make me unfit to live with, if you talk like that," she said, after a moment. "You know I only came here for a year anyway; and besides, when you are in college, you'll be right where I can see you often."

"But you'll stay till we're ready to enter?" urged Danforth eagerly.

"I can't tell," she answered slowly. "For most reasons I'd like to stay, for I have enjoyed my being here; but my mother may want me at home again. Of course I'd rather finish you up myself, instead of leaving you to another tutor or to Mr. Dufferin."

"I won't go back to Duffy, anyway." And Danforth's brow wrinkled into a sombre frown, at the thought of his former tyrant. "I never did anything under him, Miss Davis. Do you know what he told Uncle Jerry about me?"

"What was it?"

"He said I was very dull, and that my worst fault was my perfect indifference. I couldn't do anything to suit him, no matter what 'twas." And Danforth's scowl grew deeper, as he crossed his legs and began to pick at the sole of his shoe.

"Stop scowling at me," said Margaret playfully. "How can you expect me to talk to you if you glower like that? But really, Dan," she went on more seriously; "I don't think Mr. Dufferin was quite fair in what he said to you and about you. He didn't understand you, and I think he frightened you a little bit more than he meant to do. I haven't found you either indifferent or dull, Dan; but a good worker."

Danforth's face brightened under her praise; then it grew thoughtful, as she went on, —

"Dan, my boy, may I tell you just what I think about you? Remember, I'm not the tutor, tonight, only the friend you said I might be; and it's because I care for you that I want to talk this over."

"Go on, please." And Danforth bent forward to stir up the fire; then he drew his chair a little nearer to Margaret's side.

"I don't know just how to begin," said Margaret, as she looked into the dark blue eyes which met hers so honestly. "You see, Dan, you are just where you've proved that you can do splendid work; and I want you to keep up to it, when it isn't quite so easy. You have a good mind, and you can work like a beaver when you are interested; but, under Mr. Dufferin, if you weren't interested, or if he was a little cross, you didn't tell half you knew. Isn't it so?"

"He did use to rattle me a good deal," confessed Danforth penitently.

"I know it; and, as soon as you were rattled, you lost your head and didn't feel sure that you knew anything, and that made you shut your mouth tighter than ever, and frown as you did at me, a few minutes ago. You see I know all about it, just as if I'd been there." And Margaret smiled mischievously.

"I suppose I did, but I don't get rattled with you; do I?" Danforth asked meekly.

"No; that's just it, and yet I don't give you half so easy lessons as Mr. Dufferin did. The first week or two, you weren't quite so ready to tell what you knew; but, since then, you've done splendidly. And now I want to know what's going to happen when you go into college. There you'll be under all sorts of men, some of them pleasant and kindly, some very stern; but you must do good work under each one of them."

"Why can't I keep on with you?" demanded Danforth. "I'd learn as much, and more too."

"I'm not so sure of that," she answered; "and besides, you need just the training that college life will give you. 'Twill be good for you to be thrown among other boys; it's like shaking glass beads together, to break off the rough edges. You'll get some hard knocks, Dan," she went on half-pityingly, as she pictured the sensitive boy launched into the rough-and-tumble existence in which the average freshman delights; "but it won't hurt you in the end, if you make up your mind to hold your own and come out of it all, a man. No matter what the boys say, no matter whether your professors like you or not, I know I am right when I say that you can go through college with a good standing, and be graduated with honor."

"But who wants to be a dig, all his days?"

inquired Jack, who had come into the room just in time for her last words.

"You and Dan both, I hope," answered Margaret promptly. "I've no patience with a boy who hasn't the dig in him. 'Tisn't the bright fellows, it's the ones who can work that make the men of whom our colleges are proud to say, ' He was one of our boys.' But because a boy digs, he needn't give up all the fun of college life; that would make him as uninteresting as the valley of dry bones. Some of the finest lessons of college are learned outside of the class-room, as all of us who have been there know."

"What's the use of college, anyhow?" asked Danforth.

"What are you going to college for?" she responded, meeting question with question.

"Fun," answered Jack laconically; "and because the other fellows all do."

"Such a noble ambition!" And Margaret laughed, in spite of herself. Then she returned again to her serious manner, as she went on, "There's a great deal of fun in college life, Jack; some of it is funny and some of it isn't, as we know who live close to a great university. I should hate to have any boy friend of mine go

through college and miss all the fun; but before
he goes, he ought to make up his mind, once for
all, where his fun should lie. Because a young
man is a student, in these days, he seems to feel
privileged to be a young ruffian, and to get himself into all sorts of scrapes which he would scorn,
if he were living at home. Have all the fun you
want and can get, while you are in college, provided you steadfastly turn your backs on everything that is dishonorable and low and, above all
else, everything that is unclean in thought or act.
You'll go into college as boys, to come out as men.
Beyond and above your class-work comes the question of your real lives; and I want my boys to
make such a record that the best and truest
women may always be glad to welcome them into
their homes."

Danforth's face had grown very thoughtful
while she was speaking, and even Jack. looked
serious for a moment. Then he gave Margaret a
whimsical, sidelong glance, as he inquired
meekly, —

"Digs and prigs, Miss Davis; what else?"

"I like prigs almost as well as you do, Jack,"
she answered. "If there's anything despicable in
this world, it's a saint who is too inefficient to be

anything else. I'd rather have a good vigorous
sinner like you, for there's more chance of making
something of him, in time. A prig isn't a boy
who prefers honorable fun to low jokes; but one
that's too indolent and finicky to appreciate any
fun at all. But, about the dig, if you're going in
for any education at all, you want to do it well.
You boys can both take a good stand, if you'll
work for it; and if you work, heart and soul,
while you do work, you'll have ever so much time
left for fun, outside. And it's in the outside life,
as I say, that you may get the greatest good of all;
for the square pegs of boys who go into college,
have to get their corners rubbed off until they can
fit into the round holes of the life beyond. The
most glorious lesson of all, better than Greek or
Latin, better than 'all the 'ologies of the colleges,'
is to know and trust our brother men, and be kind
in our judgments of them all."

She had spoken more earnestly than she realized, and as she paused, a hush fell on the room.
Both the boys were staring fixedly at the fire, and,
for some moments, neither of them moved. Jack
was the first to recover himself.

"Yes, 'um," he said pensively. "That's a beautiful sermon, 'most as good as Mr. Huntington's

that Laddie stole; but isn't it almost time for the benediction?"

"Impertinent boy!" And Margaret pulled the brown ear nearest her. "No," she added suddenly; "it isn't time yet. I've something more to say."

"Let her go, then, and get it over," said Jack, clasping his hands in mock resignation.

"This last was a general sermon, and fits every day," said Margaret laughing. "Now I am going to add another, just for to-day, and say that you were a pair of lazy boys this morning. You knew it then, and I have a general idea that you are ashamed of it now."

"I 'spects we are," responded Jack cheerfully. "I didn't mean to be a beast, now honestly, Miss Davis; but I didn't feel like working, one little bit."

"Evidently not," said Margaret; "but every day you are lazy now is doing just as much harm to the fine work you are going to do later. And when there comes a day like this, it makes me feel as if all my time were thrown away, and somebody else could do better by my boys than I am doing."

"Not much," returned Jack heartily, as he rose and stood on the hearth-rug, facing her. "Nobody else could be half so jolly; and I only wish you were related to us, somehow, so you would have to sta here alwa s."

CHAPTER IX.

DANFORTH.

"Say, Dan, what are you doing?" asked Jack, coming suddenly into the room which the two boys occupied.

It was the day before Christmas, and Grandma Atherton was busy with the preparations for the next day's festivities, while Bobbie and Pen were decorating the drawing-room, hall and dining-room with sprays of holly and mistletoe. Outside the house, the rain was pouring heavily down from the dull, leaden sky, and the bare trees tossed and writhed in the wind. Danforth cared little for the weather, however, for he was all-absorbed in a new book; and Jack had come in, to find him lying face down across his bed, with his open book as near to the window as possible, his chin in his hands and his heels in the air, a picture of perfect contentment. At Jack's question, he only gave a grunt of recognition, and then returned to his reading.

"I say, wake up there!" remonstrated Jack.

"What business have you to be up here, loafing and spoiling your eyes in that dark corner, when we've been wanting you more than you were worth?"

"What did you want?" inquired Danforth, reluctantly shutting his book and rolling over to face Jack, with a prodigious yawn.

"Grandma wanted some more lemons, and I had to wade over to Riverton for them. If you'd only been round, you could have gone, instead," responded Jack, with calm audacity.

"Needn't think I'm going to do all the errands," objected Danforth. "I'd been out, more than half the morning, and 'twas your turn."

"Turns don't count, this weather," said Jack, going to the window and tapping thoughtfully on the pane, as he looked out at the wind-swept landscape. "Tell you what, Dan, it's a juicy day. I was 'most blown off the bridge, coming home."

"'Tis pretty bad, worse than I thought," said Danforth, as he tumbled himself off the bed, and crossed the room to his brother's side. "Say," he added suddenly; "don't you wish Miss Davis would come back?"

"Come back? Why, she hasn't been gone but two days," said Jack.

"Can't help it; it seems a week, and there isn't anything to do, when she's out of the way."

"She is good fun, that's a fact," admitted Jack; "and she never acts too busy to do what we want. I don't see how we ever managed to get on, without having her round. Think of the times we used to have with Duffy!"

"You came out of that O. K. I was the one that had the worst of it," said Danforth. "It's over now; there's one comfort. But I wish 'twere time for Miss Davis to come back again."

"She'll be here, next week," remarked Jack consolingly. "Besides, if you go to New York, that'll take some of the time."

"Are we going?" Danforth looked up in surprise.

"You are, I'm not in it; no such luck for me," said Jack enviously. "But I supposed you knew it. I heard Uncle Jerry telling grandma that he was going to take you down, next week, to see Dr. Heinrich again. Maybe, if you tease hard enough, you can get him to plan to come back on the train with Miss Davis."

"Great head!" said Danforth approvingly. "That's a good scheme, Jack, and I'll see what I can do. I hate going down, though, and I wish I could et out of it."

"What for?" And Jack stared at his brother in surprise. "I should think you'd have immense fun. I wish Uncle Jerry would take me, instead. But let's go down now, and help Bobbie and Pen. They sent me up to call you, and I forgot it."

"What's the use?" inquired Danforth indolently. "Girls are bores, anyhow. If we stay up here, we can have a little peace; but if we go down there, they'll keep us running all over the house for them, and I get so sick of their gabble."

"Pen doesn't get sick of you, though," said Jack, laughing. "When you're round, she doesn't have half an eye for anybody else. It's 'Jack this' and 'Jack that'; but she doesn't lose sight of you, the whole blessed time."

"Honestly?" And Danforth looked up incredulously. "I never noticed it. I didn't suppose she liked me overmuch, since that time I shut her white kitten's tail in the door crack. She gave me fits then; but really I wasn't to blame, for I didn't see the little beast at all. How Pen did rage, though! I've never dared go near the house since."

"You watch her and see," counselled Jack. "I don't see how you haven't noticed it before."

"All right, I will; but she'd better let me alone, if she knows what's good for herself," said Danforth pugnaciously. "I don't want any more girls round in the way; Bob is all I can manage, and she generally manages me."

In the meantime, down-stairs, Bobbie and Pen were chattering busily over their bunches of red and white berries.

"I think your grandma is just lovely, to give us a Christmas party," Pen was saying.

"Isn't she? And I've the sweetest gown to wear. It just came home to-day."

"What is it?" And Penelope suspended operations while she looked enviously up at Bobbie, who was standing on a tall step-ladder, to hang a branch of mistletoe from the old-fashioned chandelier.

"It's light pink, with great big puffed sleeves and a perfectly e-normous sash. Miss Davis helped me to plan it; it's such a care to get a new gown." And Bobbie sighed in what she considered a very womanly fashion. "Jack says it's fine," she continued, after a pause; "but Dan makes fun of it. He says I look like a balloon in it; but that's just because he don't like pink. Blue is his color."

"Is it? I'm so glad, for my gown is blue." And Penelope beamed at the thought.

"You needn't be too set-up," returned Bobbie crushingly. "Yours is pale blue, and he wants it dark, Yale blue, you know, the color Miss Davis wears so much. Besides, he doesn't like girls, anyway. Jack is a great deal more fun."

"He's more waked-up," assented Pen doubtfully; but Bobbie shifted her ground, with characteristic suddenness.

"But Dan is the easiest to get along with, for he doesn't get cross and tease, as much as Jack does. Don't you ever tell I said it, Pen Stoddard; but really I do have the dearest pair of brothers in the world," she added, in a quick outburst of affection, for the approaching festival had made her feel unusually at peace with the world. "Jack's the brightest; but Dan is so sort of lovely that he makes up for it. Did I ever tell you about the day I left the cage door open, and let all the white mice get away?"

"No; when was that?" asked Penelope, while she tried to decide whether holly or mistletoe looked better about the marble cupid.

"It was one day last fall, and I told the boys I'd feed the mice, for they were both busy. Miss

Davis called me, just then, and I forgot to shut the door, and went off and left them. I felt dreadfully about it, for the boys thought everything of their mice. Jack found it out first, and he was very mad; he did scold me awfully."

Bobbie had dropped her berries, and sat down on the top step of the ladder to tell her story, while her bright little face grew sober and then very gentle in her earnestness, as she went on, —

"Well, I was up in my room, crying just as hard as I could cry, when I heard somebody knock. I wouldn't answer one single word, for Jack had made me pretty mad, my own self, and I had cried till my eyes were as red as a pair of tomatoes, so I just kept still. Then the knob turned, and the door opened softly; but I wouldn't look up nor speak till, all at once, I heard Dan say 'Bobbie.' I thought he'd come to scold, too; but he didn't, a bit. He sat down and pulled me over on to his knee, and kissed me and stroked my hair. His eyes looked blue as could be, and he laughed a little; but he didn't say anything at all, only just 'Poor little Bob! Don't mind so much.' That's the kind of a brother that Dan is." And Bobbie nodded emphatically, as she sat looking down at Pen.

"I think he's lovely, truly; only I'm kind of afraid of him," said Penelope, who had listened intently to Bobbie's story. "He's always so quiet and so proper that I expect to shock him."

"Dan proper?" And Bobbie laughed at the idea. "And you needn't think, because he's quiet, that he hasn't a will of his own, Pen. When Danforth Spaulding really makes up his mind to do anything, you might as well try to — to climb out of the big pot-hole down by the river, as to stop him. But here they come now. We ought to have been at work, instead of sitting here talking, all this time, for it's getting dark already. Don't you ever tell what I've been saying." And scrambling to her feet, Bobbie caught up her berries and resumed her work, just as Jack came into the room.

The next evening found the old house brightly lighted, and gay with music and the voices of young people; for Grandma Atherton had taken advantage of the Christmas festival, to give a little party for her grandchildren and their friends.

"If only Miss Davis were here, 'twould all be fine," Jack had said for the third time, while he was restlessly wandering about the rooms, waiting for the guests to arrive. "It's good weather, and grandma has a jolly spread; but somehow we need her to set us all going."

"Just wait an hour," said Bobbie, waltzing down the hall in her excitement. "When they begin to come, you won't want Miss Davis or anybody else, except just us. Now really, Jacky," and she paused, with her head on one side and her face turned coaxingly up to her brother; "how do you like my gown? Did you ever see one much prettier?"

"N-no; I don't know as I did," admitted Jack, smiling down at his sister with manifest pride. "There's a good deal of flummery to it, but it suits you, somehow. Where's Dan?"

"He's still prinking. Did you ever see such an old Betty?" asked Bobbie, laughing. "He just called me to come in and tell him what tie to wear. He had about a dozen spread out in a row, and I believe he'd been trying them all on. He is the funniest boy I ever did see. Oh dear, I do wish somebody would come; I can't wait much longer, before I see the tree. I know one thing you're going to have, though," she added triumphantly.

"What is it, a printing press?" asked Jack
ea er¹

"That's telling. It's something you'll like. But there goes the bell, at last; I do hope it's Pen." And Bobbie darted to the door to greet her friend and drag her away upstairs, for a long, whispered conference.

It was a most successful evening, and everybody said so. After the first little stiffness had worn away, and the latest comers had made their appearance, the good time began. Mrs. Stoddard had come with her daughter, to help Grandma Atherton in entertaining the young people; and she entered into the frolic as heartily as Penelope herself, now starting a new game and bringing them all into it, now sitting down at the piano to play a simple quadrille or a waltz, while the children danced. Bobbie, with her eyes shining like stars and her cheeks as pink as her gown, was in her element, and flew about the room, infecting them all with her spirits. Even Danforth, after his sister had routed him out of various obscure corners, rose to meet the emergency, and played the host with a quiet grace which won as much enthusiasm from the girls, as did Jack's more rollicking fun; and Bobbie could not keep from giving him a nod of approbation, as she whispered to Jack, in the midst of ladies' chain, —

"Do see Dan! Isn't he too dear, to-night?"

And Jack answered, as he glanced across the
room to where his brother stood talking with
Penelope, in the pause of the figure, —

"Dan's always a trump, when he forgets and
lets himself go; but seems to me Pen looks
unusually fine. How she does smile on Dan,
though!"

The dance ended and that duty done, Danforth
abruptly turned his back upon the pretty face and
dainty gown of his young partner, and strolled
away into the library, leaving Penelope standing
alone in the middle of the floor. She looked after
him with an ill-concealed disappointment, for at
heart she greatly admired Bobbie's quiet brother,
and was secretly much elated by his having asked
her to dance. She had been doing her best to talk
to him and to make him talk, so it was doubly
mortifying to be left without a word. Fortunately
she could not follow Danforth into the library,
and hear him say, as he threw himself down into a
chair beside Uncle Jerry, —

"Wish I could stay here with you! It's an
awful racket in there, with so many girls. They've
all put on their best clothes; and they don't do
anything but shake out their ruffles, or whatever

you call 'em, and look cornerwise into the glass, whenever they get in range."

Uncle Jerry laughed, as he looked up from his paper.

"Which of you took longer to dress, to-night, Dan," he asked; "you or Bobbie?"

Danforth was spared the necessity of making any reply, for Jack appeared on the threshold, at that moment, and descended upon his brother like an accusing spirit.

"I say, Dan Spaulding, what'll you take for your manners? Ask a girl to dance, and then walk off and leave her, the minute you're through! You ought to be ashamed of yourself."

"Great Scott! I forgot her." And Danforth looked up with a startled light in his blue eyes. "I didn't mean to, anyhow; but I was so glad that rigmarole was over, that I bolted as soon as I could. No matter; it's nobody but Pen, and she ought to know I don't like girls and only asked her because I had to."

"You're a great lad!" And Jack surveyed his brother with unmixed scorn. "Pen never'd speak to you again, if she did what you deserve."

"I wish she wouldn't,"-murmured the culprit feebly.

"You don't wish any such thing," returned
Jack. "Now you just come back into the parlor
and behave yourself. I'm going to take Pen out
to supper; but you must ask her to dance again,
or else philopene with her, or something, to show
you want to make up."

"Just my luck!" sighed Danforth, as his brother
vanished once more. "Bob said I must dance with
Pen, and I did it; but I supposed that was all that
was necessary. Bother the girls, anyway!" And
he disconsolately followed Jack, while Uncle Jerry
hid his amusement in his paper.

"Dan will never be a society man," he thought
to himself. "Perhaps it is just as well, for Jack
has enough of it for both the boys. Still, it may
come in time."

Prophetic Uncle Jerry!

Two hours later, the children were gathered in
the drawing-room for one last dance. The simple
supper was over, and the tree had been shown,
then admired, then pillaged. Countless pretty
trifles were scattered about the room, for each
young guest had been generously remembered;
while the more substantial gifts of the Spauldings
lay on the library table, to be opened when the
others had gone. Uncle Jerry, in the dress of

Santa Claus, stood in the doorway, looking on at the lively picture; then, answering a sudden call from his mother, he crossed the hall to the dining-room, where Grandma Atherton and Mrs. Stoddard were packing two little baskets of goodies and gifts, for the two guests who had been unable to come to the party.

Meanwhile, the young people, eager to have the music start up, and excited with their long evening of pleasure, were dancing up and down the great room, their bright faces and pretty gowns making a brilliant contrast to the quaint, old furnishings of the place. All at once, Jack whistled a few strains of a waltz, and Bobbie, seizing Penelope, whirled her away across the floor. A moment later, there came a crash, followed by a cry of fear which quickly changed into a shriek of pain. The two girls, heedless of where they were going, had collided with a small table at the farther side of the room, upon which stood a large banquet-lamp on its tall pedestal. It swayed to and fro for an instant, but not long enough to allow the frightened children to catch it, or to spring away; then it fell on its side, throwing the reservoir from its place and over upon Penelope. The next moment, she was enveloped in a blaze of the burnin oil.

What happened after that, Penelope never knew. She had a vague memory that the room rang with cries of fear and calls for help; that her friends were running wildly about her, and then that some one pushed her roughly to the floor, and held her there under a pile of heavy clothing, while she writhed with pain and terror. That was all she could remember, and that came back to her mind, bit by bit, when she waked to find herself in Bobbie's bed. Her head felt tired and confused, and she was surprised to find her hands and neck bandaged and smarting painfully, while across a chair by the bed lay the ruins of what had been her pretty blue gown. Then it all came back to her, and she cried out again, as she felt the wild terror of those few seconds which had seemed like years. At the sound, her mother came forward to the bed.

"What is it, dear?" she asked gently.

"I don't know." And Penelope began to cry, in weak, hysterical pity for herself. "What happened? Was I burned to death?" she asked, as soon as she could speak again.

Her mother did not even smile at the odd question; she shuddered a little, as she bent over her daughter.

"No, dear; but you might have been, if it hadn't been for Danforth."

"Danforth!" And Pen looked wonderingly up into the loving eyes above her.

"Yes; the others were too much frightened to help you; but he ran out into the hall, and caught an armful of the boys' coats, and held them over you on the floor. There was no one else near enough to do anything; and if he hadn't been quick to think and to act, —" Mrs. Stoddard paused, and a hot tear splashed down on Pen's cheek.

"Did Dan do all that for me?" said Penelope, looking solemnly up at her mother.

"He not only did it, but he did it at the risk of his life, almost."

"And was he burned?" Pen asked the question with an odd little catch in her breath.

"Only a little, on one hand and his cheek. But now you must try to go to sleep, dear. It is almost midnight, and I want you to get some rest, so you can be able to be taken home to-morrow."

"But I don't feel as if I could ever sleep again," said Pen restlessly. "As soon as I shut my eyes, I keep seeing the blaze -all - around me. Oh, Mamma Stoddard, wasn't Dan splendid? I never supposed he'd do such a thing for me. You're sure he wasn't burned much?"

Late the next afternoon, Danforth sat by the library fire, nursing his burned hand and poring over the pamphlets which had come with his new camera, the day before. His white face, with a small burn on his left cheek, and his bandaged hand were the only signs of his experience of the preceding night; and beyond a little annoyance at the inconvenience it was costing him, and a curiously unsteady feeling in his knees, Danforth thought little about the matter, though every one else in the house, the night before, had gone away with a new respect and admiration for quiet Dan. Jack and Bobbie, in particular, had prostrated themselves before their brother, who had received with an ungrateful disgust their attempts to lionize him; and he had blushed and stammered and wriggled while Mrs. Stoddard was trying to thank him, until, in mercy to him, she had left her gratitude quite unspoken.

Now, however, she came into the room and roused him from his blissful study of lenses and plates, by saying, —

"Danforth, the carriage will be at the door in a few minutes now, and Pen has asked to

see you, before she goes. Will you come up-
stairs?"

Feeling strangely like a culprit, Danforth rose
and followed Mrs. Stoddard out of the room. He
had been dreading some such summons, and he
felt no wish to see Pen until they could both
ignore the past. Boy as he was, he had realized
that they stood together in great danger, the
evening before; but, boy-like, he had no idea
what to say about it, and regarded any words as
being quite superfluous. Moreover, his hand
smarted, and he felt tired and cross after the
excitement. In fact, the hero had returned to
the normal boy again, and the normal boy was a
little out of temper and extremely ill at ease.

Penelope was lying on the sofa, listening for his
step. Her face brightened as Danforth came into
the room, although he looked rather forbidding, as
he reluctantly advanced to her side.

"I don't know how to thank you, Dan," she
began slowly.

"What's the use of trying?" responded Danforth bluntly, while he stood frowning down at
her.

"But you kept me from being burned to death,"
she said, "everybody says so, and the last I re-

member is your holding me down, under the coats.
How could you be so brave?" and her eyes filled
with tears.

But Danforth was dumb. He found no words
to say, just then, for a sudden memory of the
scene rushed back to him, as he stood looking
down at the girl before him. It seemed to him
that he had never before known how pretty she
was, how yellow her hair and how pink her
cheeks; and only last night, she had almost —

All at once, Penelope and the sofa grew misty
before his eyes, and, to his intense mortification,
he felt two great tears rolling down his cheek.

"Don't be cross about it, Dan," Penelope was
begging him. "I only want to tell you how good
you were. You see, if it hadn't been for you, I
should have been dead to-day."

"Bother take it all, Pen! What's the use of
making such a fuss about it? I didn't do anything
more for you than I had to, and I'd have done it
for anybody else in the same scrape, so you needn't
feel so everlastingly grateful to me." And Dan's
face turned scarlet, as he pulled off his glasses
and rubbed away the offending mist upon them.

"I know that, Dan; but 'twas for me, and I do
thank you," persisted Pen seriously. "But if you

won't let me talk about that, can't we say we'll be good friends after this, and shake hands on it?": And she held up her small hand, enveloped in its wrappings of old linen.

Danforth took it awkwardly, and stood looking as if he really did not know what to do with it. Then, of a sudden, his face changed, and he said huskily, —

"We are friends, Pen, and we'll stand by each other. I'm sorry I shut your cat in the door, and I hope you'll be all right, in a day or two."

He felt Pen's fingers give his hand an answering squeeze ; then he escaped from the room, with the uncomfortable conviction that he had been ex-tremely ungracious.

CHAPTER X.

HIDE AND SEEK.

A FEW days later Margaret's vacation came to an end, and early one winter afternoon, she and Molly were pacing up and down the long platform of the station, talking busily while they waited for the train which was to carry Margaret back to her pupils once more. It was a clear, cold winter day, and the yellow sunshine gleamed over the waves of the harbor and the scattered schooners lying at anchor there, and beautified even the old wharf with its border of shabby buildings, and the great gap in the roof of the station where the tower had been eaten away by a recent fire. Far down the bay, a Turkish man-of-war showed its dark outline above the dazzling surface of the water; and, nearer the shore, two saucy little oyster-boats were puffing to and fro, with the air of having the concerns of a nation hanging upon every revolution of their wheels. Then there came the sound of a distant whistle, followed

by another close at hand, and, a moment later,
the train rolled up beside the platform, shutting
out the whole bright picture with the dingy outline of its sides.

Margaret glanced up indifferently, while she
waited for the crowd to move away, then her
whole face brightened, as she caught sight of a
boyish figure capering up and down on the platform of one of the cars, and waving his hat to
attract her attention.

"Dan! Where did you come from?" she exclaimed, forsaking Molly to hurry forward to greet
her pupil.

"New York, of course; where'd you s'pose?
Uncle Jerry and I came down yesterday, and I
knew we'd find you here," responded the boy
gleefully, as he seized her bag and umbrella, and
handed them to the sable porter. "Uncle Jerry
took a place for you at New York, so as to make
sure of it."

Margaret turned back to introduce the boy to
Molly, and to speak one last word to her sister;
then she followed Danforth into the car where
Gerald was waiting for them.

"Tell you, this is fine," said Danforth contentedly, as Margaret took off her jacket, and settled

herself in her seat. "I was so afraid I'd miss you,
somehow or other."

"You should have come up yesterday and spent
the night here," said Margaret, turning to wave
her hand to Molly who stood watching them as
the train slowly moved away. "But tell me, how
is everybody at home?"

With the undisguised interest which every one,
in travelling, feels privileged to manifest in his
neighbor, the people about them had smiled at the
boy's eager greeting of this pretty young woman.
Now, from behind the safe screen of novel or newspaper, they listened with amusement to the quick
chatter which followed, while they speculated
vainly as to the relationship existing between
the members of the little party. Uncle Jerry
sat silent, for the most part, watching Margaret's
bright face as she replied to Danforth's questions,
and any one looking closely at him, might have
seen a little look of weariness or sadness in his
pleasant, kindly eyes. But Margaret's face was
turned a little away from him, and Danforth was
too much interested in her, to pay much attention
to his uncle who could study Margaret unobserved. How sweet and bright she was, he
thought. No wonder that she had completely

won his quiet nephew; and Uncle Jerry smiled a little to himself, as he listened to Danforth's eager flow of words. Then he grew grave again, and after a few minutes he excused himself and went away out of the car.

"But what sent you down to New York?" asked Margaret, after she had replied in detail to Danforth's manifold questions.

"Uncle Jerry wanted me to see Dr. Heinrich again. We had a fine time, though, for we went to the theatre last night, and went pretty much all round the city this morning. Don't you think the 'L' is immense, Miss Davis? It's such fun to ride along, and peek in at everybody's up-stairs windows."

Unknown to herself, Margaret's face grew suddenly grave, as she recalled her last ride down through Third Avenue and the Bowery, on one of those warm, breathless days of late summer when the very plants in the windows seemed to be gasping for air. The crowded, noisy, littered rooms, as she flew past them, had made her long to escape from that vast Bedlam into her own clean, cool little home city again. The glimpses of life she had seen that day, the roar of the streets and the suggestive fumes of chloride of

lime had scarcely been according to her idea of
fun. She had wondered whether one could be
happy to live anywhere within the limits of a
city known to have such horrors inside it. And
yet, she did not fully believe that Rivington
Street offered the one open door, through which
all these wretched, swarming multitudes were to
pass on into ways of pleasantness and peace.

Something of this was in her mind now, as she
sat looking at the quiet, snow-covered country
across which they were rushing. She was
roused by Danforth's asking, —

"What is it, Miss Davis? You look as if something didn't suit."

She turned back to him, with the quick smile
which he knew so well.

"It doesn't, Dan. I was deep in social problems, ever so far from here. But I want to forget
all that, and hear more about your Christmas
vacation. What have you been doing to yourself?" she added, as, for the first time, she caught
sight of his bandaged wrist and the long red scar
on the back of his hand, from which he had just
pulled his glove.

"I burned me a little, the other night. It's most
well now, though," said Danforth evasively.

Margaret stretched out her hand and drew his toward her.

"What a terrible burn!" she said pityingly. "How did you do it, Dan?"

To her surprise, the boy blushed crimson and dropped his eyes, as he answered, —

"We tipped over that tall lamp in the drawing-room, and I was helping put it out. 'Tisn't much now. My hand is almost well, but my wrist is pretty bad. Want to see?"

"Oh, don't," interposed Margaret. "It makes me sick to think of it, even, for you must have suffered so much. Why didn't you tell me?"

"Pen was burned more than I was," said Danforth, with a second blush. "She's been ill, ever since then; but they say she's almost well again now, and she isn't going to be scarred any, that's one good thing."

"Tell me all about it, Dan," Margaret urged. "What was it?"

"Truly, there isn't much to tell," he answered, with some confusion. "The lamp tipped over, and Pen's gown caught fire. We were both burned some; that's all."

At a loss to explain his unwillingness to speak of the affair, Margaret could only conclude that

Danforth was in some way to blame for the accident. Accordingly, she changed the subject and, for the next hour, they talked of other matters. Then Uncle Jerry came back to them again.

"I didn't mean to be away from you so long," he said apologetically, as he dropped into his seat; "but I found a friend in one of the cars back here, Thornton, the man who's running our electric line. You may have heard me speak of him. He came up from Hartford to Springfield, and I was talking with him and didn't notice how the time went."

So Hugh had been on the same train with her, and she had never suspected it. Margaret leaned back in her chair and stared hard at the rugged outline of Mount Tom, under whose shadow they were passing. She wondered if Gerald had mentioned her name, and Hugh had not taken the trouble to say he had known her. Would this wearisome game of hide and seek never come to an end? It was bad enough to have him go away and leave her so suddenly; it was even worse to have him within reach, where she was in constant expectation of meeting him again, without knowing whether her anticipations were those of hope or fear. She was just beginning to breathe quietly again, when her attention was caught by Gerald's next words.

"What do you think of our young hero?" he asked, with a glance at Danforth, who had walked to the door of the car and stood there, looking out.

"What do you mean?" she answered.

"Hasn't Dan told you? I thought you'd have noticed his burn."

"He hasn't told me anything, except that the lamp was upset, and he and Pen burned."

"That's a small part of the story," said his uncle, bending forward and speaking quickly, as Danforth started to come back to them. "The children were alone in the room, and they lost their heads completely, all but Dan. Penelope would surely have been burned to death, if he hadn't buried her under a pile of overcoats, and held her there by main strength until the fire was smothered. 'Twas a wonder that he wasn't more seriously burned, himself. But what do you think of our boy now, Miss Davis?"

A smile was Margaret's only answer, for Danforth was within hearing again; but that smile, so happy and tender with her pride in her boy, said more to Uncle Jerry than eloquent words could have done. Then she turned to Dan.

"Why didn't you tell me, my boy?" she said impulsively. "You ought to have known how proud of you I should be."

"I didn't s'pose you'd care," he answered, in a low voice, while he picked nervously at a loose thread in the edge of his overcoat.

"That's not quite fair to me, Dan," she replied gently. "Did you really believe that?"

"No; I didn't," said Danforth honestly, as he raised his eyes to her face. "I knew you'd like me to do it; but what was the use of making such a time about it? The others have harped on it till they have made me tired; and 'twas no great affair anyhow. But I'm awfully hungry."

It seemed very pleasant to Margaret to settle back into her peaceful routine, the next morning. Her vacation had been a most enjoyable one; but the time had been almost too fully occupied, for she was a favorite in her own particular circle of friends, and every moment that she could spare from her mother, was claimed for the endless succession of teas and dinner-dances, in which her sisters delighted. Two weeks of this rushing existence had made her glad to go back to the quiet, restful atmosphere of the Atherton house again; though it was almost with a feeling of shame that she admitted to herself how much more interesting she found the bright chatter of Bobbie and the boys, and the gentle, old-time flavor of Grandma Atherton's conversation, than the society nothings of the acquaintances she had been meeting so constantly. She did not realize that it all came from having a personal, practical interest in life, from her earnest wish to make the most and the best of these young people in her care. Instead of seeing how her life was daily broadening and deepening from her contact with her pupils, and her study of their characters and needs, she only told herself, again and again, that she was growing narrow and dull. The strong instinct of motherhood, which is latent in every true woman until circumstances develop it, had sprung into active life, in the presence of these motherless children; and, all unconsciously, Margaret was giving them her best and truest self.

Life was at its smoothest, for the next two or three weeks. Their short separation had taught the children how much they had grown to depend upon their tutor, so they welcomed her back with enthusiasm, and plunged into their lessons with a will. Bobbie was wrestling with the Greek alphabet, now, and groaning over it, as every normal child has groaned before her; while the boys were making havoc of the finest lines of much-abused, long-suffering Virgil, or elaborately tattooing themselves with their pencil-points, as they pondered upon the problems of reversion of series, for preliminary examinations were looming up in the near future, and college, the first step to full-grown manhood, was but a year and a half away.

The days passed pleasantly and all too quickly, to Margaret's mind. She enjoyed the sterner winter of northern New England, the bright, bracing days when she could go out for long walks and drives, the furious storms which swept down the valley, piling the snow high over the fences and heaping great drifts in every sheltered corner, while the wind roared about the old house and made the warm place by the fireside doubly attractive, after going out with the boys to battle with the storm. It seemed to her that, until they had spent the long, cosy evenings together, she had never really known the family. Grandma Atherton was always the same sweet, motherly little woman; but over the blazing hickory logs even Grandpa Atherton thawed out and told stories of the days of his far-off boyhood; while, viewed in the flickering light of the fire, Bobbie became more gentle and womanly, more considerate of her grandparents and her brothers. Ever since Christmas, she had treated Danforth with a new deference quite unlike the little air of superiority which she had formerly assumed toward him; and during the first few days after his burn, she had hovered over him with the quick pity of girlhood for any wounded creature, to the manifest discomfort of Danforth who had a boyish antipathy to being coddled. But bright as Bobbie always was, lovable as she could be when she chose, Margaret's real enjoyment lay with the boys, in Jack's proud, manly spirit, in Danforth's gentle affection. And the boys responded generously to her love, showing in countless little ways their hearty admiration for her, their enjoyment of her society and their willingness to be guided by her judgment.

She saw more of Gerald, too, at this time. A troublesome cold and cough kept him at home in the evenings, and he usually formed one of the group about the drawing-room fire, where they gathered to listen to Margaret's singing, and to devour the vast pans of popcorn which formed a part of Jack's nightly program. Margaret found the young man a charming addition to their circle, and, moved by a shy, nameless pity for him, she watched over him, quick to anticipate his wishes and minister to his comfort, all unconscious of the new, deep look of pain which sometimes crossed his pleasant face.

They were all sitting there in the drawing-room, one night, Gerald and his mother reading at one table, while Margaret and the children were playing stop, at the opposite side of the fireplace.

"Just fancy the feelings of my respected great-grandma," suggested Jack wickedly; "if she could see us playing cards on top of her table! I'm glad she can't appear to us."

"What for?" inquired Danforth, looking up from his hand. "Most likely she played cards herself."

"Don't you believe it," returned Jack, with conviction. "She was too near puritan days, and probably thought cards were a sin."

"Nine of spades! Ten of spades!" proclaimed Bobbie. "Is it a stop?" And she looked inquiringly about the table.

"'Tis, for all me," said Jack.

"And me," added Danforth. "How is it with you, Miss Davis?"

But Margaret had lost all consciousness of the

game, for she had overheard Gerald's last remark to his mother and, of a sudden, the voices of the children had grown faint and far-away.

"Oh, by the way," he had said, looking up from his book; "Thornton is coming over here to-night. He came to the office, just as I was leaving, to get me to help him out of some sort of a muddle about their right of way. I told him to come over, this evening, and we'd talk it up, at our ease. I told Maggie to bring him in here, when he came, for I thought you'd like to meet him. He's a thoroughly good fellow and a gentleman."

"Is it a stop, Miss Davis?" demanded Bobbie impatiently.

"N — no, — yes, — I'm not sure." And Margaret stared blankly at her cards.

"Have you the jack of spades? We want him," explained Jack, looking in amazement at his tutor, for she was usually quick to think.

"No; it isn't here," responded Margaret hastily, while her unseeing eyes rested upon the jack, which lay uppermost in her hand.

Five minutes later, Bobbie challenged her for playing the missing card, and Margaret roused herself from her dream.

"Forgive me, Bobbie," she said contritely. "I

didn't mean to; but I forgot. I'm not feeling
quite well to-night," she added, with a wan little
smile; "and, if you'll excuse me, I'll go up into my
room and lie down for a while."

She was but just in time, for, as she went wearily
up the stairs, she heard the bell ring. Mechani-
cally she paused for a moment in the dark upper
hall, to listen to Maggie's steps as she went to
admit the guest. Then, turning suddenly, she
fled to her room and closed the door, as if she
dared not trust herself to hear the well-known
voice which was asking for Gerald.

For some unexplained reason, Grandma Atherton felt a quick liking for the stranger who came
into the room. To be sure, Grandma Atherton's
hospitality and her liking for young people were
almost boundless; and the mere fact that it was a
friend of Gerald's would have led her to adopt a tone
of cordiality to any one whom he chose to introduce.
However, this young man was quite to her taste.

It would be hard to say wherein lay the attraction, for Mr. Thornton was far from being handsome.
In fact, his dark face was undeniably homely; but,
apart from all that, there was such an air of simple
sincerity and manliness about him, that one forgot
his face in listening to the hearty ring of his voice

and in feeling the firm grasp of his hand. And yet, tall and strong and athletic as he was, there was nothing about him that seemed to dwarf Gerald into insignificance, as sometimes happened with large men. There was nothing aggressive about his personality. On the contrary, under all his healthy, vigorous physique, there was a lurking suggestion of gentleness and quiet.

He was but just seated before the fire, answering with an easy courtesy to Grandma Atherton's welcome, when there came a strange interruption. Laddie, who had been dozing in the library, had wakened at the sound of the bell, and lifted his head in a dreamy curiosity. He had just let it drop back again on his yellow paws, and nestled down to sleep once more, when he heard Mr. Thornton's voice in the drawing-room. He started up, listened eagerly for a moment until he heard the voice again, then he dashed into the drawing-room and threw himself upon the stranger, licking his face and crying aloud in his joy over the unexpected meeting.

Fearing that Mr. Thornton might resent Laddie's excited demonstrations, Jack had sprung forward to pull him away. To his surprise, he saw the young man bending over the dog, stroking his golden head and calling him by his name, with apparently as much pleasure in the meeting as Laddie himself had shown.

"Why, do you know Laddie?" he asked, in amazement.

"You can see for yourself," answered Mr. Thornton, with a smile. "But do tell me how you came to have him."

"He isn't ours," explained Gerald, who was looking on in surprise at the dog's wild greeting. "He is only a guest, for he belongs to the children's tutor, Miss Davis."

"Miss Davis!" Mr. Thornton gave a quick start of surprise, which was hidden by a fresh onslaught from Laddie.

"Yes; Miss Margaret Davis. Do you know her?"

But Mr. Thornton had already mastered himself, and he answered, with seeming indifference, —

"Yes; that is, I met her a few times, two or three years ago; but she has probably forgotten me. I used to see the dog often, though, and I petted him a good deal. You see, he remembers his old friend."

"Miss Davis was here till just before you came in," said Bobbie, who had been casting admiring

glances at the stranger; "but all at once she
didn't feel well, and went to lie down. I'll call
her, if you'd like."

"Oh, no; it would be too bad to disturb her.
I will wait till some other time; that is, if your
grandmother will allow me to come again." And
he looked at Grandma Atherton, with a face
which had suddenly lost all its genial smile.

A little later, Danforth left the drawing-room,
where Jack had subsided into a book and Bobbie
was posing before the fire, with one eye upon the
guest. He went softly up the stairs and along
the hall to Margaret's door where he paused for
a moment; then he knocked gently.

"Come in," said Margaret's voice.

"I only came up to see if you didn't want something," said the boy, as he opened the door into
the dark room.

"Oh, Dan? Come in, dear; I only want you."
And she sat up on the sofa, where she had thrown
herself.

"I'm afraid I'll disturb you," he said, drawing
back as if to go away.

"No; 'twas good of you to come, and I wish
you'd stay a little while," said Margaret, touched
by his evident wish to do something for her.

"If I'm not in the way." And he came forward to her side. "I was afraid you were ill and might need something, and the others were busy, talking with Mr. Thornton."

To his surprise and alarm, Margaret's head went down on the pillow, and he heard a smothered sob. It had never before occurred to him that a grown woman could cry, least of all, his bright, merry Miss Davis.

"What is it?" he asked in dismay. "Shall I call grandma?"

"Oh, don't," she begged, choking back her tears. "I'm only a little tired and nervous. Just don't say anything about it, dear. Stay here and talk to me for a while, and I shall feel better. I was lonely, truly," she added wistfully, as the boy dropped down beside her on the sofa, never dreaming how deep was the loneliness of which she spoke.

CHAPTER XI.

JACK'S SKATING.

"OH, Miss Davis, the funniest thing!" And Bobbie dropped into the nearest chair, as she pulled off her mittens and unfastened her jacket.

"What now?" asked Margaret quietly, for Bobbie reveled in superlatives and, whenever she was at all eager or excited, her conversation was thickly sprinkled with exclamation points.

"Why, grandma sent me over to Riverton for some more yarn, and I just stopped in at Pen's for a minute or two, and there sat Dan. Did you ever?"

"Ever sit there?" queried Margaret, with a smile, though at heart she was as much surprised as Bobbie could have wished, at the thought of quiet Dan's going of his own will to call on any girl, least of all, the irrepressible Penelope, whom he had always treated with such indifference.

"No; you know I don't mean that," said Bobbie a little impatiently. "But the idea of Dan, our Dan, going to see Pen, all his lonesome!"

"Perhaps he went on some errand or other," suggested Margaret, laughing at Bobbie's sisterly incredulity that her brother could find any other girl attractive.

"No; he didn't." And Bobbie shook her head in violent dissent. "He didn't act so a bit, for his overcoat was off, and he was sitting down his whole weight, with Pen's everlasting old white cat on his knee. You know he hates cats. I tried to make him come home with me; but Pen teased him to stay a little longer, and he just wouldn't budge." And Bobbie paused to sigh over the unwonted situation.

"But why shouldn't he run in to see Pen? He's known her so long and so well," urged Margaret, much amused by Bobbie's excitement.

"Yes; only it's so funny," responded Bobbie, returning to her original proposition. "But won't I give it to him when he does come home." And springing up, she danced from one toe to the other, laughing exultantly to herself, meanwhile.

"No, Bobbie; please not." And Margaret looked up suddenly.

"Why not?" asked Bobbie maliciously. "It's such a joke, and 'twould make Dan wild."

"Just the reason you ought to keep still about it, little girl," said Margaret. "Remember how sensitive Dan is, Bobbie, and that what may seem a good joke to you or Jack, may really hurt him. You do hurt him oftener than you know," she added gently. "Dan is too kind to do it to you, and it's not quite fair for you to tease him so unmercifully."

"But I don't tease him, Miss Davis," protested Bobbie, as she threw herself into the chair again, with a pout. "He's babyish, and makes a fuss over every little thing."

"Babies don't usually save their friends from being burned to death," observed Margaret, holding up her work to survey the bunch of nasturtiums she was embroidering on Bobbie's new tablespread.

"I don't mean that way," returned Bobbie quickly. "Dan has sand enough, as Jack calls it; but he's more than half girl, after all, and if you scold him or tease him the least little bit, it upsets him."

"Then, if you know it so well, what makes you do it?" asked Margaret promptly. "You really can't enjoy hurting Dan, Bobbie. I supposed you only did it by accident. Dan is very fine, and sometimes, after your sharp words, I have seen him draw back as if you had struck him. You keep teasing him, and yet, he would do anything he could for you."

"Well," Bobbie was beginning defensively, when she was interrupted by the sound of Jack's voice from the library.

"I don't care, I shall go," he was saying excitedly.

"But I tell you the ice isn't strong enough," Grandpa Atherton answered, in the overbearing tone he sometimes used with the boys, and which invariably roused Jack to rebellion.

"The fellows are all there, and there's no danger." And Jack made a little, impatient motion which set his skates to clicking against each other.

"It makes no difference to me what the other fellows do. As long as you stay in this house, I shall insist upon your minding me," said his grandfather, with unnecessary sternness.

Margaret could fancy just how Jack's dark eyes were flashing, and she longed to go in and break up the angry conference; but she dared not interfere.

"But I told Ellie I'd come down, and he'll wait for me," begged Jack. "It's perfectly safe, grandpa; they've been skating there for two days. I don't see why you won't let me go."

"Because I say that it isn't best," said Grandpa Atherton angrily. "That is all you need to know about it. You are here to mind me, and I expect to have prompt, ready obedience."

For a moment, Jack glared at his grandfather without speaking; then he muttered, —

"I'll skate if I choose, there or somewhere else." And he stalked out of the library, jerking aside the portière with an impatient regret that there was no door to bang, as an outlet for his exasperated feelings.

It was a clear, crisp day in late January. A sudden thaw, followed by a few days of unusual cold, had covered the river above the dam with a smooth sheet of ice, which had aroused the admiration of every owner of a pair of skates, and already the broad surface of the river was thick with a crowd of boys and girls. On his way to Riverton, that morning, Jack had encountered Ellsworth Pierson who had started for the ice; and Jack had rushed off home for his skates, promising to meet his friend at the end of the bridge.   The snow had come early, that year, and this was the first good skating of the season, so it was doubly provoking to be stopped in the hall, and forbidden to have a share in the sport. If only Grandpa Atherton had not been quite so decided about it, Jack could have borne the disappointment more easily; but there was something very irritating about his grandfather's tone and manner, as if he were expecting direct disobedience and were prepared to combat it to the last moment.

Margaret always dreaded these contests, for, although Jack's conscience was tender and he suffered the pangs of remorse later, in the time of them, he was too angry to care what he said. Moreover, she felt that they gave a wrong impression of the boy to Grandpa Atherton who, by reason of his deafness, lost much of Jack's conversation in his gentler moods, and rarely saw him during the fits of penitence, which followed his outbursts as inevitably as the hush follows a violent thunder shower.   Now she crossed the room to the window, and stood looking after Jack as he walked slowly down the drive, with his collar turned up about his ears, his skates slung about his neck and his little gray cap on the back of his dark hair. Already the reaction had come, and his very walk showed his dejection, though he did his best to cover it under an assumption of scornful indifference. Then he disappeared below the edge of the hill, and Margaret returned to her work; but through all the rest of the long morning, she never once lost the little feeling of regret and discomfort which Jack's outburst had caused her.

Lunch-time came and went without Jack's appearing; but that fact caused no comment for, on Saturdays when the children had no lessons, they were often irregular at the meal. Nothing had been said to Grandma Atherton or Gerald, in regard to the morning's discussion; and yet there seemed to be a little cloud resting over the table, and Bobbie was too much out of spirits even to tease Danforth about his sudden interest in Penelope.

· Margaret had promised to go for a ride with Danforth, that afternoon; so, soon after lunch, they set out, with Duke prancing and pawing the snow, and the gay little sleigh heaped high with fur robes. Tempted by the bright, cold day and the fine sleighing, they were out longer than they had intended, and it was already sunset when

they drove up to the door again. Grandma Atherton met them on the steps, looking strangely
excited.

"Miss Davis, where is Jack?" she asked
quickly.

"Jack? I've not seen him," answered Margaret, in some surprise, for, in her enjoyment of
the drive, she had forgotten the conversation
which she had overheard, that morning.

"He hasn't come home yet. It is so late, and
Mr. Atherton says they had some sharp words, just
as he was going away. I am so afraid something
has happened to him." And she looked piteously
at Margaret, as if begging for a word to reassure
her.

For some reason, Margaret felt her heart grow
heavy with a sudden fear. Jack would never
mean deliberately to disobey his grandfather; but
he was always rash and quick-tempered, and he
had gone away from home in a dangerously reck-
less mood.

"He said something about Ellie," said Bobbie,
who had followed her grandmother to the door
and stood watching her in awed silence. "Maybe
he'd know where Jack is."

Margaret turned to Danforth.

" Dan, will you — ? "

But Danforth was already half way down the hill, and Margaret turned back to Grandma Atherton again.

" Come in to the fire, dear," she said gently. " You are shivering, and I am afraid you'll take cold. Jack is probably with Ellie, and he will come back with Dan, in a few minutes."

But though she tried to smile, Grandma Atherton was too anxious and sorrowful to respond to Margaret's efforts to soothe her. She stood by the drawing-room window, looking after her grandson as he went flying across the distant bridge, and then was lost to sight between the buildings on the farther side of the river.

" If he would only hurry a little !" she said almost impatiently, although the boy was urging Duke forward at the top of his speed.

In less than half an hour afterward, he was back again, breathless and chilled.

" Ellie hasn't seen him since morning," he said, throwing himself into the nearest chair. " He promised to go skating on the river with Ellie, and Ellie waited for him ; but when he came he was rattled about something and wouldn't go to the river at all. He said he was going up to the

reservoir, and wanted Ellie to go with him; but
Ellie wouldn't.   He tried to make Jack stay here,
for 'twas so far, and he'd heard that the ice wasn't
safe up there.   Jack stuck to it he'd go, and went
off alone; and Ellie hasn't seen him since."

"The reservoir!"   And Gerald came hastily out
from the library. "Jackson's men were telling me
to-day that the ice there isn't good for anything.
Jack never would walk up there, either."   Nevertheless, he was pulling on his coat while he was
talking.

"Where are you going, Jerry?" asked his
mother anxiously.

"I think I'll walk up that way," he said reassuringly. "We may meet him, or else he will be
here before we get back.   You'll come, won't you,
Dan; or are you too tired?" he asked, turning to
his nephew who had risen and was restlessly walking up and down the hall. "We shall be back by
seven, at the latest; but don't wait dinner for us."

The hour that followed was a long and anxious
one.   In vain Margaret tried to convince herself
that it was a false alarm, that Jack would come
back to them, safe and well.   She could only re-
call the dull foreboding with which she had
watched him go down the hill; and she was con-

scious that her words had the ring of insincerity,
as she endeavored to encourage Grandma Atherton who sat by the window, staring out into the
gathering darkness and starting nervously at every
sound. Grandpa Atherton was tramping up and
down the hall, and Bobbie was roaming about the
house, too restless to settle to any employment, although she insisted upon it that she knew Jack
would be at home before Uncle Jerry.

Slowly the moments dragged away. It seemed
at times as if the clocks must have stopped; then
again they could hear the solemn *tick, tick* of the
tall old clock in the dining-room, as it told off the
seconds, in just the same tone it had used when
Grandpa Atherton's first shrill cry broke the stillness of the ancient rooms. It had ticked a monotonous welcome to the baby boy; it had ticked a
slow, sad farewell to the young mother, and, from
that day to this, it had gravely ticked out its message in the stillness which accompanied every
family crisis. What was it saying now?

Seven o'clock came, half past seven, eight; and
still no one appeared. At length steps were heard
outside. Something in their sound told Margaret
that they were the bearers of no good news. A
moment later, the door opened, and Danforth and

his uncle came into the hall. There was no need for words; their white, set faces, the weary hopelessness of every gesture told the sad truth, that the time for watching and waiting had ended, and that for endurance had come.

When the first outburst of grief was over, Gerald told his short story: how, fearing the darkness, they had stopped at a strange house to borrow lanterns, and then pressed on to the pond, as rapidly as they could; how they had found the ice thin and broken about the edges, and with a great, angry-looking dark hole in the middle, and how Danforth had caught sight of a small, light object floating there; how they had torn away rails from a fence near by, and carefully worked their way over the ice until, with a long pole, they had drawn the object towards them, to find it a little cap of pale gray cloth. That was all. They said no word of the long, dreary walk homeward, when their hearts were breaking with their own sorrow, and with their knowledge of the anguish they were carrying to those who watched at home.

Slowly the night wore away. No one had thought of dinner; no one thought to go to bed. It seemed as if the routine of the house had suddenly stopped, and its life were ended; only the old clock went on, on, as if its tale were not all told. Up-stairs in the Wilderness, surrounded by the countless treasures which Jack had stored there, Danforth and Bobbie were huddled together on the floor, now sobbing convulsively, now still, and holding their breaths to listen yet once more for the well-known step and voice. Down in the library, Gerald was trying to quiet and comfort his mother, holding himself outwardly calm for her sake, though he shuddered as he thought of the dread work in store for him, with the first light of day. Margaret did what she could for Grandma Atherton; then she went away and left the mother and son together, for she felt she had no right to intrude upon their sorrow, and she knew that the children were longing to have her come to them. As she passed the drawing-room door, she paused for a moment, wondering whether she ought to go to Grandpa Atherton, who sat alone by the dying fire. Then she heard his voice, husky and broken, —

"Oh, Father, if I have caused this, punish me, not him! Nevertheless, not as I will —" His words died away, and Margaret could hear the old man sobbing like a little child.

One after another, the old clock chimed out the hours, every one of them carrying bright, merry Jack farther into the past, away from their present lives. Up in the Wilderness, Bobbie had cried herself to sleep on the sofa; but Danforth and Margaret still sat before the fire, talking of Jack and trying to realize the blow which had come upon them. In his sorrow, the boy had drawn even closer to Margaret; and as she sat stroking the yellow head resting against her shoulder, and speaking a few words from time to time, she felt that here was her return for the care and love she had given him, the ability to meet him in his grief and, in a measure, to share it with him.

At length the new day showed, faint and gray, through the eastern windows. It was not so bad in the night, for then it seemed as if the whole world were sharing in their darkness, and lying silent in sympathy with their sorrow. But the morning would bring in the familiar sights and sounds of their every-day lives, which as yet they were powerless to meet. Danforth was so still that Margaret hoped he had dropped into a doze; but, as she stirred slightly, he looked up, and she saw that he had not been sleeping. Down-stairs, all was quiet, except for the clock which still continued its measured strokes, on and always on. Slowly the gray light in the east grew stronger; then its lower edge was tinged with a rosy glow, which broadened and deepened into a band of dazzling scarlet, until, from its very midst, rose the flaming circle of the sun which shone pitilessly in upon the mourning household. It had just left the horizon, and Margaret was stealing quietly across the room to draw the curtains, that the sudden flood of light might not arouse Bobbie, when she caught the sound of the quick trot of a horse's feet. The next moment, the outer door flew open, and a boyish voice was heard shouting, —

"Where are you, everybody? Grandma! Uncle Jerry! *Breakfast!*"

Bobbie and Danforth were on their feet in a twinkling, and rushed down-stairs just as Grandma Atherton, pale and trembling, caught her grandson in her arms. It took only a moment for Jack to tell of his adventures. Unwilling to disobey his grandfather, but determined to skate in spite of him, he had gone to the reservoir, where the ice had broken under him. Fortunately for Jack, some wood-choppers had seen him sinking and rushing to the spot, they had succeeded in catching him, just as he was going down for the last time. They had taken him out, drenched and shivering, and had hurried him away to their rough cabin; but by the time that his clothes were sufficiently dry to allow him to put them on once more, it was too late for a return over the rough mountain roads; but, with the first light of the dawn, they had set off for home. The risen sun of the new day looked in upon the rejoicing family, while the old clock ticked its welcome to the wanderer.

The first glad murmur died away and a hush fell upon the little group, as Grandpa Atherton extended his hand above their heads in benediction, while he said brokenly, —

"For this my son was dead, and is alive again; and was lost, and is found."

Then he bowed his head upon his clasped hands.

CHAPTER XII.

THE MEETING OF OLD FRIENDS.

EVER since morning, the clouds had been hanging low over the hills. By noon they had settled down in a solid, dark gray pall, and the air from time to time was thick with a flurry of fallen flakes, while a biting wind swept down through the valley, whirling the white particles before it in a cloud.

"Even if 'tis late in the season, this is going to be the storm of the winter," Gerald had said, as he was buttoning his coat, preparatory to returning to his office after lunch. "I'm glad our electric line is through; I shouldn't care to walk over to Riverton and back twice to-day."

An hour later, Jack came into the library where the others sat cuddled over the fire.

"Anybody here that wants to go out for a walk?" he inquired. "I'm going over to Riverton; want to come, somebody?"

"Catch me!" And Bobbie shook her head in scorn.

"What's struck you to go out, such an afternoon, Jack?" asked Danforth lazily. "You must be hard up."

"Evidently you're no good. Well, I suppose I shall have to go alone," said Jack, with his eyes fixed suggestively upon Margaret.

She took the hint and rose.

"I believe I'd like to go; that is, if you'll let me," she said.

"Good for you! But I'm going to walk, I warn you, and I want to go clear over to the printing-office, to get some ink and ask Mr. Merrill how to take my press apart to oil it. It's getting dreadfully squeaky."

"Ought you to go, Miss Davis?" asked Grandma Atherton. "It's snowing hard already, and I'm afraid the storm will be worse than you think."

"I don't mind storms," answered Margaret lightly. "I'll dress for it, and I am used to being out in all weathers, so I never take cold. I will be ready in a few minutes, Jack, and then I'll walk as far and as fast as you please."

"Oh, Jacky, let me go too." And Bobbie started up.

"Oh, Bobbie, I won't," he responded. "You wouldn't go, a minute ago, and now you can't."

"But I didn't know Miss Davis was going," she urged. "Let me go with you."

"Not much! You had your chance and lost it. I asked you to go, and you said you wouldn't; and now I don't want you." And Jack marched out into the hall to wait for Margaret, leaving Danforth to console his sister as best he might.

It was not entirely devotion to Jack which had roused Margaret, that afternoon. In spite of the storm, the prospect of a long walk was very attractive to her, accustomed as she was to being out every day and in all sorts of weather. For at least a part of the time between the morning lessons and the long, quiet evenings by the fire, she loved to be out in the open air. There was an almost intoxicating pleasure, to her strong, young womanhood, in fighting her way through storm and wind and rain. It had been a constant source of surprise to her, in her experience of Riverton, to find how much more the people there dreaded facing a storm, than in the larger city where she had always lived. At home, her friends went out whenever they - chose, regardless of the weather; but here in the little village at the foot of the hill, where one would have naturally expected to find a hardy race of countrymen, out-of-door life was practically suspended in a storm. Even the men and boys shut themselves up in the house and waited for the sun to shine again, before they would venture to stir from under shelter. How much real enjoyment such people missed, she thought to herself pityingly, as she dressed for her walk. There was an exhilaration in facing a driving storm, which few things else could equal.

Hastily putting on a short blue serge skirt, kept for just such occasions, and adding her mackintosh and a saucy little toque to match it, she went running down the stairs, looking such a pretty picture of perfect health and enjoyment, that Jack felt moved to express his approbation, as they went floundering away down the hill, through the deepening snow.

"It's some fun to go out with a woman that isn't afraid of the snow," he remarked, with an admiring glance at Margaret's head and shoulders which were already powdered with the falling flakes. "They generally have to have so many umbrellas and things, that they lose all the fun of being out."

"I wouldn't have missed it for anything," panted Margaret, pausing for a moment with her back to the gale. "Don't tell, Jack; but it makes me want to run, just like a cat when the wind blows."

"Come on, then; why not?" And Jack set off at full speed.

Margaret looked over her shoulder to see that she was unobserved; then, carried away by the excitement of the storm, she went flying after him, down the long drive and out into the road, where she halted, laughing and breathless.

"I repeat it, don't tell of me, Jack," she said, as soon as she could speak. "'Twas very undignified; but I always lose my head, in a day like this."

"Wish you lost it oftener," remarked Jack approvingly. "I know how you feel, though; I've often been so."

"I suppose I must be proper again, now we are in sight of everybody. Is my hat straight?" she asked, as she settled two or three hairpins loosened by her run.

"Straight enough," responded Jack, with a lofty indifference to the fact that all a woman's dignity depends upon an accurate placing of her

headgear. "Come ahead." And he tramped
away to the bridge.

Margaret fell into step at his side. In spite of
the snow and the consequent difficulty of walking,
Jack's long, swinging step was just what she enjoyed, and frequent practice in walking together
had taught them just what pace to adopt.

"There aren't many women who know how to
walk," Jack had remarked, one day, with boyish
scorn. "Some of them lop and roll and wobble
along, and the rest generally trot till it makes me
out of breath to watch them. You walk the way
the English women did, we used to see in India;
the way they did when they first came out, that
is. They lost it all by the time they'd been there
a few weeks."

Even Margaret was glad to rest for a few moments, by the time they reached the safe haven of
the printing-office. Chief among Jack's Christmas
gifts had been a little press, which now was absorbing most of his time and attention, and Uncle
Jerry had given him a note of introduction to Mr.
Merrill, the editor of the local paper. Accordingly, the kindly old gentleman could receive the
storm-beaten pedestrians into his official sanctum,
without fear of their having manuscript poems

concealed about their persons, ready to be drawn forth at a moment's notice. Their host drew two chairs up to the register, while he expressed his hospitable surprise at seeing a woman out in such a storm, until Margaret began to feel that he regarded her as being a particularly aggressive young Amazon. Then, as soon as they were seated, Jack launched forth a shower of questions in regard to the technicalities of the business. The old man listened attentively, much amused by the boy's eager interest and by the information upon the subject, which he had contrived to pick up. Encouraged by Mr. Merrill's genial manner, Jack chattered on, all-unconscious of the fact that, at home, Bobbie was revenging herself for his refusal to let her join them in their walk, by emptying into one heterogeneous pile his carefully-sorted fonts of type.

"You see," Jack explained at length, with one of his brilliant smiles; "as soon as I get a little more used to running it, I'm going to start up a weekly paper like yours, only larger. There are lots of the fellows that would take it; but I don't just know how I can get stuff to fill it. Do you write most of *The Register* yourself; or how do you get it?"

Mr. Merrill smiled, as he recalled his overflow-ing waste-basket.

"I have a good deal sent to me, one time and another," he admitted; "sometimes more than I can use."

"That's what I supposed," said Jack promptly. "Now, why couldn't you sell some of it out to me? I'd pay something, not very much till I was under way; but then, 'twould be better than it is to waste it all. I want some good lively stories, and some funny jokes, not chestnuts; and I sup-pose I'd have to stick in a few poems, just for the looks."

Leaning back in his revolving chair, Mr. Merrill laughed loud and long, as he thought of the prob-able emotions of aspirants for literary fame, who found their carefully-written lines appearing in Jack's sheet.

"Excuse me, young man," he said, as soon as he could speak. "I didn't mean to be disre-spectful; but this struck me as being a new de-parture in journalism. I'm afraid I can't give you my cast-off contributions; but I'll tell you what I will do, I'll write an editorial for your opening number."

"That'll be fine," exclaimed Jack eagerly.

"Make it real long, won't you, so as to fill up a good deal of room. What else do you have?"

"Occasionally we interview a few people, if they are very noted," suggested the editor mischievously. "Those things take pretty well, and you might try it. And now our afternoon edition is just going to press, and perhaps you and Miss Davis would like to see it put through."

Leaving the office, they mounted to the top story of the building where they lingered for a long half-hour in the room, while Mr. Merrill devoted himself to Margaret's instruction, and Jack roamed about the place at his own sweet will, convulsing the compositors with his questions and winning their liking by his bright, interested face and manner. When at length they came downstairs again and out into the street, they were amazed to find how late it was, and how the snow had accumulated during the time that they had been under cover.

"It's no use for us to think of walking home, Jack," Margaret said, as a car came down the street toward them, sending a line of fierce blue light along the snow-covered wire. "Let's take this car, and get home as soon as we can."

It was easier said than done, at least, in so far

as the getting home was concerned. Happily unconscious of the fact that, for the past half-hour, the same car had been running up and down over a few hundred feet of track, in its unsuccessful efforts to fight its way onward, they hailed it, and took their seats, congratulating themselves on their good fortune in finding it at hand. So interested were they in talking over their call on Mr. Merrill that, for a few moments, they did not notice the remarkable behavior of their five-cent conveyance. All at once, Jack sprang up and walked to the door.

"What's the matter here?" he exclaimed impatiently. "Why don't we go ahead?"

The car was certainly acting in a most peculiar fashion. Now it stood still on the track, while its wheels buzzed round and round on the rails; now it backed off to a short distance and made little, ineffectual rushes at the unbroken snow ahead; then it apparently sat down and waited, metaphorically speaking, with its hands in its pockets, while the conductor and motorman, seizing their brooms, swept a few feet of track bare and sanded the rails, preparatory to repeating the whole performance once more. At length Jack rebelled.

"This is getting slightually monotonous," he

objected, as he looked at his watch. "We've been just the even half-hour in going one block ; at this rate, we shall be till day after to-morrow morning in getting home.   Great Cæsar!"   And he remained speechless with disgust, as the car went ignominiously sliding away down the track to the power-house, half a mile away.

"Next time we want to get home, we'll take a car headed the wrong way," suggested Margaret laughing. "There is no help for it, Jack, and we may as well make the best of it," she added, as the car stopped at the power-house.

"We've evidently come back for reinforcements," said Jack, as half a dozen men, muffled to the eyes and each bearing a shovel and a pail of sand, took up their positions on the front platform.

They went flying up the track once more, and regained their former position where the fight began in earnest.   While Jack went out to reconnoitre, Margaret sat watching the workmen.   They were so enveloped in their long coats, with their collars turned up to meet the soft hats pulled down over their faces, so covered with the light snow which clung to their clothing, their beards and even their eyebrows, as to be absolutely unrecognizable. And how they did work! She noticed one of them in particular, a tall man in a long black ulster and a little blue yachting cap, who accomplished as much as any other two men, while he seemed to keep the rest in good humor by his constant flow of spirits and fun. She watched him with amused eyes, while he tossed the snow to the right and left, regardless of his fellow workmen who chanced to be within range. She wished that she could see his face. He must be an Irishman, she was sure, as she saw his clumsy purple worsted mittens. Just then Jack came back into the car.

"Lively prospect," he remarked, dropping down by Margaret's side and taking off his cap to shake away the snow. "We're stuck here, just like a little mice, till the plow can get to us. It's over at the other end of the line now, went up an hour ago, and they'll come back as soon as they can. All they're going to try to do, is to keep one track clear till it stops storming. It's 'most dark now; wish they'd hurry up."

"We might get out and walk," suggested Margaret.

"No use. You couldn't walk three blocks in this storm, to say nothing of a long mile. No;

we will stick it out, here. You wait a minute, though; I've an idea."

He left the car again, and Margaret saw him leaping through the snow to the pavement. When he reappeared, he had a large paper bag in his hand.

"Thought we might as well have something to amuse ourselves with," he said triumphantly, as he dropped his burden into Margaret's lap. "That mean little grocery didn't have much in stock; but I bought some crackers, and some dates so I could see how time went."

"We're living in deeds, not years, just now," she answered merrily, while the car backed off for a block or two, and then made a fresh lunge at the snow. "I always envied Robinson Crusoe, myself, and it's much more fun to be cast away in a wilderness that has all the modern improvements of rapid transit. We actually went ahead as much as two feet, that time," she added. "I only wish we had a few more passengers, for the sake of excitement. I don't believe in monopolies."

"Most likely they have too much sense to go out in such a storm," returned Jack impertinently. "Just think how much better off you'd be, over the fire at home with Grandma."

·"Never!" protested Margaret, rising and going to the front door of the car, to look at the workmen. "I wouldn't have missed-this frolic for anything."

"It's a blessing that Bob didn't come," said Jack thankfully, as he dived into the bag for a fresh supply of rations. "She'd have been in fifty fits by this time."

"Jack, come here a minute." Margaret spoke in a low repressed voice.

"Yes 'um," responded Jack cheerfully, as he went forward to her side.

"Who is that man ahead there, the one in the little cap? It's snowing so fast that I can't see his face."

"That? That's Mr. Thornton, the superintendent," said Jack indifferently. "He knows how to make them work, too; he just keeps his men at it, all the time."

"Mr. Thornton?"

"Yes. Haven't you seen him before?" asked Jack, with an utter unconsciousness of his tutor's change of manner. "He was over at the house one evening, you know; where were you?"

"I—I don't know," faltered Margaret, as, held by a strange fascination, she pressed her cheek

hard against the cold glass of the door, while she
stared out at her old friend. Strange that she
hadn't recognized him before, she thought, as she
gazed at the familiar figure whose every motion
brought back to her mind some memory of the
past. She no longer saw the other men; her eyes
were for him alone, and she strained them to
catch another glimpse of his face through the
fast-gathering dusk. She forgot Jack. She even
forgot to move away, when Mr. Thornton turned
to come back to the car. All at once, he
glanced up and met her gaze. She saw the color
leave his face, as he took off his cap with a
courtesy which he tried in vain to render indifferent. If only she dared call him to her, and
tell him of all the sad mistake! But there were
Jack and all those strange men, and perhaps he
no longer cared. Deep down in her heart, she
knew that she was deceiving herself, and that she
deserved to suffer for being so foolish; nevertheless, she merely gave a slight bow in answer to
his salute, and walked away to her seat.

A moment later there was heard a brisk hum-
ming of the wires, and the plow came rushing
down the track toward them, scattering the snow
before it in a fine, soft mist. It came to a halt,

a few feet away from them, the trolley was re-
versed and the men were preparing to start off
once more, when Hugh called the motorman to
him and gave him some instructions. Then the
man entered the car where Jack and Margaret
sat, patiently waiting for further developments.

"Mr. Thornton said I was to ask you if you'd
like to ride home in the plow," he said, pausing,
hat in hand, before Margaret. "It's likely to be
a good while before we get a car through, for this
one has to go back to the power-house for more
sand. The plow will go straight through, though,
and it's safe, even if it isn't a very nice place for a
lady like you. Some smoky, you know," he added,
in explanation; "but it's better than 'tis to lie
here all night."

"What a lark! I've always wanted to see the
inside of the thing." And Jack sprang to his
feet. "Come ahead, Miss Davis; we'll go home
in style."

He led the way to the great blue box on wheels,
and Margaret climbed into it, feeling as if she
were in some strange dream. Hugh stood at a
little distance, in the midst of a group of men.
She looked at him, appealingly this time; he
raised his cap again. Then the door closed

behind her, and they went rushing away into the darkness, while Mr. Thornton walked back to the deserted car, saying to himself, —

"She did flirt with me most abominably, and then threw me over like a broken doll; but, confound it! I'm just as bad as ever. If I hadn't my reputation to make, I'd give up my contract here to-morrow, rather than run the risk of meeting her any day. Well, I'll grin and bear it for a while longer." But his face had no suggestion of a grin, as he spoke.

CHAPTER XIII

"DAN SPAULDING, I've a perfectly fine scheme," said Jack, coming suddenly into the Wilderness one day, a week or two later.

"What now?" inquired Danforth, looking up from the bowl of water in which a dozen blue print photographs were floating dejectedly about, in various stages of development.

"Well, now, you see here," and Jack sat down on the edge of the low table, that he might unfold his plan at his ease. "You know I'm going to start up my paper, in a week or two, now I've succeeded in getting the hang of my press; and I want some good stuff to fill it up with."

"Write it, then," suggested Danforth indifferently, as he grasped the collar of Laddie, who was apparently seized with a suicidal desire to drink from the water in which the prints lay soaking.

"I can't write it all," objected Jack. "Besides, the first number ought to be an extra good one,

so all the fellows will think they want to sub-
scribe."

"What do you want to go into the thing for,
anyway?" asked Danforth. "It will be more
trouble than it's worth."

"What do you want to go into photography
for?" retorted Jack. "It's more trouble than it's
worth, and, besides, I'll have you arrested for libel,
unless you break that last negative of Brownie
Bell and me. It looks as if we'd both been dead
for a couple of years, and then dug up, all of a
sudden, when we weren't expecting it. Now if I
pose the whole time for you to try all your experiments on, it's only fair that you should help me
out with starting my paper. By the way, what
shall I call it?"

"The Spaulding Chestnut," responded Danforth,
with unexpected promptness. "I say," he added,
suddenly diving into the bowl before him; "isn't
this coming out finely?" And he held up a
picture of Penelope, with her white cat perched
high on her shoulder against the laughing face of
her mistress.

"'Tis good, that's a fact," said Jack approvingly.
"You've certainly caught the knack of posing Pen,
whatever you do to me. But about the paper,
now."

"What is it you're after?" inquired Danforth. "You might as well out with it, and have it over."

"It's only something that will be fine for the paper, and give us a jolly lark," replied Jack. "It's just this way; the day Miss Davis and I were at the *Register* office, I was asking Mr. Merrill what to do to fill up, and he said I'd better interview somebody. Don't you know how all the papers are interviewing Cleveland and Ward McAllister and that kind of people, about all sorts of things? Everybody wants to know what they'll say about it, and it sells the paper. Now, that's what I'm going to do."

"Whom will you interview?" asked Danforth, beginning to grow interested.

"That's what I couldn't tell, for ever so long; but, last night, I happened to hear Uncle Jerry talking about that Mr. Smithson, who's just come to Chester to live. He said he's the one that wrote *Breeze of the Prairie and Breath of the Sea.* You know we thought 'twas fine, when we read it, last year."

"Really, is he that one?" And Danforth's face lighted with genuine enthusiasm.

"Yes. I want most awfully to see him, myself, and I think he'd be a splendid one to interview, as a starter. He must be fine, if he could write a book like that, one of these great, big men, with lots of stories to make your hair stand on end. He might be cross, just at first; but we'd tell him we liked his book, and then he'd be willing to talk, you know."

"We?" echoed Danforth interrogatively.

"Yes, we," replied Jack firmly. "You needn't think I'm going to put it through alone; you must help me. Besides, reporters always hunt in pairs, one with a note-book and the other with a camera. You'd just do for it, you see."

"But I don't see, one little bit," protested Danforth. "I don't want to get into any such scrape, and you know Uncle Jerry never would let us go."

"I'll fix all that," said Jack easily. "It's only twenty miles to Chester, so we could go at ten and get back at six. We would just tell him that we were going on an errand that would take us all day, and we'd tell him all about it when we came home. If I'll settle that, will you go down with me, next Saturday?"

"I don't half want to."

"Just think of talking with the man that wrote *Breeze of the Prairie!*" urged Jack. "Don't you

remember, when we read it, how we both wanted to
ask him piles of questions?"

"Yes, I know; but— And then, what if Mr.
Smithson shouldn't like it?"

"But he will," responded Jack, with conviction.
"That kind of people always do. I suppose it
makes everybody read their books. Come, Dan,"
he added persuasively, "I'll promise to have the
whole bother of it, and all you'll need to do is to
come along with me. It's ever so much more fun
to go together, and I won't make you talk any,
only just snap your camera at him, when he's talking to me and doesn't notice it. You ought to be
willing to do so much. Won't you go?"

Danforth yielded, as he always did when Jack's
voice took on that tone, half-laughing, half-caress-
ing, wholly irresistible.

"I'll go," he agreed; "only, if we get into a
scrape, I won't be responsible. I'm only going as
special artist of the expedition. Now do let me
finish these, before they get spoiled."

"All right; let's see your catalogue, though."
And Jack caught up the little book in which his
brother kept recorded the list of his pictures.
"Five of Miss Davis, two of Bob, nineteen of
Pen, seven of Laddie, and ten of me. Jupiter

Ammon! That's hard on Pen. I thought I'd had the worst of it." And Jack departed, whistling.

Five days later, the boys started upon their first professional errand. Just how Jack had arranged it with Uncle Jerry, it would be hard to say; but he had explained their prospective absence for the day, quite to his uncle's satisfaction. At least, the weather was in their favor. It was one of the clear, bright mornings of late March when spring seems close at hand. The two boys looked unusually manly, as they stepped on board the train. Both were tall for their age and well-formed, and both had the little ease of manner which comes with good birth and good training. Jack's face beamed with smiling assurance, as he patted his pocket wherein lay the shining new note-book, and thought over the generous store of information he had gained as to the tricks and manners of the interviewer. Danforth followed him, grasping his camera a little nervously, for he had a faint, a very faint doubt as to the propriety of their errand, and he remembered hearing somewhere that great authors were not always very courteous to their lesser brethren of the pen. Nevertheless, he forgot all that as soon as the train started, for Jack proceeded to unfold his plan of campaign, and Danforth could only admire his brother's brilliant tact in arranging the speeches he would make to the great man whom they were so soon to behold.

"You see," said Jack, as the train went rushing across the meadows above Chester; "we'll go to the door and ask the servant if we can see Mr. Smithson on professional business. That'll get us in, for he'll probably think that we are a publisher or something, after more books. Then when we get into his library, I'll give him my card and say that we're from *The Riverton Junior Review*, and think his books are the best ones in the world. By that time, he'll get pretty good-tempered, and I'll pepper him with questions; and while I am writing down the answers, you turn on the camera, and count the books and the pictures on the walls, and see if he's gray any. He most likely is, for, in *Breeze of the Prairie*, he said he was fifty when he landed in America. Here we are! Come on."

A moment later, the boys stood on the platform, looking after the train which was fast vanishing in a cloud of dust and smoke. Then Jack turned to the elderly baggage master.

"Can you tell me where Mr. Smithson lives?" he asked.

"Never heerd of him, sonny,' the man replied, as he picked up the pole of his truck.

This was a double blow to Jack. To be addressed as sonny was bad enough; but it was nothing in comparison with the disappointment of finding that his hero was unknown to his very neighbors.

"Never heard of him!" he repeated blankly. "Why, he's a great author and wrote *Breeze of the Prairie.*"

"Never heerd of that, either," said the man, with an apologetic chuckle. "Say, Jim," he added, raising his voice; "know anybody round here named Smithson?"

"Nobody but that queer chap that's just built, up on the Hudson place," answered Jim, lounging up to the little group. "Don't you know the one that has the great greenhouse? come up here last fall."

"That must be the one," said Jack eagerly. "Please tell me how I can find him, and I'll make it worth your while," he added, with a fine assumption of being a man of the world.

But Jim drew back.

"Don't want your cash, bub. Chester folks are ready to do a stranger a good turn for nothin', once in a while. Just go up this street here, till you come to a bank; then turn to your left and keep on for a piece, till you get to an iron watering-trough. Most likely you'll see some yaller hens in the road there. Then turn to your left again and go through a stretch of woods, and pretty soon you'll come to the place. It's a great big red house with lots of corners, not a farmhouse, but a new-fangled one with colored glass and things, and a greenhouse beside it larger'n the house. No; no thanks." And he walked away, leaving the boys to set off on their wanderings.

"He must be awfully rich," said Jack, whose eyes had sparkled at the description of the magnificence in which his hero lived. "He'll probably have a butler, or a footman, or something. I 'most wish we'd hired a carriage to take us, Dan."

"If it's as far as that man said, we shall wish we had a carriage to bring us back," returned Danforth, giving a rakish poke to the, dignified Alpine hat, which replaced the cap he usually wore. "If we get out into the howling wilderness, Jack, where'll we get anything to eat? I'm about starved now, and I never can stand it till night."

"Maybe he'll ask us to stay to lunch," suggested Jack, hopefully.

On they went, through the pleasant old town and out into the quiet country roads beyond. Apart from the excitement of their errand, it was delightful enough to be out in the air, on such a day as this. They had plenty of time before them, and they strolled slowly along, pausing now and then while Danforth took a snap shot at some especially attractive bit of hill or wood, or Jack threw aside his professional dignity long enough to leap over a fence, and peer into the depths of the little brook which tumbled and raced along by the roadside. They had passed the watering-trough, which they had no difficulty in recognizing from the yellow hens wandering aimlessly about it, and they were just entering the little patch of woodland, when Jack caught the sound of a distant jingle of bells.

"Say, Dan," he exclaimed; "here comes a baker's cart; see if 'tisn't. If it is, I'm going to get something to eat, for I can't stand it much longer. We'll have time to eat it, before we get through these woods."

"Good scheme," said Danforth. approvingly. "What'll we get?"

"Doughnuts," responded Jack promptly; "those great round, sugary ones that Bob says are so swinicky. She'll never let us have any, and I think they're fine. Now's our chance."

A few moments later, they continued their journey, each with one of the despised delicacies in his hand, while Jack carried a paper bag containing the rest of the half-dozen. There was something so irresponsible, so unexpected in their position, it was such fun to wander along, talking of a hundred things and munching their doughnuts, that the boys determined to prolong their enjoyment as much as possible. They were still far from the end of the woods, when they were startled to hear a violent crashing of the underbrush. The next minute, a young man leaped over the fence into the road before them, and paused, as if waiting for the boys to join him.

" Does Mr. Smithson live near here?" Jack asked, by way of opening the conversation, for the young man evidently expected them to speak.

" Yes," he answered, with a sudden smile; " he lives about a quarter of a mile from here. Were you going up there?"

" We started for there," said Jack, nudging

"Thank you, I'm as hungry as a wolf."

—Page 256.

Danforth to call his brother's attention to his politic reply. " We were stopping here in town for a few hours, and so we thought we'd walk out this way."

" I'm going that way, myself," said the stranger quietly; " and I can show you where he lives. Do you know him?"

" No; but we know his books," said Danforth, in a sudden burst of enthusiasm which roused him from his wonted quiet.

" His books?" The stranger looked a little puzzled.

" Yes; he's an author, you know, and wrote *Breeze of the Prairie*," explained Jack kindly. " It's a splendid book, too, the best I almost ever read."

"I've heard of that," the stranger said, with a slight air of embarrassment which Jack attributed to the fact of his never having read the great author's great book; " but I supposed — at least, I've heard that he hadn't ever written anything else."

" Then he'd better," returned Jack indignantly. " A man who can write stories like that, ought to keep at it the whole time. You read it when you get a chance. But, I say, won't you have a doughnut?" And he hospitably extended the bag.

The stranger accepted his offer gratefully.

"Thank you," he said; "I'm as hungry as a wolf, for I've been out ever since breakfast, and it must be nearly noon."

As they walked on, from time to time Jack glanced slyly up at his new companion. He was a tall, slight young man, not more than twenty-five or twenty-six at the utmost, with light hair, great blue eyes and a complexion as fresh and rosy as that of a girl. In spite of his shabby brown suit and the great tin box which he wore slung over his shoulder, he was unmistakably a gentleman. There was something very attractive, too, in his easy, off-hand manner, and he soon had both the boys talking with him, as if they were the oldest and best of friends.

"This is Mr. Smithson's house," he said at length, pausing at the gate which opened upon a broad, rolling lawn.

"This?" And Jack gazed with reverent eyes upon the scene before him. Then he looked up at the young man, who was turning in at the gate. "And are you his gardener?" he asked, with a new respect in his tone.

The stranger smiled a little.

"No; not exactly," he answered; "but I live here on the place. Is there anything more I can do for you?"

Before Jack could beg the stranger to gain him the coveted privilege of interviewing the author, a man, working on the lawn, had come up to the spot where they were standing.

"If you please, Mr. Smithson —" he was beginning; but Jack heard nothing more. He could only stare at the stranger, with amazement written on every line of his face. At length he asked slowly, —

"Are you the real Mr. Smithson?"

"I'm afraid I am," confessed the stranger, smiling at the boy's surprise.

"The one that wrote *Breeze of the Prairie?*"

"The very one."

Alas for Jack! During the past few days, he had often fancied himself brought face to face with his idol, had fondly pictured the ease with which he would open the interview, the graceful words he would say. Now that the expected moment had come in such an unexpected fashion, he could only stare blankly at Mr. Smithson for a seemingly endless interval, and then ejaculate slowl ,—

"Great Scott! And I offered you a doughnut, and you — you *took it!*"

The young man laughed.

"I hope you don't grudge me the best lunch I've had, in many a long day," he said gayly. "I'll own that I played you rather a shabby trick; but at first I never dreamed that you wanted to see me, or knew anything about me. Still, 'twas very good to find that at least two boys like my story, and wish that I would try again. Now come up to the house, and tell me what you wanted of me."

"We wanted to interview you," explained Jack, with an uncomfortable feeling that he was not approaching the subject as easily as he had expected to do.

Mr. Smithson looked as if he did not quite understand. He was used to reporters and their ways; but even the dreaded word *interview* did not lead him to connect these attractive boys with that much-hated race.

"To — what?" he inquired.

"To interview you. We're reporters, you know," said Jack, producing his card on which he had written, "Editor of *The Riverton Junior Review.*"

There was a sudden, almost imperceptible stif-
feuing of the author's manner. Then, as he glanced
at the card in his hand, he smiled again in his old
pleasant way.

"And so you are Mr. John Bennett Spaulding,"
he said; "and editor of *The Riverton Junior Review.* I don't think I know the paper. What is
it, a weekly?'

"It isn't, yet," responded Jack honestly,
although he shrank from the admission, fearing
that it might be disadvantageous to the coming
interview. "It's going to begin next Saturday,
and come once a week. We wanted to have an
interview with you, to start off with. This is my
brother Dan," he added, turning to Danforth, who
stood gazing at Mr. Smithson, in an unconscious
attitude of admiration and fear.

"And you were going to serve me up on your
camera plate; were you?" asked Mr. Smithson,
as he gave his hand to the boy. "Now," he went
on, while he led the way to the piazza and settled
his guests in some large rocking-chairs in a sunny
corner; "sit down here and tell me all about this.
It's an immense joke, whatever it is; and I want
to hear about it."

And Jack told him, entering with boyish enthusiasm into the details of his press, his prospective paper and his plan of interviewing their genial host; while Mr. Smithson leaned back in his chair, and laughed till the tears came into his eyes, with his enjoyment of the caper.

"Suppose we make a bargain," he said at last. "I've never yet been interviewed, and I've always said that I never would be. What if we leave it this way : you stay here to lunch with my mother and me ; and, before you go, I'll write just a little scrap of something for your first paper, on condition that you won't say anything about me, — except to say that you came here to lunch with me," he added, seeing Jack's sudden look of disappointment. "But don't say anything else, please. Only," he laughed again, "you must count me as one of your regular subscribers. But come in and see my mother." And he led the way into the house.

A week later, the opening number of *The Riverton Junior Review* made its appearance. Its first page bore, in the place of honor, a rhymed greeting to the new periodical, signed with the well-known name. Beneath it was a short note, informing the public that the little poem was written by Mr. Smithson, the last time that the editors had the pleasure of taking lunch with him, in his own house. A marked copy of *The Review* went flying down to Chester, by the earliest possible mail, and appeared to Mr. Smithson just as he was leaving the breakfast-table, for a long morning in his library.

"Jove!" he said, with a laugh, as he read Jack's letter which accompanied it. "That boy has the go-ahead in him, and he'll make something, some day. 'Twas almost too bad to put him on his honor about showing me up; and it would have been good fun to see what he'd say. I believe I'll turn the tables, and write him up, — only I could never do him justice. I wish I could be sure that all my public liked my first attempt as well as he did." And he whistled gayly to himself, as he sat down and took up his pen.

CHAPTER XIV.

DANFORTH'S ROMANCE.

"WILL you be good enough to tell me what you're up to, Dan?" asked Bobbie's voice at the kitchen door.

Danforth started violently, nearly dropping the flatiron from his hand, while the color rushed to his face.

"I'm busy," he answered curtly. "I wish you'd go away."

Bobbie pushed the door wide open and came in.

"What in the world —?" she began slowly.

"Can't you see for yourself?" he responded impatiently. "The crease is all out of my trousers, and I'm trying to put it back in again. Nothing strange in that; is there?"

Bobbie gave one comprehensive glance at the garment on the table, at the fast-cooling iron in Danforth's hand and at the dark red flush on Danforth's cheeks. Then she burst out laughing

262

and ran away out of the room. Five minutes later, she knocked at Margaret's door.

"Oh, Miss Davis, Miss Davis!" she exclaimed, as soon as she was admitted. "What do you think? Dan's caught it at last."

"Caught it!" echoed Margaret, while there rushed into her mind direful visions of scarlet-fever or small-pox.

"Yes, I know now. He's in love!" And Bobbie dropped into a chair and nodded conclusively.

"What nonsense, Bobbie! Dan is nothing but a child."

"I don't care," responded Bobbie coolly. "I know what I know, and you'll think so too, when I tell you. He's in love, and it's with Pen."

"Bobbie dear, I'd rather you didn't talk about such things," said Margaret quite decidedly. "Dan and Penelope are good friends, just as you and Ellie are; but people don't get in love at fifteen, and you know that Danforth would be very angry, if he heard what you are saying."

"I can't help that," persisted Bobbie. "It's true, every word of it, as true as true can be. Now you see here, I've kept still ever so long,

and now I must talk. You'd rather I'd say it to
you than to Dan. What's the harm? I think
it's just lovely, only I like to plague them about
it a little."

Margaret made no reply, so, after a short pause,
Bobbie went on, —

"It's been going on for ever so long. That
Christmas fire 'started it up, I suppose. I didn't
think much about it, at first. I knew Dan was
there ever so much; but I s'posed it was so he
could take Pen's picture. Then Dan began to
act queer, and I kept my eyes open. He used
to wear his best suit every day; and wouldn't
ever put on his cap, but wore his hat the whole
time. When Grandma sent him on an errand,
he always went round by High Street, no matter
how much of a hurry he was in. Then his hair
began to look dark and sort of shiny; and, one
day, I found my bottle of violet hidden in his
bureau drawer. Now, to-day, I've just found him
all alone in the kitchen, trying to iron some new
creases into his trouser legs." And Bobbie paused
to laugh again at the recollection. " Well, all
this showed something was going on; but I
wasn't just sure, till a day or two ago. You
know that pretty bracelet Pen had Christmas,

the dark silver one? All at once she stopped
wearing it; and when I asked her where 'twas,
she just blushed and wouldn't say a word. Night
before last, when Dan was frolicking with me, I
looked up his sleeve, and there was Pen's bracelet,
way up inside his cuff. Now what do you think?"
she concluded triumphantly.

"Think? I think that you are an excellent
detective," said Margaret lightly, although she
was secretly amused by Bobbie's ferreting out the
mystery which she had long since suspected.

"And then there's something else," added
Bobbie, with a fresh laugh. "This time it's Pen.
Five or six of us walked down the river, a week
or two ago, you know. I didn't see much of
either Dan or Pen, for I was ahead, with Jack
and Charlie Prentiss; but, coming home, Pen
came rushing after me and caught hold of my
arm. Her face was as red as could be, and she
looked all swelled up, ready to cry; but 'twas
ever so long before she'd say anything. By and
by she began in a queer voice, as if the words
were a good deal larger round than her throat,
'Bobbie,' — no, I remember; she said 'Roberta.'
She never calls me Roberta, unless something is
very much wrong. Well, she said, 'Roberta, I

want to ask you something.' Then she stopped
and puffed, like this." Bobbie illustrated Penelope's agitation, with unsympathetic amusement.
"Then she went ahead, 'I want to ask you something a friend of mine wanted to know; 'tisn't
for me, you know, but for this friend. If a lady
insults a gentleman, ought she to apologize, or
ought she to wait and make him?' Wasn't that
the greatest idea? I told her that her friend
ought to be ashamed of herself for not having
any more sense. Then she flared up, and said
I was mean as mean could be. I didn't know
what she meant then; but Dan came home sulky
as anything, and blue as your gown, and Ellie
said they'd been having a perfectly dreadful
fight." Bobbie's tone was darkly suggestive of
dirks and cutlasses. "They must have made it
up in a hurry, though, for Dan was there the
next day. But wasn't he glum, that night! I
believe I'll go and see if he's finished his ironing."
And she went away as abruptly as she had come.

Much to her regret, Margaret was forced to
agree with Bobbie's conclusions, though she
smiled to herself, as she thought of the premises
upon which they were based. For the past two
or three months, in fact, ever since Christmas,

she had been surprised to see Danforth's increasing devotion to Penelope; and she had been the more astonished at it, because heretofore Danforth, partly from shyness, partly from indifference, had always treated Bobbie's girl friends with supreme contempt. Moreover, Pen was not at all the girl whom it seemed likely that Danforth would fancy, her irrepressible words and ways were so contrary to his own quiet gentleness.

At first, Margaret had rejoiced in the new friendship, for she found that it was giving Danforth an ease and assurance which he had always lacked, while his overflowing spirits testified to his own enjoyment of the unwonted interest. However, she discovered that, little by little, his lessons were beginning to suffer from his absorption in Penelope; and, as week after week went by, he slowly dropped behind Jack who was working finely, spurred on by the approach of June and the long-talked-of preliminaries.

It was hard to know just where lay the real trouble and its remedy. Danforth worked his full time; but it was in a listless, half-hearted fashion, quite different from his previous enthusiasm, and he took all of Margaret's little lectures and rebukes with a most exemplary meekness. Still, she was at

her wit's end, for she disliked to appeal to Uncle
Jerry, knowing but too well that such a course
could only lessen Danforth's liking for her, and
her consequent influence over him. Exhortation
and command had no effect, beyond the moment
of their being uttered; and, meanwhile, Danforth
was steadily dropping backward. What was to
be done?

Moreover, she had noticed the new desire to
beautify himself, of which Bobbie had spoken.
In an older man, she would not have been slow
to attribute it to its proper cause; but it seemed
impossible that Danforth, her shy, shrinking boy,
could be already emerging from his chrysalis and
entering upon one of the phases of the full-grown
butterfly. She dismissed the thought as absurd,
and yet it was true, painfully true. Even Bobbie
had recognized the fact.

For the next week or two, Margaret watched
the boy closely. Except for the increasing neglect of his lessons, it seemed to her that he had
never before been half so lovable, for in addition
to the old, gentle, winning ways which she knew
so well, there was a new brightness and fun that
she had never seen until now. Pen was evidently stirring him up; but unfortunately she

was, at the same time, ruining his chances for passing a creditable examination, and Margaret felt that it was time for her to interfere. Accordingly, one noon after Jack and Bobbie had left the library, she told Danforth that, for the present, she should give him an hour of work, each afternoon. The boy faced her abruptly, with a little hurt look in his blue eyes.

"What's the matter, Miss Davis!" he asked quickly. "Won't my work go as 'tis?"

"Not quite, Dan," she answered. "You've been running behind a little, and I want to go over some of this last work, to make sure that you're all right. You can't afford to run any risks; and we can both take the time well enough. A few weeks will straighten you out again."

For a moment, Danforth looked at her doubtfully; then he said reluctantly, —

"All right; only I don't think I need the extra time. I'm getting on well enough, as 'tis; and I can work a little harder, mornings, if you want."

"I think the afternoons will be better, Dan," she answered, in a tone of quiet decision which she rarely used.

And so it came about that Margaret and Danforth took possession of the library, for an

hour each afternoon, and devoted the time to a
thorough review of the work of the past few
weeks. It was the best training that the boy
could have had; but he failed to accept it in all
gratitude, since it shortened his afternoon calls
on Penelope, and kept him at work when his
friends were all taking their recreation. It was
particularly hard, in the warm, tempting days
of early spring when the others were all off on
some ride or walk; and as the days went by,
Danforth's face grew longer and longer, and his
hours grew shorter and shorter. But if it was
hard for the boy, it was harder still for Margaret,
since she saw so plainly all his side of the matter,
all the causes which had tempted him to neglect
his work. At length, one day just before Easter,
came the final issue. Margaret had gone to her
room, directly after lunch, when she heard Danforth's step in the hall. A moment later, he
knocked at her door.

"Come in, Dan," she said hospitably, as she
opened the door.

"I can't; I'm in a hurry," he answered nervously. "I — I came to see if you wouldn't let
me off this afternoon."

"But I told you I couldn't, Dan," she said,

trying to speak quietly, though she saw, from the
set look of Danforth's lips, that at last she was to
engage in a contest of will with her favorite
pupil. "You know you asked me yesterday,
and I told you then that you would have to take
your regular work."

There was a long silence. Margaret was the
first to break it.

"What is it that you want to do?" she asked.

"I wanted to take Pen Stoddard for a drive,"
he answered desperately, while his color rose
at the admission. "Uncle Jerry is going to sell
Duke, this spring, and I may not have another
chance. He's likely to go, any day."

"Have you made an engagement with Penelope?" inquired Margaret slowly. "I thought
you knew that you were to have your usual hour."

"'Tisn't a real engagement," Danforth replied.
"I only wanted to go."

There was another prolonged silence. This
time Danforth spoke first.

"What if I don't come?" he asked.

Margaret hesitated. She disliked to give in;
and any appeal to Uncle Jerry to uphold her
authority, would be childish, she felt. She could
read the boy well enough to see that he was fully

determined to go; but that he could not be quite
satisfied to do so without her consent. She looked
out at the clear, yellow sunshine, and her heart
urged her to relent; then she remembered that
this was not a question of to-day or to-morrow
but of Danforth's whole future ability to deny
himself, if need be, and she hardened her heart.

"You are not a baby, Dan," she said slowly, as
she looked straight into his great blue eyes;
"and you know, as well as I do, that I have no
real authority over you. You know, too, how I
feel about this. You must do as you think best,
only remember that I absolutely disapprove of
your going."

The pause which followed was a critical one.
Each was conscious of the tension of the other's
mood, and each, while secretly resolving not to
yield, yet felt uncertain how the contest would
end. Danforth had set his face as rigidly as
he could, but his chin was quivering a little.
Unwilling as he was to give in, it was hurting
him more than he had supposed it would, to
oppose Margaret's wishes and incur her disapproval. As she watched him, Margaret felt a
nervous desire to laugh and cry at the same time,
to laugh at the mock seriousness of this tempest

in a teapot, to cry with a childish disappointment
in her lack of influence over the boy. It seemed
as if he would never speak. At length he asked
a little impatiently, —

"What difference does this one day make, Miss
Davis? There are plenty more coming."

"It isn't just for to-day," she answered gently;
"only, if you give up, to-day, and run off when
you ought to be working, it will be just so much
harder to begin again to-morrow. You are making
up now for time when you have been doing half-
work; and you know I told you that I must have
this afternoon hour, so that I can get you back
even with Jack, before I go home at Easter. If
you give up to-day, and another to-day, and still
another, it will surely end in your losing your
year. I have told you just what I think; now I
can only leave it to your sense of right."

Still the shut teeth, but the quivering chin, as
Danforth looked at the floor, at the walls, at the
folds of Margaret's gown, everywhere but at her
face which, in spite of the anxious light in her
eyes, never once lost its friendly smile. Then, all
of a sudden, he looked her full in the face, as he
said unsteadily, —

"I think I'll risk it."

"Very well," she replied, although with a surety
that it was not very well, that the battle was lost
for both sides.

She stood on the threshold, watching the boy as
he went down the stairs. There was nothing about
him to suggest the victor; he was much more like
the vanquished, for complete and utter dejection
was written on every line of his face and figure.
His conscience was not active enough to make
him yield a point; but it was sufficiently active to
render him extremely uncomfortable, now that his
point was gained.

Danforth was unusually silent and grave when
he appeared at the dinner-table, that night,
although Margaret's manner to him was quite as
if nothing unusual had occurred; and, for the first
time, he failed to join the others in the library,
later, when they were reveling in the Van Bibber
sketches. Jack was reading, that night; but
Margaret heard little of the charming stories, for
her thoughts were with her other boy, wondering
whether to keep up her unconcerned manner, or
to say a word or two, and then dismiss the affair
into the past. She knew Danforth well enough
to see that already he was feeling ashamed of
himself. It would doubtless be good discipline

for him to let him suffer the pangs of remorse for a little longer. But, on the other hand, she disliked to do anything to hurt the sensitive boy; and she was unwilling to allow their warm friendship to be scarred by a longer coldness between them. After all, perhaps the victory was on her side; she felt that she could afford to be magnanimous.

She saw little of Danforth during the evening. When she and Jack went back into the drawing-room, Danforth had gone up into the Wilderness; and although he reappeared later, he took up a book and apparently buried himself in its pages, though she was conscious that he was watching her out of the corners of his eyes, while she played bézique with Jack. Earlier than usual he started up, book in hand, bade them all goodnight and left the room. Half-way up the stairs, he heard Margaret speak his name.

"Well?" he said reluctantly, as he turned to face her.

She slowly went up to him, and sat down on the stair below him.

"Come, Dan," she said; "don't go off to bed just yet. It isn't time; and besides, I want to make up, first."

This was unexpected, and Danforth's face showed his surprise. Then he controlled himself, and dropped back into his old indifferent manner. At heart, he longed to respond to her friendly advances; but the very intensity of his feeling made it hard to speak out. His face only grew more and more grim, as he asked briefly, —

"Make up what?"

"I think you know what I mean," she answered gently. "You were vexed because I wouldn't let you off this afternoon; isn't it so? You haven't been like yourself, ever since you came home; and you were running off to bed, to get out of sight of me. Come, Dan," and she held out her hand; "we've been too good friends to quarrel, and the longer this goes on, the harder it will be to end it; so let's shake hands on it, say there's been a mistake somewhere, and then forget all about it and begin again."

Her look and manner were not to be resisted, and Danforth's coldness suddenly melted, as he dropped down on the stairs at her side, and seized her hand in a grip which nearly forced a cry from her lips.

"I was mad, Miss Davis, for I wanted to go like fun; and I'd promised Pen I'd take her. I thought then that you hadn't any business to keep me in, and I wasn't going to knock under; but," he hesitated; then he added, in a lower tone, " but I about came' to the conclusion, while I was gone, that I hadn't any business to go. I am sorry, truly; and another time, you can count on me."

It is always hard for a boy to acknowledge himself in the wrong, and Margaret realized all that this avowal was costing Danforth. The stairway, where they sat, was too dark to allow her to see his face clearly; but his voice and the little hesitation in his manner told of the difficulty he was having in confessing his small sin. Margaret found it hard to add one word of rebuke, for this short contest had taught her how dear the boy was to her.

" Dan," she said slowly, as she rested one hand on his shoulder; " I did what I thought was best for you, and the doing it hurt me more than it did you, for I knew just how you wanted to go. But lessons have to come first, dear, whether it's before we go into college, or after we come out, and I felt that I'd no right to let you shirk, to-day, when it might make a difference to your whole life. You've been falling from grace a

little, the last month or two, and we've both of
us had to work to make it up. Now we're nearly
ready to start fair and square again, and I mustn't
be disappointed in you. You haven't much idea,
Dan, how many hopes and plans for your manhood I am making. If you'll do your part, they
can all be carried out, and my dear old Dan will
be a man of whom I shall be proud, some day.
Now let's turn our backs on the past, and on
to-day's horrid little disagreement, and look at
the future and work toward it, like true men
and women, sure that every day of real, faithful
work will bring the goal nearer and still nearer
us."

Through the dim light, she could see Danforth's
eyes fixed upon her face, and his own face was
very serious and gentle, as he said, —

"I will try, Miss Davis. I know I've been
acting like a jay; but honestly, you won't have
any more trouble of that kind. Give me another
chance, and I'll start fresh."

"What are you doing, mooning there on the
stairs?" called Jack from below. "I thought
you'd gone to bed an hour ago, Dan. Come
ahead; I'm sleepy."

Two days later, Bobbie came into Margaret's

room, with excitement and mystery written on every feature.

"They've had another dreadful quarrel," she announced, without further preface. "It was day before yesterday, when Dan was taking her to ride I don't know what's happened; but Dan's given back her bracelet, and Pen says she doesn't mean to speak to him again, forever and ever, because he's a stupid and a Miss Nancy. I told her that Dan was a great deal too good for her, and if she didn't speak to him, I wouldn't speak to her, so there! But what do you think could have happened? Seems to me I can't stand it, unless I find out. Pen Stoddard knows what I think of her, though; and that's one comfort!"

CHAPTER XV.

"FACILIS DESCENSUS AVERNI."

HUGH THORNTON sat musing by the fire in his room, one evening early in April. A gentle shower was pattering down on the piazza roof outside his window, and the monotonous, dreary sound made a most suitable background for his thoughts, since his mood was as gloomy as the night outside. That afternoon, he had chanced to meet Margaret on the street, and she had given him a bow so chilling that, as soon as she had passed him, he had involuntarily turned up his collar and plunged his hands deep down into his pockets. Now, for an hour, he had been sitting with his book closed on his knee, while he viciously gnawed his mustache and scowled at the open fire. He was fond of that fire, too. In fact, it had been one of the chief reasons for his choosing the room, but to-night it seemed uncommonly fractious. It persisted in smoking at intervals, while, in spite of his efforts, the sticks on the andirons refused to lie cris-crossing at the proper angle, but packed themselves into a firm, solid pile which was death to a cheery blaze. He had promised to dine with his cousin, Mrs. Pierson, that night; but when dinner-time came, he had not found himself in a mood to be an agreeable guest, so he had sent a messenger boy with a note of apology for his non-appearance, and dined alone instead. It was the first time, for nearly a year, that he had allowed himself to stop and think just how miserable he was; and now that he was deliberately giving himself up to the contemplation of his woes, he began to think that he had never before half realized how great they were.

"It's a beastly place to put me in," he was saying to himself. "Here I am, likely to meet her any minute; there's no chance of missing her, in this two-inch hole of a town. 'Twasn't enough for her to flirt with me and then drop me; but she had to come up here after me. No; come to think of it, she was in ahead of me, and I followed her." And he laughed at· his own inconsistency. "But why, in the name of all the laws of chance, did we ever happen to strike Riverton at the same time? I should as soon have thought of finding her in Patagonia, as over at Atherton's, that night. I wonder what sent her up here, anyway. However, that something I'm not likely to find out. If she were a man, I could ask her, point blank, what she meant by treating me like a worn-out pair of shoes; but you can't do that kind of thing with a woman. If I dared" — He rose and walked up and down the room, still venting his impatience upon his long-suffering mustache. At length he stopped abruptly, as he said aloud, "By Jove, I'll do it, and take the consequences."

The next day was one of the most perfect days of early spring, and Gerald came home to lunch, declaring that it was a disgrace to anyone to stay in the house, in such weather as that, they must all go for a long drive together. As invariably happened, Gerald's will carried all obstacles before it, and shortly after two o'clock, the great, three-seated carriage was driven up to the door. Grandpa and Grandma Atherton were snugly packed away on the back seat, Margaret and Danforth took the middle and Bobbie settled herself in her usual place at her uncle's side. Then there came a sudden inquiry for Jack; but Jack, strange to say, was nowhere to be found.

"We can't wait any longer," said Uncle Jerry, after they had searched and called in vain. "He knew we were going; and if he isn't here, that's his look-out." And gathering up the reins, he drove down the hill, out into the road and then northward, up the valley.

Quarter of an hour later, Jack cautiously emerged from the hay-loft of the barn whither, for reasons of his own, he had retired directly after lunch. It had not suited Jack's convenience to go to drive, that afternoon, although he was perfectly contented to have the others go and leave him alone, for he had important business on hand, and he had no wish to be interrupted. Two days before this, Bobbie had run off with his silver penholder, and refused to give it up until he promised to get one like it for her. To-day, Jack had resolved to take justice into his own hands by rummaging among her possessions until he found it. Then, if there were any time left, he promised himself the pleasure of rearranging her bureau drawers for her, a favorite employment of his, whenever Bobbie had been particularly exasperating.

It had cost him something to give up the drive, that day, to watch the others starting off without him and to know that, if he chose, he could have a place on the front seat and, perhaps, drive the span, after their spirits had quieted down a little. Still, justice was justice and must triumph, so he resolutely refused to answer their calls; but, as soon as they were well out of sight, he had climbed down from the fragrant loft and marched toward the house, to wreak vengeance upon Bobbie.

To his extreme surprise, he found the back door closed and locked. Unknown to him, Grandma Atherton had given both the maids permission to go out for the afternoon; and the old house was quite deserted, except for Jack who wandered up and down, as anxious to enter as any prowling thief, and as powerless. In vain he tried the front door, the side door, the hall window. Then he came around to the back door again and shook it. The clatter of the old-fashioned latch startled him with its noise; but his efforts produced no other effect. He backed off to a little distance and looked up at the windows. Bobbie's was left temptingly open, as if to mock him. If he could only get up there! But he might as well wish to call on the Man in the Moon, while he was about it; a pair of wings would be necessary in either case.

Once more he prowled around the house, trying all the windows within reach from the ground. They were all made fast on the inside, as Jack had, supposed, for Grandpa Atherton's hobby was a continual fear of burglars, and he had enough bolts and bars on his house to enable it to withstand an ordinary siege. Finding his efforts of no avail, Jack came around to the front of the house again, and threw himself down on the broad porch at the door, to rest at his ease while he planned what to do with himself, all the long afternoon. If he had only gone with the others! But there was no use in his wishing for an impossibility. The mischief was done, and he must make the best of it. Still, it was provoking to miss both the drive and the chance to revenge himself upon Bobbie. He wondered what he would better do next.

He was still glancing meditatively about and revolving various plans in his fertile brain, when he chanced to catch sight of a low, narrow window opening into the cellar, and a sudden brilliant idea came into his head. The window was very small, the sash only held two square panes of glass and was swung on a hinge; and he saw from the crack at one side that through some carelessness it had

been left unfastened. He chuckled to himself as
he thought of his grandfather's horror, if he could
see it. Just below the window, he remembered,
stood Grandma Atherton's shelves of preserves;
and, by careful management, anyone who should
succeed in crawling in through the window, could
use those shelves as a ladder by which to descend
to the floor. Once on the cellar bottom, his course
was clear. Ten feet from the window, the stairs
led up into the kitchen, and from there it was easy
enough to reach Bobbie's room, find his pen, make
hay of her possessions and then retire by way of
the front door. Jack hesitated no longer. He
pulled off his coat, threw it on the floor of the
porch and, approaching the little window, he
pushed it wide open.

The hole was a tight fit for a boy of fifteen, and
Jack surveyed it rather dubiously. Then he put
in his head and looked about him. The sudden
change from the bright sunshine to the dim light
of the cellar made it impossible for him to distin-
guish anything below him; but he took it for
granted that everything was in its usual place.
Accordingly, he drew out his head, turned around
and prepared to wiggle in, feet first. Half-way
through the window, he stuck fast, and for a few

moments it seemed more than probable that he would have to spend his afternoon in that undignified position. However, after he had writhed and kicked and pushed until his courage and strength were both becoming exhausted, he at length succeeded in forcing his way through the opening and hung by his hands, while he swung his feet this way and that, in search of the shelves which were nowhere to be found.

The old cellar was ten feet deep, and Jack realized with an uncomfortable keenness .that it would be no pleasant experience to drop from the little window at the top, down on the hard earth floor beneath. It was impossible to pull himself up again, and work his way out through the window once more; so he could only cling to the sash, while there flashed through his mind grewsome tales of broken ribs and sprained ankles and similar uncomfortable experiences. At length his wrists could bear the strain no longer; be felt his hold weakening, and he fell with a thud down upon a great pile of wood ashes which had been placed there, only the day before.

Beyond the blow to his feelings, and the cloud of ashes which filled his eyes and mouth, Jack was not hurt in the least. He lay still for a

moment, to collect his scattered ideas; then he
rose and brushed himself off, while there came
into his mind a vague memory of having heard
Uncle Jerry tell the man to save all the ashes
from the wood fires, that winter, since they were
so good to scatter over the lawn, in the spring.
However, he was unable to discover what had
become of the shelves which ordinarily stood
there, until, glancing across into a dark corner
near the stairway, he saw the familiar gleam of
the well-filled glass jars.

Once on his feet again, he realized that there
was no time to be wasted, especially since to his
former program was now added the necessity of
removing all traces of the ashes from his person;
and this, he felt convinced, would be no short
and easy task. According, he marched across
the cellar, ran up the stairs to the kitchen door
and pressed the latch, only to find that all his
trials were to no purpose. With unusual care
and foresight, the maids had bolted the door
before they left the house. At this overwhelm-
ing discovery, Jack's feelings overcame him, and
he gave vent to a prolonged whistle.

"Treed like Davy Crockett's coon, by Jove!"
he said to himself. "Here is a mess! I must

get out, or I'll never hear the last of it from
Bob. She's never forgiven me for having to
fish her out of the pot-hole, last fall, and she'll
just fatten on this." And quitting the stairs,
Jack returned to the ash-heap, where he dejectedly sat down to ponder upon his situation.

It was not an encouraging prospect before him.
The cellar was dark and damp; the afternoon
would be a long and tedious one, for he had no
possible occupation; and, most of all, he had the
certainty of being well laughed at, when the
others came home and discovered him in his
absurd plight. He was perfectly well aware that
he deserved being laughed at, that he would have
laughed at Danforth or Bobbie in the same pre-
dicament; but that made it no easier for him to
bear their ridicule. And yet, sitting there in the
ashes, he laughed at himself, laughed till the
tears came into his dark eyes, so keenly did he
realize the comicality of his position. No; it
would never do to be discovered there. He must
get out, in some way or other.

He started up again and began to explore the
cellar, in the hope of discovering, in some dark
corner, a ladder or else some boxes which he
could pile up under the window, and so climb

out into the light of day. Nothing of the kind was to be found; the cellar was barren of all such waste lumber, and swept and garnished as was all of Grandma Atherton's domain. For one short moment, Jack even meditated taking all the glass jars from the shelves, and moving the shelves across to the window. Then he dismissed that hope. It would be a long piece of work, and he would be unable to come back again to replace the jars, so their changed position would inevitably lead to discovery. If he must take the ridicule in any case, he would not put himself to all that trouble as well. He returned to his ash-heap and waited.

The afternoon passed very slowly. In the intervals of thinking of the others and picturing their enjoyment of their drive, he had plenty of time to meditate upon his past, his present and his future. He went back to India, even, and to the memory of one long day of solitary confinement he had undergone, where his *ayah* had remorselessly told tales of his misdeeds to his mother. Bobbie had been in the same scrape, too, and he remembered that he had gained some comfort from the knowledge that she was just as badly off as he was, that he was not alone in his suffering. But to-day Bobbie was triumphantly riding off at Uncle Jerry's side, and he was sitting there alone in the dark, gloomy cellar. He thought of the Prisoner of Chillon and the Man in the Iron Mask, and reflected that never before had he felt half enough sympathy for them. The Princes in the tower didn't count, for there were two of them, and they could keep each other company.

He had apparently been sitting there for hours, when he heard a step approaching the house, and he held his breath to listen. If it were only one of the servants, all would yet be well, for Jack had a generous allowance and he had already tested the effect of small bribes in covering the manifestations of his sins. But the person, whoever it was, evidently was not a servant, for the steps went directly toward the front door. Should he throw himself upon the mercy of a guest? Jack hesitated. If it were a woman, she would be powerless to help him out; moreover, she would be much more likely to tell tales of him. All in all, though, he thought he would take his chances, so he called as loudly as he could, —

" Who's there? I want some help."

There was a short silence, while the caller

evidently looked about to discover the source of this unexpected salutation. Then, to Jack's infinite relief, the answer came back in an unmistakably masculine tone, —

" Where are you ? "

" Down cellar. Come and help me out."

After his experiences of the afternoon, to Jack's mind there was but one way of approach to the cellar. Apparently the stranger did not possess the key to the mystery, however, for there followed another pause of uncertainty.

" How shall I get there?" he called, at length.

There was something so absurd in this interview, carried on at the tops of their lungs, although in reality they were but a few feet apart, that Jack had to stop and laugh, before he answered, —

" Through that window by the front door, the little, low window. But don't you come here; I want you to get me out, not come in, yourself."

A moment later, Jack saw the window suddenly darkened. Looking up, he discovered the face of Mr. Thornton staring down at him with unfeigned amazement.

" If I might inquire — " he was beginning, as he gazed down upon this nineteenth-century Job, still seated in the ashes, when Jack interrupted him, —

"Don't inquire. Help me out, Mr. Thornton, and do your inquiring later. You get me out of this, and then I'll tell you all about it."

"But is Miss Davis at home?" Mr. Thornton asked a little nervously.

"No; there isn't anybody at home. That's the reason I'm here," replied Jack petulantly. "Can't you get me out?"

"I'm not sure how to manage it," said Mr. Thornton, who was apparently dazed by this unexpected call upon his mercy and his inventiveness. "Why don't you go up those stairs and around through the house?" he suggested feebly, after a prolonged contemplation of the scene of action.

"Oh, come off there!" said Jack irreverently. "Don't you suppose I'd have done that hours ago, if I could? I'm locked out and I tried to get into the house this way; don't you see? That door at the head of the stairs is fastened, and I can't get back out of the window. I don't know when the others will be home, and, naturally, I want to get out of this ·place before the crack of doom."

"Oh, I think I am beginning to understand," said Mr. Thornton, upon whom a new light had dawned. "You're caught in here, and you want to get out before the others come home to laugh at you; is that it?"

"Now you've struck it," said Jack approvingly. "Next thing is, how are you going to strike me?"

"Isn't there a ladder around here anywhere?" inquired Mr. Thornton, looking about him.

"Two little ones in the barn, left hand side as you go in," replied Jack concisely.

"Wait till I get them." And the head vanished.

It was gone for a long time. At last there came a sound of bumping and scraping, and then Mr. Thornton's voice called, —

"All right? Keep out of the way till I let this down." And the end of a ladder came slowly in at the open window.

It was but the work of a moment more to let down the ladder and to arrange it in position. Then Jack slowly crawled forth to the light of day, and drew the ladder out after him. But such a Jack! Coated with ashes from head to heel, he came out as gray as the proverbial miller, for the dust had powdered his hair, begrimed his face and changed the complexion of his clothing until it might easily have been mistaken for penitential sackcloth. The boy looked down at himself, then at Mr. Thornton who was dressed with more than usual care, and he burst out laughing so heartily and infectiously that his companion joined him.

"I really must be going," Mr. Thornton said, a little later, after Jack had told him the full story of his woes. "Please say to Miss Davis that I called, and that I am extremely sorry she is away. You'll not forget?" he added anxiously.

"Trust me!" returned Jack. "You don't know how grateful to you I am, Mr. Thornton. You've helped me out of a bad scrape to-day, and maybe sometime I can do the same for you. I hope so, anyway." And as the guest went away down the hill, Jack departed to the barn, to find the horse-brush and the carriage-sponge, and remove as much as possible of the ashes from his clothing and skin, that he might be able to get to his room unobserved, as soon as the house was opened again.

CHAPTER XVI.

DUKE AND DANFORTH.

"ANYTHING you'd like before I go, Grandma?" asked Danforth, coming into the dining-room where Grandma Atherton and Margaret sat lingering over their lunch, long after the others had left the table.

"Nothing, I think," she answered, looking up at the boy who stood, cap in hand, in the doorway.

"Where are you bound, my dear?" inquired Margaret, rising and crossing the room to his side.

"Off for a ride; that's all," he replied, smiling down at her, for in the year he had completely outgrown his tutor, and took great pride in looking over the top of her head. "I wish you felt like coming, too."

"I wish I could," she answered fervently. "You know I'd like nothing better than a scamper with you; but I played, all yesterday afternoon, and to-day I must write to mother, or she'll think I have forsaken her. Take good care of yourself, little boy." And she patted his arm in the motherly fashion which Danforth liked so well.

" Trust me to look out for number one," he said, laughing, as he came forward to the table and helped himself to a handful of crackers. " If you won't come with me, come out and see me mount, at least. Remember your first experience in that line ? "

"Saucy boy!" said Margaret, laughing at the recollection. "I've redeemed my reputation, so you ought to be generous and forget my early sins. Wait till I get some sugar for Duke, and then I'll come and see you off."

" I do wish Jerry would sell that pony," said Grandma Atherton uneasily. " I don't think he's safe for you to ride, Dan."

"You don't need to worry, Grandma," he answered carelessly. " Duke is cross sometimes; but he knows I'm his master, and he has to come to terms."

Duke certainly was cross, that day. His eyes showed an angry gleam, as he came out of the stable, and he pawed the ground restlessly, while Danforth was buckling the saddle girths, even the sugar he accepted haughtily, as if he were in no mind to be bribed into a good humor. The next moment, Danforth leaped lightly into the saddle and grasped the reins, as Duke reared and kicked in a way to send a less experienced rider to the ground. But Danforth kept his seat easily enough, and with a quick touch of the whip, a quick turn of the curb-rein, he brought Duke to the ground again, and sent him bounding forward at a gallop. Then he turned in .his seat, and waved his cap to Margaret. For one instant, she saw the bright, boyish face, the sparkling blue eyes and the smooth yellow hair uncovered in the sunshine; then the horse and rider vanished under the brow of the hill.

For some reason, Margaret's letter progressed slowly, that afternoon. Perhaps the warm, clear day made her long to be out with Danforth; perhaps she was in that melancholy condition, common to us all at times, of having nothing to say. However the case might have been, she found herself, pen in hand, dreaming over her paper, as she sat by the front window of her room. Grandma Atherton was taking her afternoon nap, down-stairs, and Jack and Bobbie were out, so the old house was very quiet. What a dear old house it was, and what good times she had enjoyed in it! At Easter, it had been arranged with her mother

that she was to come back for one more year, to
finish preparing the boys for college. They had
all rebelled at the idea of her leaving them in
June, and Mrs. Davis had given her consent to
Margaret's return, moved partly by Gerald's urgent
letters, partly by her daughter's evident happiness
in her work. The boys were doing splendidly, too,
so that she could take genuine satisfaction in the
results of her teaching.

Since Danforth's little romance had ended, and
he had returned to common sense and the plain
prose of living once more, he had worked with a
will, anxious to efface the memory of his recent
failure. What a dear child he was! As Margaret
looked back over the year, she could see how, all-
unconsciously, her thoughts had centered in him;
and she recalled the many good times they had enjoyed together, walking, riding, or talking lazily by
the library fire. He was always so companionable
and interesting, always the gentleman in look and
word and act. She acknowledged to herself to-day,
that he was the real cause of her wanting to come
back for another year, that she was unwilling to
leave him to another tutor, whom she would dislike,
if he failed to win the boy's liking; of whom she
would be mortally jealous, if he quite took her
place.

However, this was not writing her letter; so she resolutely dipped her pen into the ink, wrote three lines and stopped again, while she sat with her eyes dreamily fixed on a tree far down the valley. Should she tell her mother that Hugh had called, the day before? As yet, she had never mentioned him in her letters; there was really nothing to tell. Now that he had called, she felt even less inclined to write of him, for she could form no idea of his motive in coming to see her. Her heart had throbbed with a sudden hope when Jack had given his message, the afternoon before; and she had lain awake most of the night, trying to imagine his reasons for calling upon her, after all these months when he had been so near her and made no sign. Probably it was a mere formal call, such as he would make upon any acquaintance; and he had made it to avoid any comments, now that he had admitted to Gerald that he used to know her at home. If that was his real reason for coming, she was rather glad, after all, that she had been away at the time.

So absorbed was she in her musings, that she did not notice a closed carriage which turned into the drive and came slowly up the hill, while the driver carefully held in his horses, to keep them from breaking into a trot. Her first sight of it was not until it was stopping, just below her window; and, rising, she ran quickly down-stairs, to go to the door, for the maids were busy and Grandma Atherton was asleep. As she passed the hall window, she saw something inside the carriage which made her throw the door wide open and rush out across the porch, just as the driver sprang down from his seat and came toward the step.

"What is it?" she asked breathlessly. "Is something the matter?"

To her surprise, the carriage door opened quickly, and Hugh Thornton's face looked out at her. Her woman's eye told her at a glance that he was very grave, and involuntarily she looked beyond him, toward the figure which had caught her eye from the window, while he said, with an accent of relief, —

"Miss Davis, I am so glad that you chanced to see us first. I had been hoping it might be so. There has been a little accident — "

"Is it Dan?" she interrupted impatiently. "Tell me, quick! Is he — badly hurt?"

The pause showed her unspoken thought, and Hugh hastened to reassure her. He had hoped to see her first, since she would doubtless be the one least shocked by his errand; but her sudden pallor and her ill-repressed excitement told him his mistake, told him, too, that in the presence of this great sorrow, she had lost all thought of him and of their past.

"It is Dan," he answered, trying to speak lightly. "His pony threw him; but I don't think he's seriously hurt, at least, I hope not. He hasn't really come to himself yet; but I brought him right home. Can I carry him in now, or do you want to prepare his grandmother first?"

"She is asleep and won't hear you," said Margaret, forcing herself to speak quietly, though she could scarcely stand, and the lawn and the river and the valley were dancing before her eyes. "You'd better come now."

For a moment, he thought she was going to fall, and, springing out, he caught her. At his touch, she rallied.

"Don't think of me," she said, with a wan little smile. "I can go through it all. Come."

"Better take him right to his room," said Mr. Thornton, as he went back to the carriage door. "That will save moving him later, and I think I can carry him easily."

Margaret nodded slightly; then, not trusting herself to speak or to look back at Hugh's burden, she led the way up-stairs into the boys' room, and paused beside the bed until he joined her there, and gently laid Danforth down among the pillows. For a moment, Margaret looked down at the still, white face and the closed eyes; then, bending forward, she smoothed the disarranged hair and, for one instant, laid her cheek against the boy's forehead, in a mute caress, while the tears came fast. Then she turned to her companion, with a piteously appealing look.

"Tell me, Hugh," she begged; "I can't seem to think or to know anything. It's as if everything had all stopped. What ought I to do?"

As he met her eyes, Mr. Thornton's face grew radiant with a new hope; but this was no time for pleading his own cause, neither would he take an unfair advantage of her excitement. She had spoken as if the past fourteen months were all a blank. For the present, that was enough for him, and he would meet her upon her own ground; and yet, no power on earth could keep him from using the little old home name, as he answered gently, —

"Poor little Peggy! It is hard for you all. I

never dreamed that you cared so much for your boy, or I would have prepared you more. But now I will stay with him while you go down and tell Mrs. Atherton; then I'll drive over, as fast as I can, and bring back a doctor. Truly, it may not be so bad as you think."

"Oh, my Dan! How can I bear it!" And in spite of her efforts at calmness, the tears rolled down her cheeks; but she rubbed them away, and left the room.

An hour later, she was roused by a knock at Danforth's door. Opening it, she found Maggie, who whispered softly, —

"Mr. Thornton wanted me to say he's waiting here, Miss; and can he do anything more?"

"Tell him I'll come."

As Hugh rose to meet her, he wondered at her perfect quiet. She was using all her self-control to keep back her tears, and to meet him as she would have done another man, in his place.

"Forgive me for disturbing you," he said penitently; "but I couldn't bear to go away without knowing what the doctor has said."

"He said so little, so dreadfully little," she answered, dropping into a chair. "Dan has come to himself, at last, and the doctor says he hopes it will be nothing serious; but he can't tell until he makes another examination to-morrow. In the meantime, Dan is to be kept very quiet, not even allowed to see Jack and Bobbie. I am to be chief nurse, I believe, for he asked for me at first, and is restless if I leave him."

"Don't let me keep you." And Mr. Thornton rose, as if to go.

"Please stay a little longer," she said slowly. "I haven't said yet how thankful we are for all you have done. I can't seem to find the words I am trying to say; but — you know. And I must hear how it all happened."

"It was the fault of that pony he rides. He's a vicious little fellow, and too much for anybody, though Dan has managed him splendidly. They were coming up through the other end of River-ton, when the pony was frightened at one of the cars by the power-house. He shied, and then he ran. Dan stuck to him like a burr, and I thought he'd conquer the beast; but the pony swung round a corner so suddenly that he threw Dan off against the curbstone. He struck on his back and head —"

"Oh, don't!" The words came like a cry of pain, as Margaret's head fell forward on her hands.

"What is it?" Hugh asked anxiously.

"That's what the doctor was afraid of. I know now, and it may be worse than we feared."

"You don't mean his spine?"

Margaret gave a slight sign of assent.

"Anything but that!" And Hugh's face grew even more grave, at the thought.

"That is what he meant; I'm sure of it. It can't be, to have it come all in a minute, when nobody was there to help him."

"It may not be so, after all. I wish I could comfort you; but only Dan can do that. Go back to him, please; I am selfish to keep you."

She rose and took his hand.

"Thank you so much," she said huskily, "for all you've done for us to-day. You have been so good."

He looked steadily down into the sad, white face below him, as he stood holding her trembling hand in his two firm, muscular ones.

"May I come again," he asked, in a low voice; "come again when Danforth is better, and you can spare a little time from him?"

There was a hush, only broken by the ticking of the old clock across the hall. Then Margaret raised her eyes to meet his.

"Yes," she said simply; "you may come again."

When she went back up-stairs, it seemed as if years had passed since she had left Danforth, only a few moments before. Grandma Atherton and Gerald were still sitting by the bed, looking so sad, although they forced themselves to smile whenever the boy opened his eyes. Only a little while before, she had shared their hopeless mood; now she felt a new, involuntary hope springing up within her. Life was so good to her, so kind, in spite of all her fears. It had brought back to her what she had most desired, and it could not be that she must lose her Dan, just at the very moment when she had regained so much. He must live and get well, she told herself over and over again. No matter what the future brought her, it would only be an imperfect gift, if Danforth were to be taken from them. If he lived, her life looked full of promise; without him, even the joy of finding Hugh lost half its delight. But if only to-morrow would come, and the doctor give them his final verdict! This suspense was worse than all the rest.

As she came into the room, Gerald rose from his place at the head of the bed.

"Danforth has been asking for you," he said, in a low voice, as he looked wonderingly up into her face which, in spite of all its gravity, was lighted with a new, sweet joy that he had never seen there before. "He says you know best how to make him comfortable."

She went quickly forward to the bed and bent over the boy, who opened his eyes and smiled faintly up into her face.

"Don't go off again," he murmured. "You know just how."

She laid her hand caressingly against his cheek.

"I won't leave you, Dan," she promised. "As long as you want me, I'll stay here with you."

Late that night, they were alone together. Jack had been sent into his uncle's room to sleep, and Margaret had begged Grandma Atherton and Gerald to go away for a little rest. There was nothing to be done but to wait until morning should decide the future; Danforth was content to have her with him, and she was stronger than they, to bear the strain of the long night. At length, they had reluctantly gone away and left her alone with the boy. The darkness of the room was only broken by the faint glow of the fire and the one shaft of light which came stream-

ing in from the lamp in the hall. Margaret sat
in a low chair by the bedside, with her head resting against the end of the pillow and her fingers
lying lightly upon Danforth's hand, while her
brain throbbed with the day's excitement.

One after another, a series of pictures seemed
starting out of the darkness before her: Danforth, cap in hand, riding away in all his boyish
strength; Danforth, limp and unconscious, being
brought up the stairs, in Hugh's strong arms;
Danforth, as she had seen him in the twilight,
lying there so white and still, while the grave
face of the old doctor bent above him, seeking to
know the full extent of his injuries. Her passing
hour of courage had fled again, and into the
future she dared not look. Hugh's account of
the accident had sent a quick fear into her mind,
the sickening thought that death, even, might
not be the worst thing which could come to her
boy. Any injury to the spine might mean that
the time would come when they would all wish
that Danforth had never roused from his stupor.
Involuntarily her hand closed upon his, as if to
shield him from such a fate. Danforth stirred a
little.

"What is it, dear?" she asked.

"My back hurts me a good deal," he answered wearily; "and I can't seem to get comfortable."

"Perhaps I can make it easier," she said. "Let me try. So; isn't that better?"

Seating herself on the side of the bed, she placed one arm under the pillow and drew it gently toward her, until Danforth's head and shoulders rested against her side.

"That's fine," he said gratefully. "What time is it?"

"Only eleven," she answered.

"Eleven; why don't you go to bed?" he asked wonderingly. "I don't want you to stay here, just for me."

"I'm not sleepy, at all," Margaret replied gently. "I am going to stay with you, to-night, in case you want anything. Now, can't you go to sleep?"

"I wish I could, for I can't lie still, and it hurts me to move."

"Poor old Dan!" And Margaret drew her hand slowly across the boy's forehead and cheek.

"That feels good," he murmured; "go on, if it doesn't tire you."

She kept up the motion, with a slow, even touch which told no tale of her unstrung nerves. It was all she could do for the boy who, all-unconscious, was lying between life and, perhaps, something worse than death. Instinctively her arm grew tighter about him, and her touch on his cheek became more and more gentle.

"Sing something," he said, in a whisper.

Without a moment's hesitation, she began to sing a little cradle song which she had often sung, two years ago. Hugh had been so fond of it, in the old times, and it had never crossed her lips since the day she had last seen him. Now, all-unsought, it came into her mind, and she sang it, softly and low.

> " ' Slumber, and dream of the fast-coming years,
> Which are unfolding before thee;
> Dream thou of those whom love endears,
> Who now so fondly watch o'er thee.' "

Hugh's face seemed to be looking down upon her, out of the darkness. She could see it again, just as it had been, that afternoon, with a whole unspoken story in its brown eyes, and a little glad note of exultation thrilled in her voice, as she went on, —

> " ' Gathering storms may not fail to o'ertake thee;
> Only a true love will never forsake thee.
> Bide but a little longer!
> Bide thou —— ' "

Danforth's breath was coming with a deep, gentle regularity, and she could feel the relaxation of his whole figure, as he yielded to her soothing touch and voice. If he could only rest to-night, to be ready to bear what the new day had in store for him!

> "'Slumber, and dream of the splendor of spring;
>   Joy to o'erflowing is given.
>   Hark! how the birds so tenderly sing,
>   Love reigns on earth, as in heaven.'"

Again the new note of happiness in her low voice. Down-stairs in the library, Gerald stopped his restless pacing of the floor, and held his breath to listen. The words were speaking to him more eloquently than the singer was aware; and it was as well, perhaps, that Margaret could not see him, as he stood on the threshold, resting his head against the portière, while she went dreamily on to the end of the song.

> "'Seasons pass o'er thee, but thou art not heeding;
>   Thy time of promise toward thee is speeding.
>   Bide but a little longer!
>   Bide thou, bide but a little longer!
>   Slumber!'"

Her voice slowly sank away into silence, and the old clock took up its monotonous refrain.

Down-stairs, the man had fallen into a chair and covered his face with his hands, as if to shut out the sight and sound of temptation; above, in the dark, quiet room, Danforth had fallen asleep.

CHAPTER XVII.

THE REPEATED MESSAGE.

"Miss Davis?"

"Yes, Dan." And Margaret rose from her place by the window, and crossed the room to the bed.

"I wish you'd tell me something, tell me honestly."

"What is it, dear?" she asked, with a little feeling of dread of the coming question, for the boyish face before her, while it looked very young and childishly delicate, yet had a strange expression of anxious determination.

"I want to know just what the doctor said about me, last time he came. Am I going to get well?"

"Oh, yes," she answered, trying to force herself to speak lightly.

"Perfectly well?" he asked slowly, as he looked searchingly up into her face.

314

For an instant Margaret hesitated; then she said gently, —

"I hope so, Dan."

For his only answer, the boy drew the sheet up over his face for a moment, and lay very still. Then he asked steadily, —

"What are the chances?"

Margaret sat down on the side of the bed and took his hand in hers.

"We can't tell yet, Dan. Duke gave you a bad fall, that day; and it may be a good while before you are quite your old self again. Still, that's only a maybe, and the doctor said you might come out of it all right, in a little while."

"And if I don't?"

"We won't look at that if, Dan," she said cheerfully. "The other is what we're going to hold on to, and we'll try to forget this."

"What's the use?" he asked quickly. "I'd rather be told all about it now, Miss Davis, for I know something's wrong, or grandma wouldn't look at me the way she does. I've been in bed more than a week, now, and I'm able to hear how I'm coming out. Please tell me. If you don't, I shall think it's ever so much worse than it really is."

It was a hard moment for Margaret, and she longed to run away from the boy's gaze and from his questions. Then she nerved herself to the sternest of all duties, that of speaking the truth.

"Dan," she began slowly; "I wish you hadn't asked me, for we none of us know just what to tell you. It will be a few days longer before the doctor can know how soon you will get over this. You may be all right in a very few weeks; it may keep you here some months, perhaps a year. But we'll all of us hope that it won't be so long, for we must have our Dan his old self again. It is very lonely without you, down-stairs."

As she paused, Danforth's grasp on her fingers tightened nervously, and he looked straight up into her face, saying, in a low, breathless tone, —

"That isn't all, I know. No matter what happens, will I be able to walk again, some day?"

Before Margaret could speak, he had read the answer in her eyes, and, withdrawing his hand from hers, he covered his face and was silent. The sight of his suffering was more than she could bear, and she laid her hand on his again, as she said pityingly, —

"Don't feel so badly, Dan. It's only a chance, one little chance, and you will probably be as well

as ever.   The doctor doesn't feel at all sure, so we
must hope all we can."

Danforth uncovered his face and looked up at
her again.   A sudden outburst of noisy grief
would have been much less unnatural, much easier
to meet than his perfect quiet, and the hopeless
look in his dark blue eyes.

"Don't mind so much, Miss Davis," he said
drearily, as a hot tear splashed down on his hand.
"We'll get used to it in time, and then it won't
seem so bad. You'll have to stay round here a
little longer, though, for I can't get on without
you."

There was a short silence, while Margaret
struggled to regain her self-control.   All at once,
Danforth asked, —

"Where's Duke?"

"He hurt himself, the day he ran," Margaret
answered reluctantly; "and he had to be put to
sleep."

Danforth had borne the rest in silence; but
when he heard of the loss of his old friend and
companion, his courage gave way, and he suddenly began to cry, with a grief all the more
intense for his previous calmness. Margaret still
sat by his side, stroking his hair and speaking a

few words of comfort, now and then; but she felt
that it was of little use. Danforth was fighting
out his battle alone, and she was powerless to
help him. At length he quieted himself again,
and turned to her gratefully.

"You were good to tell me," he said. "I'd
rather you did it than anybody else, for you've
been my friend through thick and thin, and you
used to go out with me, so you know how fond I
was of Duke, and of riding,—and all the rest.
I'll be good now, and won't be a baby again;
but you won't go off and leave us just yet,
will you?"

Late that same afternoon, Mr. Huntington was
sitting beside the bed. Several times since the
accident, he had called to inquire for Danforth,
and to-day the boy had insisted upon seeing him
for a few moments, although as yet no one but
the family had been allowed to go into his room.
Margaret had led the way up-stairs, and stood
leaning on the foot of the bed, watching the
young man as he bent down to speak to Danforth,
with a quiet cheeriness very different from the
lugubrious bedside manner assumed by too many
members of his profession. All his usual shyness
had vanished, and he shared a quick perception of

the right word to say which made Margaret feel quite at ease, as she went away and left them together.

After their first greeting, there was a short pause as Mr. Huntington sat down by the bed and looked at the face on the pillow before him, the same face he had known so well, only it seemed to him even more young and delicate and refined, while its pallor made the great blue eyes look unnaturally large and dark.

"And they tell me that you are gaining a little, every day," said the young man cheerfully.

"Yes; I'm ever so much better than I was at first, and it's good to see somebody again."

"I feel immensely honored at being allowed to come up," said Mr. Huntington, with a bright little laugh; "but it won't be long, I hope, before you're round with us once more."

"I don't know," answered Danforth, with a sudden gravity. "I'm afraid it may be a good while, and maybe, even then — " All at once, he asked abruptly, "Mr. Huntington, just suppose you had to stop, all of a sudden, just when you were in the middle of everything? Seems as if I shouldn't have minded it so much, a year ago; but now there are so many things I want to do."

Mr. Huntington understood him, without more words.

"That's the hardest part of it all, Dan," he said quietly. "It takes more courage to drop out of the ranks, and sit down to watch the rest march by, than it does to go forward into the fight. But sometimes we have to step to one side, for a while, and let the others go on without us."

"If it hadn't been just now," said the boy unsteadily. "Ever since I've been here in America, I've had hard work to keep on my feet. Things went all wrong, somehow, and nobody quite understood. Then, last fall, Miss Davis came, and since then everything has seemed so much easier. I don't know just how 'twas; but she gave me a start and helped me to keep on, and I began to think I might amount to something, after all. College was coming, in a little over a year; but now —"

Mr. Huntington took Danforth's hand between his own, and held it firmly.

"No matter when it comes, Dan, whether early or late, there is always the same feeling that you need a little more time. Our stopping-place never is found until we are ordered to halt and lay down

our arms.   Sometimes we have to lay them down
entirely; sometimes we drop them, only to take
up others, as you may have to do.   It's useless to
say that, if we're resigned and all that, it doesn't
hurt us.   The hurt is always there, until we have
grown so used to the pain that we can look under
it, and see the good which comes with it.   But
that comes later; now we can only shut our teeth
and try to bear it as well as we can, for courage is
one of the first lessons we have to learn."

"I know; only it's so hard to begin," said Danforth, looking up into the kindly brown eyes above
him, which grew suddenly sad, as Mr. Huntington
went on, —

"We all of us have to begin, and to begin early,
Dan.   None of us can go through life just as we
would choose; but one of us has to give up one
hope, another another.   Sometimes it takes all our
pluck to do it, for our plans are the very best
parts of our lives, and often it seems as if 'twould
be easier to give up life itself.   But when the time
comes, the courage comes with it, and helps us
through even the hardest places.   It will come to
you, Dan, if you need it; but I hardly think you
will, just yet.   From what I can find out about
you and about what the doctor has said, I think a

few weeks will see you about as well as ever; and you may be sure that not one of your friends will be happier then than I."

Danforth's face had brightened during the last words; and, as Mr. Huntington paused, the boy looked up with something of his old smile.

"I'm awfully glad you came up, Mr. Huntington, for you've said just the right thing. I'll try to keep up my pluck, whatever comes; and maybe 'twon't be so bad, after all. At first, it seemed as if I couldn't get out of it; but now I'm not so sure."

"Here comes Miss Davis, and I must run away," said the young man, rising as Margaret entered the room. "I'm afraid you'll wish Laddie had stolen my sermon again to-day," he went on, with a mischievous glance at Margaret.

"How unkind of you to suggest it!" she said, blushing, while Danforth laughed outright. "I carefully shut Laddie up, when I saw you coming up the hill, for fear he would get into fresh mischief. I don't know about the sermon; but you have certainly done my patient good," she added, as she saw the new light in Danforth's eyes. "I think I can safely urge you to come again."

Mr. Huntington's call certainly had done the

boy good, and for the next few days he gained rapidly, while he seemed to have recovered something of his former spirit. Margaret was with him during the greater part of the time, for Grandma Atherton was not strong enough for the long hours of care, and Danforth was more than satisfied to have Margaret in her place. Accordingly, lessons were practically suspended, and except for an hour, each morning, Bobbie and Jack were allowed to have a holiday, while their tutor gave all of her time and much of her strength to their brother.

Little by little, as Danforth's strength came back to him, his hopefulness came with it; and, as the days went on, he could talk over the future with Margaret, making bright plans for his restored health, or speaking of the other possibility with a quiet courage which roused in his tutor a new admiration for her boy. The long hours they spent together were not all sad ones; and as they passed away, each one brought the young woman and the boy into a closer friendship and understanding which nothing could ever destroy or lessen.

Slowly the days dragged away until, at length, came the time for the examination which should determine Danforth's future life. All that long

morning, Margaret never left him ; but when the
doctor came, at noon, she went away and shut
herself in her own room, alone. It seemed as if
the next half-hour would never end; then she
heard the doctor's step, as he went slowly down
the stairs and into the library where Gerald was
waiting for him. A little later, she heard the
front door shut, and the quick trot of the horse's
feet as he hurried away down the hill. Then she
went down to the library. Gerald stood opposite
the door, and one glance at his face was all she
needed. She sank into the nearest chair, and her
breath came a little quickly, as she asked, —

"It is really so?"

"Yes; the danger is over, and Dan will be as
well as ever in a comparatively short time. You
may tell him; it is your right, for you have been
his faithful friend."

Margaret rose and went over to his side.

"Thank you," she said impulsively, as she held
out her hands to him. "I have meant to be good
to our boy, as I promised you; and I have found
it an easy task. Whatever came to-day, you
would have found Dan ready to bear it, and I
know we should both have been proud of him."

Gerald stood holding her hands in his, while he

looked up into her radiant, flushed face and her earnest eyes. Then his own eyes drooped and, letting go her hands, he turned and walked away to the fire, saying quietly, —

" Then you will tell Dan ? "

The days that followed were a time of perfect happiness to them all. Now that the cloud was lifted, they realized more keenly than ever how dark it had been, and how great was their present joy, in comparison with it. Day after day, the spring came on and ripened into summer; day after day, Danforth gained new strength and new interest in his old life. Then came the sixteenth birthday of the twins. It was a great festival for them all, for Danforth made his first expedition down into the old drawing-room once more, and took his place in the family circle about the fire. He was only a ghost of the former Danforth, as yet, for he had grown thin and pale from his long illness, and he could walk but a few steps at a time, clinging to the arm of Jack or Margaret, while Bobbie followed him about, laden with pillows and foot-rests. Still, now that he had started on the upward journey, his progress would be rapid, and the doctor had promised them that the last of June should find him as strong as he had ever been.

It had been agreed that, as soon as he could bear the journey, he should be taken to the seashore for a month, in the hope that the salt air would hasten his recovery. Accordingly, Gerald had engaged rooms in a little cottage, at a summer resort where the hotels were not yet opened, and now they were only waiting for the time when Danforth could safely take the long day's ride.

"I shall ask you to go with him, Miss Davis," Gerald had said to her, one evening after the boys were in bed. "Nobody else will be half so good for Danforth; and the change won't hurt you, for you have been too devoted to the boy for your own good. Jack will go with you, to run errands and wait on you both, and I shall insist upon it that you and Danforth do nothing more arduous than sit in the sun and make sand pies."

"But what about Bobbie?" asked Margaret, with a momentary feeling that the present outlook before her was too blissful to be true, and that she must have the drawback of Bobbie's restless presence to make up for the perfect delight of a month of seaside idleness with her two boys.

"Bobbie would be nothing but a care for you, and I'm afraid she would annoy Dan, so I shall put her back into school, to keep her out of mis-

chief till you get home. You'll be down there till
the middle of June; then you can come back here
for two weeks and, if the boys are in good condition, you can freshen them up for their preliminaries. But, until you do come back, remember
that you are to have no lessons at all." And he
shook his head at her warningly.

During the past three or four weeks, Hugh
Thornton had called three times at the Atherton
house; but he had not seen Margaret since the
memorable afternoon when he had brought Danforth home. At the time of his first call, Danforth
had been asleep, and she had given orders that on
no condition was she to be disturbed; and on the
other occasions, she had been out driving with
Jack, for Gerald and Grandma Atherton insisted
upon her going out for an airing, every pleasant
day. Still, Hugh was not discouraged. He had
learned the truth, and now he could afford to wait.

Early one evening in May, he was crossing the
street near the post office, when he saw Jack run
into the building to mail some letters. As the
boy came out, Mr. Thornton met him at the steps.

"How is Danforth?" the young man asked,
although he was secretly-longing to hear, first of
all, from Danforth's nurse.

"Better, ever so much better," responded Jack.
"We're going down to Pleasant Harbor, to-morrow morning, and the doctor says that will set
him up on his pins again."

"Who is going?" inquired Mr. Thornton
eagerly. "All of you?"

"Oh, no; only Dan and Miss Davis and I.
We're going down for a month on Dan's account,
and because Miss Davis is pretty much tired out,
taking care of him. I'm going along as a body-
guard."

Mr. Thornton bit his lip thoughtfully, for a
moment. Then he said, —

"Jack, are you willing to do me a favor, and
say nothing about it?"

Jack looked up with a laugh.

"You'd better believe I will! Didn't you fish
me out of the cellar and not give it away? One
good turn, you know; so come on. I'm your
man, and I never tell tales."

Mr. Thornton looked down into the dark, handsome young face before him.

"I'll trust you," he said simply. "It's a matter
of a good deal of importance, Jack; and I am
throwing myself upon your honor as a gentleman.
Come and do an errand with me, first of all."

He led the way to the nearest florist's and carefully selected a great bunch of roses, whose greenish white petals, just unfolding, offered a rich
promise of their future beauty. He watched them
while they were being packed into the box; then
he took out his card and wrote a few words on
the back of it, but, with a little frown, he crumpled it in his hand, and turned to Jack instead.

"Now, Jack," he said, in a low voice, as he put
the box into his hands; "will you give this to Miss
Davis to-night, when she is quite alone, and say to
her that she will know what it means? Say too,
please, that I shall be at the station in the morning, when you go, but that I may not have an
opportunity to speak to her. Can you remember
the message? Of course, you needn't say anything to the others."

Jack nodded in perfect comprehension; then,
tucking the box under his arm, he darted away up
the street, at a pace which endangered the necks
of the heavy-headed roses within.

Fully an hour before time for the train, next
morning, Mr. Thornton was wandering restlessly
up and down the platform of the station, nervously
snapping the case of his watch, and responding
with unwonted curtness to the salutations of his

friends, who finally respected his evident desire to be alone, and left him to himself. A dozen times he told himself that he had mistaken the hour and that the train had already gone; but at length he saw the Atherton carriage driving down the hill to the station, just as a faint, distant whistle told of the approach of the Boston express. He retreated to the safe refuge of the baggage-room and peered anxiously out through the door-crack, as the carriage stopped.

Jack leaped to the platform, followed by Gerald, and they both turned to help Danforth out of the carriage. Then came a long succession of air cushions, bags, umbrellas and wraps until Hugh's patience was well-nigh exhausted; but at last he saw Margaret rise and step down on the platform. She had on a light spring gown which just matched the color of her hair, and although she stood with her face turned away, he could see that she was looking unusually happy and bright. Would she never get through fussing with that everlasting boy, and turn around, he asked himself petulantly. Just then the train came in, and, giving Danforth her arm, she walked toward one of the forward cars. As she passed near his place of concealment, Hugh caught a glimpse of something white at her belt.

Regardless of the crowd about him, he pushed his way toward her. Just as she was about to enter the car, she saw him standing not far away, and she blushed scarlet as, with a little half-unconscious gesture, she pushed aside her jacket, and exposed to view a great bunch of white roses fastened into her belt. The next moment he was at her side, and their hands and eyes had met, before the train moved slowly away and left him standing beside Gerald, on the empty platform.

The little man looked up at him, with a smile of perfect unselfishness.

"I know what that means," he said, as he offered his hand to Hugh. "I congratulate you most earnestly; you have won a glorious woman."

CHAPTER XVIII.

DOWN BY THE SEA.

THE month that followed was a happy one for Margaret and the boys. The spring had come on early, that year; and now, by the middle of May, the weather was perfect, day after day of clear, warm sunshine when Danforth could lie stretched out on the sand, in sheltered nooks of the shore, and grow strong and rosy and brown. After the long winter of study, followed by the month of anxiety and care, the lazy, out-of-door life just suited them all, and they enjoyed it to the utmost.

Pleasant Harbor was only a long, curving stretch of shore, with three or four great hotels at one end, and a strangely primitive little village at the other. At this season, but one of the hotels was open, and since Danforth was as yet unable to bear any excitement, in preference to its noisy rooms and many stairs, Gerald had hired quarters for them in a pleasant cottage at the nearer end of the village. The place was charming, and in it they

could be as free as at the hotel, and as quiet as in
their own home. Their landlady, too, was a character in her way, and the boys derived much
amusement from her conversation at the table,
where she artlessly sipped her tea from her saucer,
as she told them stirring tales of the old times
when Pleasant Harbor was a thriving fishing
ground, and summer hotels and their inmates were
a thing unknown.

. Except at mealtimes, they saw but little of the
hospitable soul, who had put her whole first floor
at their disposal and retired to a little room under
the roof. However, in some manner known only
to himself, Jack had contrived to learn the way
to the kitchen, and to coax Mrs. Larrum into
letting him have an occasional taste of the goodies
she cooked so well; but Margaret and Danforth
were content to rely upon his accounts of the good
times he had behind the scenes, and leave him to
enjoy them by himself.

Margaret never wearied of the long days on the
shore. Directly after breakfast, they used to start
away from the cottage, Jack marching ahead with
his arms full of gay-colored cushions and rugs
while Danforth and Margaret followed more slowly.
There was one particular strip of sand, facing the

south and protected on two sides by a high bluff,
where they liked best to camp, and they spent
many a long hour there, reading aloud, talking, or
resting idly on their cushions, listening to the
dreamy *splash! splash!* of the bright waves before
them. In this quiet, out-of-the-world existence,
they found a thousand things to interest them:
the changing tides and the floating clouds, a passing sail, a flight of sea-birds, or a school of por-
poises tumbling over and over at the surface of the
water. It was pleasure enough just to feel the
sun beat down upon them, as they leaned on their
elbows and let little handfuls of sand sift slowly
through their fingers.

The stragglers from the hotel who passed by
their little nook, soon learned to watch for them,
and to exchange a smile of greeting with the
pretty young woman and the tall, delicate-looking
boy. Jack they saw less often, for he was too
restless and active to stay with the others for long
at a time. By the time he had been three days at
the cottage, he knew half the old fishermen of the
Harbor, and was made free of their boats and their
wives' kitchens. He was as popular in the one
place as the other; so, while his brother and Margaret spent their time on the sand, he was coming

and going, afloat and ashore, now dashing past them in a white-winged yacht, now sliding down the rocks back of them and dropping down on the sand at their side, to tell of his morning's adventures and share with them the "nut-cakes" and yarns which he had collected.

The doctor had been even wiser than he knew, when he had ordered sea-air for Danforth. Each day, the fresh breeze was bringing new strength to the boy, whose cheeks began to fill out and grow rosy and brown with the sunshine and the simple, out-door life. Within an incredibly short time, too, he could turn his back upon Margaret's supporting arm, and walk off again with his old, firm step, slowly at first and only for a little way, then for increasing distances, until, long before the month was over, he was quite his old self again, and ready to join Jack in his explorations of the harbor and the village.

"I wish your uncle could see our pensive invalid now, Dan," said Margaret, one evening when their month was drawing to a close.

They were out on the piazza of the cottage, enjoying the warm twilight as it stole up from the sea before them. Margaret lay comfortably stretched out in the canvas hammock, and the

two boys, shoulder to shoulder, were pacing up
and down the piazza in front of her. As she
spoke, Danforth paused, with a little laugh.

"Why for?" he asked. "Is anything wrong?"

"No; on the other hand, it's very much right,"
she answered contentedly. "Do you remember
that you couldn't walk ten steps alone, when you
came down here?"

Danforth whistled thoughtfully.

"That's so; but I can hardly believe it. Let's
see, I've walked five miles to-day, and I haven't
had enough yet. Come down to our corner and
see the moon rise," he added persuasively.

"I'm afraid you have done enough for one day,"
she demurred. "Aren't you too tired?"

"Not I; I'm not an invalid any longer. Don't
I look in good condition?"

"You certainly do," she answered, smiling up
at him. "You're taller than Jack now, ever so
much. If you'll only broaden out a little, I won't
ask for anything more."

"Can't grow both ways at once, even to please
you," returned Danforth, squaring his shoulders
and standing very erect. "But come ahead; let's
go back to the shore for an hour."

Margaret rose and went into her room for her

jacket. As she passed the table, she rested her
hand caressingly upon a little basket, heaped high
with white rose petals.   Much as she was enjoying
her vacation, she almost longed to be at home
once more.   Letters were such unsatisfactory
things, at best, and particularly so now, when she
and Hugh had so much to say to each other, and
he was kept at Riverton by the absence of his
president which made it impossible for him to be
away, even for one day.   Still, life was all before
them, and she could easily afford to give up one
short month of it for the sake of Danforth, who
was just coming back into the world once more.
She gave the roseleaves a gentle touch, and smiled
happily to herself as she went on into the boys'
room, to get Danforth's light overcoat.   Then,
throwing a scarlet and blue rug across her arm
and catching up a little air-cushion, she joined the
boys on the piazza again.

"Here I am, bag and baggage,' she said gayly,
as she handed Danforth his coat. "It's so warm
to-night that we needn't hurry back, so we'll take
the key, and tell Mrs. Larrum that she needn't
sit up for us."

"All right; she's a sleepy-head, and always
wants to go to bed with the chickens," said Dan-

forth, as he pocketed the key to the front door which opened directly into their little parlor. "You're coming; aren't you, Jacky?"

"By and by," answered Jack from the hammock, where he had taken Margaret's place. "I want to go out and get some more of Mother Larrum's doughnuts. This sea-air is giving me an appetite at last." And Jack sighed pensively at the memory of his vast supper, two hours ago. "I'll come down and walk home with you," he added reassuringly; "but I smell that kettle of fat, and I know there's something good in the wind."

"Don't kill yourself, there's a dear child," urged Margaret laughingly, while Danforth put on his overcoat and took forcible possession of the rug. "Remember that no mortal boy can eat more than seven large meals a day, and then sleep the sleep of the just."

Down on the shore, the high tide was plashing up over the sand in little, curling waves, and a tiny track of light across the water led away toward the rising moon. Far off to the east, they could hear the throbbing engines of a distant steamer; and, only a mile away, they saw the dim outline of a schooner, with the swaying lights at her mast-heads. Margaret had settled herself comfortably, with her back against a great rock, and Danforth, scorning the rug, had thrown himself down on the sand at her feet, with his hands clasped under his head and his eyes fixed on the broadening path of silver light. For a long time they were silent, enjoying the quiet beauty of the evening; but at length Danforth broke the stillness.

"It's just like one night when I was ill," he said thoughtfully. "I dreamed I was on the ocean, in a little boat, and the wind was carrying me back to India. I knew papa was there, and I wanted to see him; but still I dreaded to go. Then, all at once, right up out of the sea came my mother's face, looking so young and pretty, like this picture, not as I remember her, those last few days. My boat seemed to turn around and follow her, and we went on and on till we came to the shore. She disappeared then, and when I looked for her, I couldn't see her; but you stood on the beach, waiting for me to land. It made me wonder, somehow, if she wanted to tell me she was glad you were here."

"She may have been nearer you then we any of us knew," answered Margaret gently, while she

looked down at the boy at her side, with a feeling of pity for the young mother who would have
had such pride in her son.

The moon was well up now, and its white light
fell full upon Danforth's face. She studied it
intently for a moment. It was certainly a face
of which any mother might be proud, — pure and
true and gentle, while the experience of the past
two months had given it a new character and
firmness which it had always lacked before. Unknown to all his friends but Margaret, the quiet,
reserved boy had passed through a few days of
bitter suffering, had mastered his fears and faced
a possible dark future with unfaltering bravery.
Hard as the contest had been for him, Margaret
could not regret it now, as she looked down into
his face and saw the new manliness written there.

"A penny for your thoughts," Danforth offered
her, with sudden lavishness as he rolled over and
met her steady gaze.

She laughed a little.

"I was having a most prosaic thought, just
then," she answered; "wondering whether it was
prudent to let you lie here on the ground, in this
way."

"Why not? One never catches cold in salt air

or salt water," he replied, as he obediently spread
out the rug and rolled over on top of it. "Don't
make me get up; I'm too comfortable, here in the
moonshine, and we haven't many more nights
ahead of us, if we go home next Monday."

"How are you going to like the idea of settling
down to work again?" inquired Margaret.

"I'm ready. If we stayed here, I'd never want
to do anything again; the waves make me as lazy
as a salted codfish. But when we get home, I
think I shall like to go at it once more. I only
hope I don't flunk on the preliminaries, though.
It will spoil all the fun, if Jack and I don't go in
together."

"You'll pass easily enough," predicted Margaret. "Two weeks will put you in training
again, so you needn't feel any anxiety. Next
year we can do a little extra work, to make up
for what we have lost, this spring."

"Ship ahoy!" called Jack's voice; and in another minute he came strolling along the shore
and dropped down on the sand at Margaret's other
side, remarking, "You missed it this time, sure,
I've been having a high old feast. I helped
Mother Larrum fry, and she paid me out of the
dish."

"I should think so," responded Margaret, with a sniff of disgust, for Jack had brought with him a suggestive fragrance of hot fat, which was singularly out of harmony with the moonlight and the dreamy lapping of the waves. "I can't help wishing that you hadn't come quite so straight from the kitchen to us, Jack."

"Didn't," he answered, with his mouth full. "I stopped at Captain Peleg's, on the way, and he says the tide will be right for them to empty the seine, early Monday morning, and don't we want to go? He'll get us back in plenty of time for the train, and you'd better try it, for it's worth seeing. You know I went out with him once before, when we first came."

"If he will get us back, and if you don't die of doughnuts before then," returned Margaret, laughing. "If those things were offered to you at the table at home, you'd never touch them, Jack. What's the reason you can eat them by the dozen here?"

"Don't you know you can eat anything on a picnic, even to stewed porgies?" he answered placidly. "Besides, these aren't so bad as they look, and a fellow must have something to keep body and soul together."

The last three days of their outing hurried by,
and Monday morning found the trunks strapped
and waiting on the piazza of the cottage, ready
for the journey. Margaret and the boys had been
up betimes, and by seven o'clock they were on
the beach, waiting for Captain Peleg Harding to
bail out his clumsy scow and bring it up to the
pier. Captain Peleg was the oldest and toughest
and saltest of the Pleasant Harbor fishermen. He
was looked upon as one of the leading aristocrats
· of the village, because he was sole proprietor of
the great seine which stretched out, like a giant
cobweb, above the sandbars, at low tide, and
the *Maude Annabel*, the massive, square-ended
boat in which he poled himself about the shal-
lows.

For years, ever since the hotels had been built
there, Captain Peleg had been persecuted with
requests to take the summer people out to the
seine; but he had steadfastly refused their prayers
and their more substantial bribes until, one day
on the shore, he had been attracted by Jack's face
and manner, and had invited him to come on board
the *Maude Annabel*. From that time on, Captain
Peleg and the boy had been fast friends, and Jack
had passed many long hours with the Captain in

his boat, listening to his marvellous yarns, and treasuring them up to repeat to his brother. It had needed but little coaxing for Jack to induce Captain Peleg to consent to take Danforth out to the seine; but the old fisherman was not so willing to allow Margaret on board the *Maude Annabel*, whose deck, he boasted, had never yet been trodden by a woman. However, at last Jack's entreaties had carried the day, and Margaret was to be permitted to make the voyage.

It was a gray, misty morning when they left the house, and by the time they reached the pier, the pearly fog hung low over the water, shutting out the harbor and the distant shore. Through the heavy mist, they could just make out the vague shape of the *Maude Annabel*, fifteen feet away, and of the four men who were bailing out the water gathered in the bottom of the boat. They could hear the splash of the falling drops, and see the last faint ripple of their widening circles. Then came the rattle of the oars, as the men seated themselves and rowed slowly across to the little pier, where Margaret and the boys scrambled on board and took their places on the clumsy deck built out over the stern.

"I told Jack to have you wear your oilskins,

ma'am," Captain Peleg said, with a disapproving glance at Margaret's long, light mackintosh. "It's a wettish kind of a place for a woman, an' you'll get that fancy coat of yourn spotted, I'm afraid. Sit down on them coats, though, an' maybe they'll keep off some on't."

But Margaret had reassured him as to her mackintosh, and then settled herself on the scale-flecked deck, with a boy at either hand. The men took up their oars again, and they went gliding out into the mist.

Awed by their unaccustomed guests, the fishermen rowed on in silence; and the stillness was only broken by the dull creak and rattle of the oars in their locks, or by an occasional word from the boys. Margaret herself felt no desire to talk. It was enough to watch the faces of the men before her, and the strange, unreal light upon the water, as the shore slowly vanished from sight and the mist shut down about them. Not a breeze stirred the air; not a wave broke the glassy surface of the water; nothing was moving about them but their own rude craft, which seemed to be bearing them away, out of the world. On and on they went; it might have been for rods, it might have been for miles, for there was no way to

measure their course as they drifted on, like a
phantom ship upon an unknown sea.

At length, a line of poles loomed up through
the mist. A moment later, the men dropped their
oars, as the scow floated up to the great round
pocket of the seine. Their passage through dream-
land was ended, and they had suddenly come back
again into the waking, workaday world.

The *Maude Annabel* had scarcely stopped, when
Captain Peleg leaped into the little boat trailing
at her side, and went rowing away around the
outer edge of the pocket, unhooking the net from
the poles and gathering it up, little by little, into
his boat, while the fish went sliding and tumbling
along, nearer and nearer the scow. Frightened
and confused as their trap grew more and more
narrow and crowded, they were frantically swim-
ming against each other, twisting and turning
and lashing the water into a white foam; while
slowly but surely the captain gathered up mesh
after mesh of the net, slowly but surely brought
his boat closer and yet more close to the *Maude
Annabel's* side. Then, when they lay huddled
together in a dense, throbbing mass, the men bent
over to dip up great basketfuls of them and throw
them, bluefish and whitefish, bass and shad, the

strange, balloon-like toad-fish, the beautiful sea-robin and the spotted squid, all into one vast, restless pile in the bottom of the scow. There they lay, floundering and panting, by hundreds and by thousands, until little by little their struggles ceased and all was still. But, long before that time had come, Margaret had turned away, sickened at the sight before her, which seemed to her like a blot upon the dreamy beauty of the morning. If only that writhing mass would come to rest!

Then came the rapid sorting of the fish, when all hands fell to work, counting out baskets of whitefish and emptying them into the dory which had come alongside from a fishing schooner, down the bay; throwing back the sea-robins and the toad-fish, and piling the squids into the basket of the all-devouring Italian who had rowed over from the next town. At length, when only the larger, choicer fish remained, Captain Peleg gave a short, sharp command, the men went back to their oars and rowed away through the fast-lightening mist. By degrees, the shore came into view again, first a mere dark line through the pale fog, then more and more distinct until, just as they reached the pier, the mist vanished before a glad burst of sunshine.

Their month by the seashore was ended.

CHAPTER XIX.

JUNE ROSES.

PLEASANT as the last few weeks had been, the old Atherton house looked very attractive to the three travellers, as they drove up the hill, that same evening, for bright lights gleamed out from every window, and Grandma Atherton stood waiting in the porch, to welcome them back once more. Then came the usual babel of greeting, of question and answer, while they all exclaimed at the improvement in Danforth, who was ruddy and brown as never before, or laughed at the vivid coat of sunburn on Jack's cheeks and nose. But when Gerald led the way into the dining-room where a late supper was awaiting them, Grandma Atherton drew Margaret aside for a moment, while she whispered, —

"Gerald has told me, dear. Forgive an old woman for speaking too soon, perhaps; but we are all so glad."

Promptly enough, they settled back into their

well-remembered routine, the next morning. There was much to be done in the coming two weeks, and the boys were anxious to be at work once more, to lose no chance of passing their dreaded examinations. Bobbie would gladly have joined them again ; but Gerald had decided that it would be better for her to finish the term in school, so that Margaret might be free to give all her time to the boys. Next fall, they might return to their old ways once more.

However, there was one drawback to Margaret's perfect content, in these warm June days. On her return, she had found awaiting her a note from Hugh, saying that he was unexpectedly called away upon business, and might not come back in time to see her before she left Riverton for the summer. It was a bitter disappointment to Margaret who had been eagerly looking forward to their meeting, to the long, quiet talk which they could have at last, when she could explain all the mistake which had come between them, months ago. Now she must wait again, perhaps until Hugh's vacation gave him an opportunity to see her in her own home. It was useless to try to write it all ; she would prefer to wait.

All too soon the next few days hurried by, and the

last night of her year at Riverton had come. It
had been a warm, bright day, and, after their late dinner, Margaret and Danforth had taken advantage of
the long June twilight to stroll down through the
town, and on to the rocky ledge by the basin,
where they had sat, months ago, and talked of
the boy's mother. Though neither of them had
spoken of that day, it had seemed quite natural
to them both that their last evening together
before the vacation should be spent in the spot
where they had first really known and understood
each other.

The sun was sinking toward the horizon as
they reached the place, and instinctively they
dropped down into their old positions, and watched
it for a moment in silence. Then Danforth
spoke.

"It has been a jolly year," he said thoughtfully.
"Next year will be even better, though, for we
shan't have to waste any time in getting acquainted, as we did last fall. We can start right
in, as soon as you get back. When are you coming, anyway?"

"By the middle of September," she answered.
"We always spend August in the hills, and I
must have a few days, after I get home. Still, I

shall come up earlier than I did last fall, so that we can make up for our lost time, this spring."

"Bobbie has been in a state of mind, ever since we came home," observed Danforth with a laugh. "She thinks she's not in it, because she had to stay in school, instead of working with us. I wonder when she'll get into college, anyway."

"At present rate of progress, not until two years after you and Jack do," replied Margaret, as she leaned back against the rock and looked up at the setting sun. "I'm not sorry, for she is young for her age, and it won't hurt her to settle down a little, before she starts off into the world on her own account."

"Have you heard the latest, that Pen wants to go, too?" inquired Danforth, with an amused expression in his blue eyes. "She says she can't make up her mind whether to be a doctor and go as missionary to the Turkeys, or to adopt an orphan. Fancy Pen in either business!" And he laughed disrespectfully.

"Pen did her best to adopt you, last winter," suggested Margaret, with a smile.

"'Twas about an even thing which had it worst," admitted Danforth candidly. "I had the worst of it, though, the last day I took her out with Duke, for something had rubbed her the wrong way, and she trampled all over me. Pen can be a dear; but when she's cross, you'd better stand from under."

Margaret was saved from the necessity of replying to this philosophical young lover, for she had caught the sound of a quick footstep coming along the path from the bridge, and, the next moment, she had sprung up, with a little glad outcry.

"Hugh!"

"Peggy!" And to the horror of the nnsuspecting boy on the rocks below, Mr. Thornton's arm encircled Margaret's waist, and her head rested against his shoulder.

For a moment, Danforth stared up at the picture above him, at a loss to comprehend its meaning. Then a sudden light dawned upon him, and slipping down over the rocks, he strolled off, with his hands in his pockets and his cap cocked defiantly askew on the extreme back of his head.

"Forgive me for taking you so by surprise," Hugh was saying, a little later, as they sat there in the gathering twilight. "I only came in on the six o'clock train, and I went right up to the house, but they said you had gone out with Dan. Bobbie suggested that this was a favorite walk with you both, so I thought I'd take the chances, and come on after you." He paused; then he added, in a lower tone, "Oh, Peggy, after all this time, it seems almost too good to be true."

She turned and looked up at him.

"Hugh," she began; "I've something I must tell you, something you've never understood. Do you remember that night at Mrs. Sutherland's, ever so long ago?"

He nodded silently, while a little look of pain crossed his face.

"That was all a dreadful mistake. The flowers came, but the card was left out; it didn't reach me until I had gone home, after the reception."

"What?" And Hugh started up, in quick indignation.

"Yes; it was all through somebody's careless-ness, and if we hadn't both come up here, we should never have known—"

"And if you had known, if the card had come, you would have worn the roses?"

"Yes," she answered gently. "I was ready to wear them then."

There was a pause. Then Hugh asked sud-denly,—

"But why didn't **you** tell me before?"

"**How** could I?" she replied. "**You** went away, and left no address with anyone. How was I to find you?"

"But after **we** were **up** here?" he urged. "That first night at the Athertons', when you ran away from me?"

"I couldn't," she answered simply. "After all that time, how could I be sure that **you** still cared?"

"Peggy, dear," he asked slowly, as he looked straight down into her eyes; "did you ever really doubt it?"

"No," she said with a little, happy gesture, as she let her hand fall on his. "No, I never did."

"But what became of Dan?" she asked, after a short silence. "He was here, only a minute ago."

Hugh laughed, as he pointed into the valley below, where they could see a boyish figure wandering aimlessly up and down the dusty road.

"I'm afraid I drove him off," he answered. "Shall I call him?"

"Do, please. Dan must be the first one to congratulate us, for he really brought us together again."

At Hugh's ringing call, the boy turned suddenly and came scrambling up the rocks to his old position.

"Well, I must say you're a sly pair," was his first salutation. "I'd just like to know when you settled the matter."

"It was all settled long ago," said Margaret, with a laughing glance at Hugh. "We were only waiting for a new set of roses to blossom, before we told anybody else."

"But, I say," objected Danforth suddenly; "this is going to upset everything, all round; isn't it?"

"Not a bit," replied Hugh promptly. "It's going to set everything right."

"No; but I mean you'll be carrying Miss Davis off, before we're through with her," persisted Danforth. "We can't stand that, you know."

"You needn't worry, Dan," she reassured him. "I shall refuse to be carried off, just yet. I have promised to put you and Jack into college, and I shall keep my word, so Mr. Thornton will have to wait."

"Don't be too sure of my consent," he replied, with mock dignity. "I may assert my authority, unless you hurry into Yale next fall. When do your exams. begin?"

"Day after to-morrow," Danforth answered, as he possessed himself of Margaret's other hand. "We're all going down, to-morrow morning; and Jack and I are to stay a week with Miss Davis, before we come back."

"Happy Jack and happy you!" said Hugh enviously. "You two boys have been taking altogether too much of Miss Davis's time, lately. Still, I shall have to put up with it; for if it hadn't been for you, we mightn't have been sitting here together." And he smiled at Danforth's mystified face.

The twilight had quite fallen now, and the stars were slowly coming out, in the deep blue sky above them. Down in the valley at their feet, the lights were twinkling in the windows of the lonely farm. All around them, the languid night air was fragrant and heavy with the masses of wild roses on the banks above. Hugh leaned back, and broke off a few pink blossoms from the nearest bush.

> "'Roses red and roses white
> Plucked I for my love's delight,'"

he quoted softly, as he placed them in her yellow hair. "They are our flowers, Peggy; and next June we will prove it to all the world."

Just then there came a sound of rustling and rushing along the path, and, the next instant, Laddie leaped upon them, frisking about and barking a mad welcome. Jack followed him in a more leisurely fashion, and was close by their side before he recognized Hugh through the gathering darkness. Then he cast one comprehensive glance upon the group, upon Margaret's radiant face, upon the roses in her hair and in Hugh's hand; and he gave a long, low whistle.

"Jupiter Ammon and his children!" he ejaculated, with classic fervor. "So the roses did the business; did they?"

MRS. BOLTON'S FAMOUS BOOKS.

" *The most interesting books to me are the histories of individuals and individ minds, all autobiographies, and the like. This is my favorite reading.*" — H Longfellow.

" *Mrs. Bolton never fails to interest and instruct her readers.*" — Chicago I Ocean.

" *Always written in a bright and fresh style.*" — Boston Home Journal.

" *Readable without inaccuracy.*" — Boston Post.

POOR BOYS WHO BECAME FAMOUS.

By SARAH K. BOLTON. Short biographical sketches of George Peabody, Mic Faraday, Samuel Johnson, Admiral Farragut, Horace Greeley, William Lloyd rison, Garibaldi, President Lincoln, and other noted persons who, from hu circumstances, have risen to fame and distinction, and left behind an imperish record. Illustrated with 24 portraits. 12mo. $1.50.

GIRLS WHO BECAME FAMOUS.

By SARAH K. BOLTON. A companion book to "Poor Boys Who Bec Famous." Biographical sketches of Harriet Beecher Stowe, George Eliot, H Hunt Jackson, Harriet Hosmer, Rosa Bonheur, Florence Nightingale, M Mitchell, and other eminent women. Illustrated with portraits. 12mo. $1.50.

FAMOUS MEN OF SCIENCE.

By SARAH K. BOLTON. Short biographical sketches of Galileo, Newton, næus, Cuvier, Humboldt, Audubon, Agassiz, Darwin, Buckland, and ot] Illustrated with 15 portraits. 12mo. $1.50.

FAMOUS AMERICAN STATESMEN.

By SARAH K. BOLTON. A companion book to "Famous American Anti, Biographical sketches of Washington, Franklin, Jefferson, Hamilton, Web Sumner, Garfield, and others. Illustrated with portraits. 12mo. $1.50.

FAMOUS ENGLISH STATESMEN.

By SARAH K. BOLTON. With portraits of Gladstone, John Bright, Rc Peel, Lord Palmerston, Lord Shaftesbury, William Edward Forster, Lord Beac field. 12mo. $1.50.

FAMOUS EUROPEAN ARTISTS.

By SARAH K. BOLTON. With portraits of Raphael, Titian, Landseer, Reyn Rubens, Turner, and others. 12mo. $1.50.

FAMOUS AMERICAN AUTHORS.

By SARAH K. BOLTON. Short biographical sketches of Holmes, Longfel Emerson, Lowell, Aldrich, Mark Twain, and other noted writers. Illustrated portraits 12mo. $1.50.

FAMOUS ENGLISH AUTHORS OF THE 19th CE TURY.

By SARAH K. BOLTON. With portraits of Scott, Burns, Carlyle, Dickens, Te son, Robert Browning, etc. 12mo. $1.50.

STORIES FROM LIFE.

By SARAH K. BOLTON. A book of short stories, charming and helpful. 1: $1.25.

NEW BOOKS FOR YOUNG PEOPLE.

**TOM CLIFTON; OR, WESTERN BOYS IN GRAN
AND SHERMAN'S ARMY.** By WARREN LEE GOSS
author of "Jed," "Recollections of a Private," etc. Fully illustrated. 12m
$1.50.

Mr Goss has the genius of a story-teller. No one can follow the fortunes of To
Clifton and his friends either in their experiments in farming in Minnesota or in th
Western army, without the deepest interest It is the best boys'-book of the yea
and has, besides, permanent value from a historical standpoint

FAMOUS TYPES OF WOMANHOOD. By SARAH K
BOLTON, author of "Poor Boys Who Became Famous," etc. Lives of Mari
Louise, Queen of Prussia, Madam Récamier, Jenny Lind, Miss Dix, et
With Portraits. 12mo, $1 50

Mrs Bolton here gives in an entertaining style vivid pictures from the lives c
some notable women who have won undying fame in art, philanthropy, and othe
fields of usefulness

MIXED PICKLES. By MRS. EVELYN H. RAYMOND, author c
"Monica, the Mesa Maiden." Illustrated. 12mo, $1.25.

Under this mysterious and alluring title Mrs. Raymond describes the queer an
amusing adventures of a number of bright German boys and girls and their cousin
in a quiet Quaker farmhouse.

**THE RIVERPARK REBELLION, and A TALE O
THE TOW PATH.** By HOMER GREENE, author of "Th
Blind Brother," "Burnbam Breaker," etc. 12mo. Illustrated. $1.00.

The first is the story of an episode in a military school on the Hudson, and
simply glows with life and energy. In the "Tale of the Tow Path" Mr. Green
takes the reader out of the usual environment and shows him new scenes describe
I his own inimitable way.

N BLUE CREEK CAÑON. By ANNA CHAPIN RAY, authc
of "Half a Dozen Girls," "Half a Dozen Boys," etc Illustrated. 12m
$1.25.

Miss Ray transports to the Rocky Mountains a party of her happy, wholesom
boys and girls, and depicts photographically their pleasures during a summer in
mining camp. The story is full of atmosphere and life.

THE CADETS OF FLEMMING HALL. By ANNA CHAPI
RAY, author of "Half a Dozen Girls," "Half a Dozen Boys," etc. Illu
trated. 12mo, $1.25.

Schoolboy life has not been often depicted in colors that will more surely deligh
the reader than in this volume. It is a story full of enthusiasm, with exciting ad
ventures, genial fun, and of high purpose.

THE MOTHER OF THE KING'S CHILDREN. By th
REV. J. F. COWAN, author of the "Jo-Boat Boys." With an introduction b
the Rev. F. E. Clark, D.D. Illustrated. 12mo, $1 50.

A book of much merit, quite above the average, and will do good wherever read
Especially will it deepen an interest in practical religious work.

LITTLE ARTHUR'S HISTORY OF ROME. By HEZE
KIAH BUTTERWORTH, author of the "Zigzag Books," etc. A companio
volume to "Little Arthur's England and France." Illustrated. 12mo, $1.2

No one better understands the requirements of the young than Mr. Butterwort
and his book will foster an appetite for classical studies.

SHORT STUDIES IN BOTANY FOR CHILDREN
By MRS. HARRIET C. COOPER. Fully illustrated. 12mo, $1 00.

Many teachers and parents have found that Botany may be made attraoive to ve
young children. Mrs. Cooper's little volume contains a practical demonstration c
this

Lightning Source UK Ltd.
Milton Keynes UK
UKHW020654241218
334505UK00008B/566/P